COME IN . . .

Have you met the ghost who took a lover for revenge? Or Poe's rival poet buried under the doorstep? Or the girl from the HS Yearbook entombed in the wall?

Perhaps you'd like to visit our haunted bathroom, where blood, not water, runs in the pipes. Or watch a *killer* band make a rock video. (It's guaranteed to wake the dead.)

Upstairs, in the attic, you'll find the sweetest little *thing* rolled up in a rug. Just below, there is the bedroom where Hollywood's forgotten monsters sleep. (They don't mind the howling of the gorillas in the third-floor bestiary.)

Downstairs, don't miss the killer freak in the "wreck room." If you are into body building (and disassembling), there is always the lab *below* the basement.

But forgive me for being such a poor host. You must be hungry. And something is cooking in the kitchen, especially for our honored guests . . .

Welcome to

Gahan Wilson's
The Ultimate Haunted House

Where the Dark Things Dwell

GAHAN WILSON'S

THE ULITIMATE HAUNTED HOUSE

Nancy A. Collins
Consulting Editor

A Byron Preiss Book

HarperPrism
An Imprint of HarperPaperbacks

HarperPaperbacks

A Division of HarperCollins*Publishers*

10 East 53rd Street, New York, N.Y. 10022-5299

Copyright © 1996 by Byron Preiss Visual Publications, Inc.
Introduction and illustrations © 1996 by Gahan Wilson.
Individual story copyright information appears on page 193.

ISBN: 0-06-105315-5

HarperCollins®, ®, HarperPrism®, and HarperPaperbacks™ are trademarks of HarperCollins*Publishers* Inc.

Printed in the United States of America
First printing: September 1996

Cover art by Gahan Wilson

Cover design © 1996 by Byron Preiss Visual Publications, Inc.

Designed by Michele Bonomo

Library of Congress Cataloging-in-Publication Data

Gahan Wilson's the ultimate haunted house / Nancy A. Collins, consulting editor.
      p.   cm.
"A Byron Preiss book."
Contents: The last straw / Christopher Golden—Still life with peckerwood / Ayna Martin and Philip Nutman—Reunion / Mike Lee— The head / Melissa Mia Hall—The ratz in the halls / Gregory Nicoll—An eye for an eye / Norman Partridge—Curtains for Nat Crumley / T.E.D. Klein—The inverted violin / Kathe Koja—Bundling / Lucy Taylor—Bone tunes / Wayne Allen Sallee—Afternoons with the beasts / David Arron Clark—The monster lab / Steve Antczak—Someone's in the kitchen / Nancy A. Collins.
      ISBN 0-06-105315-5 (trade pbk.)
      1. Ghost stories, American.   I. Wilson, Gahan. II. Collins, Nancy A.
PS648.G48G34 1996
813'.0873308—dc20   96-18974
                                                                                          CIP

Visit HarperPaperbacks on the World Wide Web at
http://www.harpercollins.com/paperbacks

❖ 10 9 8 7 6 5 4 3 2 1

TABLE OF CONTENTS

INTRODUCTION

by Gahan Wilson

The theme anthology has been both a great affliction and a boon to writers of fantasy.

The boon part of it is that it sells books, not so much to the reading public, but to publishers, or, to put it more exactly, to the publishers' sales staffs.

What the sales staffs of publishers primarily want to know when a book is presented to them is—quite understandably, since their whole job is to sell the thing—what there is about it on which they can pin a satisfactorily convincing pitch. Speaking in the jargon of their trade, they want to know its "hook."

Again, their strategies are not so much concerned with the reading public as with the distributors of the product, primarily the large chain bookstores who are much more comfortable if the merchandise under consideration has what is called a "tight profile."

Telling a sales staff that the book you are pitching to them is one of many in a genre does not particularly excite them. Their eyes do not gleam—again, quite understandably—if you tell them merely that your book is a collection of short stories of the mystery or science fiction or western or, as in this case, spooky persuasion.

"What *kind* of spooky stories?" they will ask you. "What are these spooky stories *about?*"

What you must do is tell them it's about something specific, for instance haunted houses, and it will reassure them enough to be able to assure the distributors, and before you know it you will have sold your book.

That's the boon part about theme anthologies.

The affliction part is that all this definitely confines the writers' options. It's no good them handing in a ghost story about haunted baby strollers (though that might not be a bad idea for some future anthology!) to an editor looking for haunted house stories.

But not to worry. As this book proves conclusively, writers are a tough, scrappy, amazingly inventive bunch, and the lot represented between the covers of this book is a sterling example of the breed. The challenge issued them was even tougher than the general theme of a haunted house; these poor devils had to confine the focus of their efforts to a particular *room* of that haunted house. There was even a list describing them, for God's sake! Yet *still* these stalwarts came though, bless their hearts, and thanks to them you hold hours of exciting, well-crafted entertainment in your hands and the distributors and the sales staffs of the publishers have found at least a tiny moment of respite from their almost unending anxieties.

Now, then—what about haunted houses themselves? What is it, exactly, that has excited such intense interest in them for so long a time?

They've been around forever in popular legends, fables, and songs, but in literature they seemed to get their jump start in the gothic novel. Gothic novels tended to feature very large and impressive haunted houses when they didn't go all the way and present the reader with an actual haunted castle—since one of the basic presumptions in gothic novels was that wealthy folk, preferably of long and ancient lineage, were much more likely to have ghosts than were common folk or serfs.

The general feeling in those highly undemocratic days seemed to be that farmers' ghosts would strike the reader as being as socially unacceptable and unworthy of any serious interest as the living farmers themselves had been. Then again it might have been unconsciously based on the notion that the lives of hardworking folks wore them out so thoroughly that when they were planted in their graves, they stayed there essentially because they were grateful for their first chance of a really good rest. On the other hand, the idle rich were well used to passing hours, years, and entire lifetimes at a specious saunter and had thus become well equipped for, and took naturally to, vague postmortem wanderings in the drafty, darkened hallways of their family homes. Also their endless groaning at the ennui of continued existence seemed a perfectly logical continuation of the sort of carping that is so often heard from those most fortunate among us.

As time went by, the Trickle Down Theory worked its magic and spectral extension slowly seeped lower and lower in the social strata. The increasingly middle-class tone of the readership prodded its authors to cause less grand gentry to stir from their graves, and before you knew it, the shades of the humblest dead found themselves prowling their shanties. At least in fiction.

Essentially, haunted houses are separated from other, more ordinary abodes in being particularly effective containers of the past. They clutch tight at old events; they refuse to forget; they carefully shelter the hopes and obsessions and miseries of the humans who died in their bedrooms or fatally fell down their stairways or expired, all forgotten, from lack of air in their hidden chambers.

Perhaps the creepiest thing about haunted houses is that, being enclosures, they not only shelter ghosts, they confine you with them. If you are unfortunate enough to come across the flickering shade of some nasty man who killed his wife and children in the moldering kitchen where he did it, you will find you are boxed in with him *and* his glittering, translucent knife. You must run from him down hallways that he knows all too well and try to find somewhere to hide in a place where he knows every nook and cranny by heart!

I've been to a couple of haunted houses—I don't know if they were haunted by ghosts because in real life I haven't a clue as to whether or not there are ghosts, I only know for certain sure there are hauntings—and I knew one of those houses was horrible from the moment I turned my car's engine off and could hear the wind soughing between the branches of the tall, dark trees that grew all around it. The unhappy stories told to me through the following weekend by my haunted hosts only served to deepen that conviction. The other haunted house was benign, totally, and had a kindness about it that I still cherish.

Of course our main haunted houses are to be found between our hats and socks. They are, every one, ghost-ridden from their epidermises on in. I wish you peace with all your specters.

THE ULITIMATE
HAUNTED HOUSE

THE LAST STRAW

by Christopher Golden

Thunderclouds rumbled outside the pristinely refurbished Victorian, casting the game room in a pallor of gray light that lay like a generation of dust. Two low windows leeched all color from the room, leaving only a heavy burden of moisture, a saturating dampness that bloated wooden sashes and doorjambs. Original Humphrey Bogart movie posters sagged in their frames, and the pool-table felt was covered in a sheen of morning dew.

It had been warm enough the night before, but the storm was armed with a cold rain. An icy chill billowed the gossamer white curtains, out of place in such a masculine room. Curled into a fetal ball in the shadow of the oak bar, Eric Shay shivered in his sleep and, with that tiny movement, began to wake.

His eyes seemed sewn shut. He sniffed and licked his lips, the stale smell and sweet taste of whiskey giving his stomach a turn. The inside of his mouth was lined with that slimy moss that only a double Jack, straight back, would wash away. He opened his eyes a crack, suddenly aware of the weather, finally truly conscious of the cold. He knew he should go upstairs and take a shower, or at least lie down in his own bed, but he lacked the motivation.

Eric pulled himself into a tighter ball, and closed his eyes.

In the dream, Helen is still alive. They are still married. It is long before Eric met April. Eric and Helen live in her family home, her mother left it to them, and Helen never fails to remind Eric of how this has eased the burden of their daily lives. Eric fucks around. Helen knows, but it is a while yet before she will do anything about it. He'll grow up one day, she knows, but not just yet.

It is an honest dream, to a point. It diverges in his conscience, for in the dream, Eric feels guilty for being a shit. He never felt guilty then. He played pool and darts in the game room, drank whiskey, and fucked Helen's cousin Cassandra on the pool table. Many times. Many ways.

He is standing in front of the window, looking out at the storm— is the storm a dream? He is looking out at the storm and feeling the guilt, the weight of Helen's death, though she is not dead yet, not in the dream. And he knows that Helen is behind him, standing there with her arms crossed, hugging herself tight, face pinched in despair, one foot tapping. Tapping.

She always does that. Taps her foot like that.

The tapping stops. Helen is still behind him. Eric can feel her there. But she's different now, not crying anymore. Not really angry either. There's something else there, something else that hangs in the air besides the humidity of the storm.

Eric is afraid.

It's only Helen, he tells himself. What's she going to do?

But Helen is dead and Eric is afraid. She is behind him, coming closer, and he doesn't want her to, now. He solves problems with his mouth or his cock, but this time is different, he knows it.

Frightened, Eric turns around, prepared to defend himself, squinting as he holds up an arm for protection . . . and then he laughs, for it is only April. There's nothing to fear.

Helen is dead.

The shrieking of the curtains opening snapped Eric fully awake. It was brighter now, though still dismally overcast, and he shielded his eyes from the wan light.

April stood by the window, one hand still on the cord that drew the curtains and the other on her hips.

"Rise and shine, sleepyhead!" she said, and her smile was as trite and false as the amused lilt of her words.

"Do you have to be so fucking chipper, not to mention so fucking loud?" Eric asked through grinding teeth.

April's smile fell away, the snarl beneath seeping with venom.

"Why do you have to be such a prick?" she asked, almost calmly considering her sour scowl. "Despite all your bullshit, I make an attempt to be pleasant, and you have to fuck that up, too. I can't take this shit anymore."

Eric pulled himself up to a sitting position and leaned against the bar, rubbing his hands over the stubble of his beard methodically. He found the abrasion soothing. "What day is it?" he asked, narrowing his eyes in confusion.

Twirling an errant finger in her hair, April hugged herself and held her breath a moment, then let it out in a rush.

"Don't worry, Eric," she squeaked in a voice drained of anger, filled instead with a quiet grief. "It's Saturday. You've got two whole days before you have to go back out and further disseminate your résumé, two days before you have to once again pretend to care that you're unemployed, pretend that you care about this marriage."

"I want to work, April," Eric said, his voice taking on a tinny rasp in his head. "But it's not like we need the money."

"Jesus," she snorted. "Money is the last thing this is about."

Eric rose behind her and turned to get a fresh tumbler from the bar. His glass clinked against a bottle of Jack Daniel's just before he poured, and then the whiskey splashed into the glass.

"I was having the strangest dream just now," Eric said, shaking his head as he recapped the whiskey bottle. He wanted to tell her about the dream, but at the same time he didn't know how she would react. In fact, Eric had been having the dream with ever-increasing frequency since the day they'd moved into the house. It came nearly every night now, exactly the same down to the smallest detail but one: each time it came, he was a little more afraid.

"The strangest dream," he said again, nodding to himself, but the urge to tell April about it had passed, as it always did.

April looked over her shoulder at him, sadly searching his eyes for a trace of sorrow, any recognition of their trouble, and finding none, glared at the whiskey glass that he held in front of him like a priest offering the host for blessing. He moved the tumbler in a slow circle, unconsciously creating a whirlpool of whiskey, and April snorted in disgust.

"What?" She laughed derisively. "You dreamed you were doing something with your life, that you had a career again? That *is* strange."

She turned and fled the room, his room, and Eric called after her, "Oh, that's fucking constructive, April! That's really helpful!"

April slammed the door, cutting off his words, but Eric merely sighed, walked to the window where she'd been standing, and lifted his whiskey glass for the hair of the dog that had bitten him hard the night before. He forced the liquid between his teeth like it was mouthwash, scouring away the grime of his hangover.

It was all gone to shit, now. The question was what to do about it.

"Bullshit," he whispered to himself. "The question is, do I want to do *anything* about it."

Truth was, he didn't know.

It had been so perfect with April in the beginning, and for a while yet after that, if Eric allowed himself to recognize the truth. He'd been kicking ass and taking names in the advertising game, pulling in a half million per, in commissions alone. Not every campaign was a hit, but none of them was a complete miss. Two or three times a day, headhunters would call, but they couldn't offer him anything he didn't have.

That was when he'd met April Chavez. She was the VP of one of his newest clients, an international fast-food chain with an enormous budget. They met for lunch. Eric could still remember how she looked the first time he saw her. April walked into Copeland's with a confident stride that molded her short skirt to her taut hips with every step. Her legs held his attention a moment, then his gaze trailed up her hunter-green skirt and jacket, her petite chest, and finally locked on her face. She had an elfin countenance, ears flaring to a point where they pinned back her stylishly short blond hair.

And she had noticed him. Noticing her. Her eyes sparkled as she approached, the corners of her mouth turning up into a bright, slightly amused smirk. "Business before pleasure," she'd said, and only then did he realize who she was. And at the same time he knew she had felt an attraction, too. It was unprofessional, but neither of them could deny it.

They were married six months later.

Together, they made more than six hundred thousand dollars a year. April, Eric discovered just before their wedding, was an heiress, worth more than fourteen million dollars just by breathing. They were set for life.

It wasn't enough. When two of the biggest names in the business broke free to start their own agency, they came after him to be their VP of creative. Just under a million in salary, not even counting bonuses and dividends from the stock they offered as an incentive. It was a risk, yeah, but a limited one when he considered the guys he'd be working for, practically brand names in the industry.

Fucking thieves. The agency closed up shop in just under a year. Some dirty dealing on their part lost a lot of money for Eric's premier client, and despite the truth behind it, industry perception hefted much of the responsibility on Eric's shoulders. Later, when it was clear he'd been duped, some industry pundits declared that was worse: better to be a cunning thief than somebody's fall guy.

Eric was out of a job, off the plane with no golden parachute in sight. With a reputation for risk taking and a lack of loyalty, none of the major agencies would even interview him. He ended up pounding the pavement like a green kid just out of college. It was humiliating. It was destroying him inside. It ate its way out of his belly until it started to consume his life, to poison his marriage. April figured he'd be better off making sixty-five thousand a year, just for the self-respect of having a regular job. She didn't understand that at that salary level, all he would feel for himself was shame, disgust, loathing.

Oh, he knew it was him. He'd driven a wedge between himself and April, no question. His self-loathing, his anger and arrogance, had curdled their love. She wasn't blameless, though, he reminded himself of that a hundred times a day. She had started to look down her nose at him the day he lost his job. She'd stopped focusing on his eyes when they conversed, his opinion having less value with each passing day. And her eyes had started to wander, hadn't they?

Eric had been home almost constantly for fifteen weeks, and April had begun to spend less and less time there, even when she wasn't working. He suspected she was fucking someone else. She sure as hell wasn't getting it at home.

Home. That's when it had all started. When they had moved into number twelve Pleasant Street. That very day Eric had begun to sense that his new job, his future, was rotting on the vine. The damned house.

Helen's house.

With April, things had gone from perfect to shit. With Helen, things had always been shit. It had been mostly his fault, he couldn't deny that now. When she'd kicked him out of the house and filed for divorce, Eric had a steaming pile of invectives to choose from when he thought of her, never mind actually speaking to her. But sometime in the head-down, worker-bee days between the divorce and meeting April, he'd grown up a little.

A little.

And six months earlier, when Helen's cousin Cassandra, whom he tried not to think about, phoned to tell him that his ex-wife had been killed in a drunk-driving accident . . . then the guilt launched a volley of fatal shots into his head and heart and belly.

After the funeral, Helen's lawyer, an old friend of Eric's named Jim Lockhart, pulled him aside. Jim had been disgusted by Eric's treatment of his wife, had stayed Helen's friend after the divorce, and as far as Eric knew, had never made a move on her. Eric often thought of him as "that noble fuck." As Helen's corpse was being lowered into the earth, Jim told Eric—just out of April's earshot—that Helen had never stopped loving him, never stopped hoping he would grow up, that they would end up together somewhere down the road. Jim had told her time and again to give it up, and she had dated a number of guys, but . . .

Well, the gist of it was she had never changed her will. Eric Shay was Helen Shay's beneficiary. There wasn't a whole lot of money, but there was the house. Eric figured April would never go for it, would never want to live in "Helen's house," or Eric and Helen's house. And her first reaction was to put the place up for sale.

That lasted up until the moment she saw it. Three weeks later they had moved in. Helen hadn't changed the game room, Eric's room, at all. Then his career imploded, after which he spent more and more of his free time in that room, surrounded by his things, comfortable, secure. Home.

Home.

"Fuck you," he whispered to himself, to April, to Helen, and poured two fingers of Jack Daniel's.

Eric rested the glass, ice clinking, on the edge of the pool table, and racked the balls. Before going to the wall to get down his cue, he took his drink to the window again and looked out at the colorless world, the dead, lifeless gray vista that reflected so closely what he saw inside his home of late.

He remembered the dream. Eric raised the whiskey glass to his lips, began to tip it back, and then he felt *her*, standing behind him, arms crossed, hugging herself tightly. Face pinched with despair. Just like in the dream. There was a flutter in his belly, empty but for whiskey and butterflies, it seemed, and the back of his neck felt cold. He shook himself like a wet dog, the motion running the length of his body.

Helen.

The thought was foolish, and he smiled into his glass, amused by his superstition. Oh, there was someone standing behind him; the feeling of another's presence, so close, so intense, was unmistakeable. And it was so much like the dream. . . .

But it was April, of course.

She must have found some more choice words with which to squeeze his balls, to give the knife another twist. Eric closed his eyes and sighed, ran a hand across his stubble. He wanted April to go away, at least for a little while. He only wanted some fucking peace, was that so hard to understand?

He looked at his reflection in the window, waggled his tongue, and raised his eyebrows, his grizzled countenance lending itself all too well to his tried-and-true Jack Nicholson impression.

"Whenever I'm in this room, and you hear me typing," he began in his best Nicholson drawl, "or whatever the *fuck* you hear me doing, it means I'm working, and I don't want to be disturbed!"

Working, how ironic was that quote. But at least it would get the message across. Get out of my face was a message he'd had to deliver to April pretty frequently in recent days, and she'd been doing an excellent job of it up until this morning. Probably off to see her Big Dick Romeo, whoever he was. Eric didn't care.

But now . . . God he could still feel her eyes boring into the back of his head. He took another sip of whiskey and sighed again. He just wanted to shoot a little pool, have another drink, go upstairs and take a shower, then come down and do it all over again.

It was Saturday, for God's sake!

"April," he started, "why can't you just leave me alone for one day, for one hour? Just leave me alone?"

No answer but the cold certainly that she stood there glaring at him. And then there was an answer, one that made Eric's balls rise in his scrotum, made him hold his breath for a moment, perhaps three.

She started tapping her foot.

Eric was rooted to the spot. The blind fear of his dream returned and froze him there, tumbler halfway to his mouth. His eyes rolled left, searching his peripheral vision, but he didn't dare turn his head.

Tap, tap, tap, tap . . .

April? Of course, April. Who else could it be?

"April, what the fuck are you . . . " He started to say as he turned, but he never completed the question.

The door was closed. He was alone in the room. The tapping had stopped the moment he turned around. But he had heard it, to be sure.

"Jesus," he groaned, then dragged a hand down his face.

Eric turned back and opened the window further, then crouched down and let the moist chill buffet his features. He took in a long breath, held it a heartbeat, and then blew it out. Leaving his whiskey on the windowsill, he stretched, then walked around the pool table to the rack of cues on one wall. His favorite had his initials on the shaft and mother-of-pearl inlaid on the handle. He stepped to the table, placed the cue ball on its mark, chalked his stick, sighted along its length, and blasted into a beautiful break, sinking the solid purple four.

Smiling, Eric circled the table, dropping balls more often than not, sipping his whiskey. When only the cue ball was left, he went to the bar to refresh his drink, dropping some ice in this time.

"Women," he snorted as he poured.

"What about them?"

Eric started as if he'd been goosed, spilling Jack Daniel's on the oak bar as he turned. He scanned the room, head jerking as if he were at a high-speed tennis match. Ignoring the sticky-sweet spill, he put down his glass and walked around the room, bent to look under the pool table, then craned his neck to see behind the bar. Half a dozen Humphrey Bogarts were the only other people in the room, drooping mournful eyes watching his every move. *The Maltese Falcon, Key Largo, The Big Sleep, Casablanca, To Have and Have Not,* and of course, *Treasure of the Sierra Madre.*

But he wasn't going bugfuck. He was not hearing the voice of his boyhood idol. It was a woman's voice he had heard, only a moment ago, there in the room.

April playing fucking tricks on him. Had to be.

Eric marched to the door and flung it open, but there was nobody in the hall. Slowly he closed the door. A voice in his head, that was all. It wouldn't be the first time. More than likely it was the voice of Jack Daniel's. He laughed to himself as he went back and racked the balls again. No doubt it would be best if he gave himself a chance to dry out, twenty-four hours without a glass of whiskey. No doubt.

Thing was, he just didn't care.

"Eric."

He froze.

"Eric?"

"Who the fuck is that?" he snarled to the room.

The door opened quickly and Eric's heart jumped as he took a step back, eyes wide with surprise.

"Listen, master of the house," April hissed quietly, "maybe you treated Helen like this, and now that you're back in her house you think you can do the same to me. But you're wrong. Your self-pity is killing us, and it's killing you. You can bet your ass that every day she turns over in her grave because she never changed her will."

Eric stared at her. It had been her all along, of course, but how had she done it? That comment earlier, and just now the first time she had called his name, it had sounded like she was right there in the room with him, speaking softly close to his ear. He could have sworn he felt her breath on his neck. Now he realized it must have been the breeze from the open window. It had felt cold after all.

April stood, looking expectantly at him.

"What?" he asked, throwing up his hands.

"You have a visitor," April said, finally, in a withering tone. "Cassandra."

Eric fought the smile that wanted to come, biting his lip. He hadn't seen Cassie since they'd moved into the house, but he'd promised if she came by that she could have a series of figurines that Helen had inherited from their grandmother. He'd completely forgotten that today was the day, and he'd never bothered to tell April. Well, fuck her! It was his house, after all.

"You can wipe that smirk off your face now, little boy. Your guest is waiting."

The good feeling of a moment ago disappeared from Eric's chest.

"There's nothing between Cassandra and me anymore, April. She's here for some of Helen's things, not to see me," he explained. "You've got nothing to worry about."

"Who's worried?" she asked.

"Obviously not you, you coldhearted bitch," he snapped. "Who is he anyway, this guy you're fucking?"

April blanched, shock replacing the anger on her face. She looked, for a moment, as if she might vomit up the cheese-and-mushroom omelette that she ate every day for breakfast. And then her face crumbled, like a sand castle under the incoming tide. The waves broke, the tears came, and April bit her lip and shut her eyes tight. She wiped them away and looked hard at Eric.

"That's the problem, husband of mine," she said, forcing a chuckle. "Once upon a time you would have been scared to ask that question for fear you might be right. Now it's just another shot in the heat of battle. You shit. Your guest is waiting in the living room. And by the way, you look like hell."

She stalked off, but her shoulders sagged, the pride with which she usually fought him, the dignity, bled out of her. Some part of Eric, a small part, wanted to feel triumphant, to raise a glass in his own honor. Instead, he grieved for her defeat, because it signified one more step toward forever losing what was between them. And despite it all, he wasn't sure he wanted that.

She was fucking someone else. He was absolutely certain of it. But was she right? Did he care about it because he loved her, or because she had dared to cross that line? He had spent hours, days, sitting in *his* room, like a teenager surrounding himself with his things and flaunting the will of his parents. He'd spent his time inebriated, playing pool instead of throwing darts for fear his besotted aim would lead to shattered glass and the ruin of his Bogart posters.

It was all part of the war. But maybe he was maturing after all, because he'd finally realized that the outcome didn't matter: wars were lost the moment they were begun. And yet if, as he was beginning to suspect, there was no way to stop the erosion of their marriage, it was somewhat comforting to know that it wasn't his fault alone. April had kicked him when he was down. Instead of giving him a hand up, she had stood on his head and watched him drown. Maybe she wanted it to end. Did Eric? In truth, he couldn't say.

But even if he made the effort, tried to salvage what they had once shared, it might be too late. Weeks ago, days, hours, perhaps even minutes, he might have salvaged their partnership, their union. But now?

Eric tried to push April from his mind, at least for a few minutes, as he went to greet Cassandra. He ran his hands through his hair several times, trying to tame its sleep-wildness. Passing a mirror in the hall, he knew it was no use. He surrendered to that knowledge. He looked like hell, as April had said. There was nothing to be done about it. Besides, Cassandra had seem him looking worse. Had seen him at his very worst.

Emerging from the wreckage of his marriage, of his life, Eric Shay stepped into his living room and was struck momentarily speechless by Cassandra's appearance. Their affair, taboo as it was, had lasted only weeks. Helen had forgiven Cassie, but not Eric.

Cassandra Broussard was just shy of thirty years old, but in size and mode of dress, she looked every inch a teenager. She was five foot two with long black hair, pulled back in a ponytail. She wore little or no makeup, a white cotton blouse, new Levi's, and a pair of white Reeboks. In that moment Eric had to struggle to remember why he had ever stopped sleeping with her. But the answer was all around him, in the house. He had loved Helen as he now loved April. He had never loved Cassandra.

"Eric?" Cassandra asked, obviously taken aback by his appearance.

"Cass." He nodded, smiling. "As you might have guessed, I sort of forgot you were coming by today. I was just about to go up and shower."

"Alone?" she asked, several meanings apparent in the question.

"Unfortunately," he answered, just as vaguely. His memories of sex with Cassandra were great masturbatory fodder, but he'd vowed never to cheat on April. If their marriage ended, he'd sow his seed far and wide, but he wasn't quite ready for that. None of which precluded flirting with Cassandra, precluded keeping that door open.

"I'm really glad to see you, Cassie, it's been much too long."

"That's not my fault," she teased.

"No," he admitted. "No, it isn't. Can I get you anything?"

"I'm fine, thanks."

Cassandra sat on a white love seat in the middle of the high-ceilinged living room. Arched windows shared the gloom of the storm and the patter of rain punctuated their words. Eric took a few steps and perched on the edge of a large, overstuffed chair that matched the love seat. It was easy to get lost in that chair, to lean back with his feet propped on the ottoman, but he wanted to give Cassandra his full attention.

Eric sniffed the air, noticing an odd smell. It was a Helen smell, a perfume she was fond of wearing. Nicole, or Nikki, something like that. But Eric seemed to remember that they'd stopped making that stuff even before he and Helen had separated.

"Eric?"

"Huh, what?" he fumbled. "I'm sorry, I'm still pretty tired."

"I don't know what's on your mind, Mr. Shay"—she laughed—"but you're a happily married man."

He frowned: "Uh-huh."

"I see." Cassandra pursed her lips, and Eric thought he knew what she was thinking.

"Look, Cass, I have some bad news," Eric began. "Ever since we moved in here, we've had a run of bad luck. I don't mean personal—well, that, too—but we've just had one accident after another and I don't know how to explain it. What it comes down to is that some of your grandmother's pieces, some of the pieces you wanted . . . well, they're trashed, hon. I'm sorry."

"Oh, Eric." Cassandra's face fell. "Not the ballerina!"

"No, thankfully," he said quickly. "Though a lot of valuable things, including most of the Lladro, were lost. We came down one morning and this entire shelf in the dining room had given way. Just last week a piece was knocked from my desk in the library. I guess I left the window open."

Cassandra's eyes narrowed. "You don't think April—" she began.

"No, no," Eric cut her off. "Our troubles have nothing to do with you. In fact. . . "

Eric smelled it again, stronger this time, as if a woman were wearing far too much of the stuff. He didn't know what he expected to see, but he looked around the room, curiosity starting to get to him. When he looked back, Cassandra was frowning, her head tilted back slightly as she sniffed at the air.

"You smell it, too?" he asked, surprised.

"Yeah," she answered. "It's so familiar. What is that smell?"

"You're gonna think I'm crazy, but I think it's—"

"Nikki, the stuff Helen used to wear," Cassandra finished for him. "But didn't they stop making that?"

"Yeah, a long time ago."

They exchanged a quizzical look, and Eric felt a chill, though no windows were open. Cassandra shrugged.

"Could be in the cushions, you know, just settled into the upholstery and stuff," she suggested.

"I never noticed it before, but I guess anything's possible," Eric admitted, though he wasn't convinced. "Anyway, the things you've asked for are in the library, and you can pick out anything else you want as well."

He got up and Cassandra followed him down the hall to where

the library door stood closed. Eric tried the knob, but it wouldn't turn.

"Eric."

"I'm trying, Cassie," he answered. "It must be swollen from the moisture."

"What?" she asked behind him. "I didn't say anything."

Eric turned to look at her, cocked his head to one side, and chewed his lower lip.

"You didn't just say my name?"

She shook her head. Eric went back to trying to open the door. The knob turned, but the door wouldn't open, as if it had grown too big for the frame and was just stuck there like Pooh bear down Rabbit's hole. Eric took a step back and held the knob as he slammed his shoulder into the door once, twice. The third time, it slammed open with a thud. A rush of freezing air followed, and Eric shivered.

"It's so cold," Cassie whined as they entered. "Jesus, I can see my breath."

Eric let out a breath and realized that she was right. It was insane, but he could see the fog of his breath in the library. The window had a sheen of frozen condensation on it, but it was closed tight. The door had been closed and Eric could hear the tick-ticking of the furnace going even as they looked about the room.

"I don't know what the fucking problem is here, but let's just get your things and go," Eric said, teeth chattering.

Lined up on his desk were seven figurines that Cassandra had specifically requested, including a Lladro ballerina she had coveted since her childhood. They each took a step toward the desk.

"Don't let her, Eric!" an urgent voice pleaded.

"Jesus!" Cassie jumped. "I heard that." She whirled on him. "What the fuck is going on here, Eric? You playing tricks on me, or is it just April? She wants to keep this stuff, my grandmother's stuff, for herself? Well, you can tell the little twat this stuff belongs to me, to my family, and she can . . . "

As Eric watched, the Lladro ballerina lifted itself off his desk and hurtled across the room at his face.

"Christ!" he yelled as he ducked, then covered his head as the figurine shattered on the bookcase behind him, raining expensive fragments of nothing down on his head. He looked up to see Cassandra standing, speechless, staring at her shattered prize, a red scratch etched by Lladro shrapnel on her left cheek.

When the other treasures began to fly off the desk, Eric pushed

Cassandra out the door and fell on top of her in the hallway. He looked up and thought he saw a figure disappearing through the door of the game room down the hall. Then he heard it, a brief, muffled cry of pain.

"Eric, what the fuck is—"

"April!" Eric shouted. "She's after April!"

"What are you talking about?" Cassandra yelled in his face. "Who's she, what's happening here?"

Eric ignored her, started down the hall at a run. What he and April had once had was probably irrevocably destroyed, he knew that. But a part of him would always love her. And whatever was happening here, whatever part of Helen was haunting him, or whoever was playing with his fucking head, April didn't deserve to be a part of it.

"April!" he yelled again as he grabbed hold of the door frame and swung into the game room. If he was being haunted, if that's what all of his dreams were, and the smashed figurines, and the fear in his heart, then he would face the consequences himself. Not . . .

April lay nude, breasts lolling to the side, spread-eagled on the pool table. She squealed with delight, and Eric felt the bile rising in his throat. A diaphanous form swirled between her legs, answering the invitation of her parted thighs. April's hands were nowhere near her sex, but her labia twitched and pulsed as though it were being touched, licked, probed.

For a heartbeat, Eric could see her, could see Helen bent over, face buried between April's thighs, and then only wisps of fog remained.

April opened her eyes and the pleasure drained from her face as she saw Eric in the doorway. Without a hint of embarrassment, she stood and took a step toward him. Eric backed away, fear and repulsion driving him in retreat. He knocked into Cassandra, who had come up behind him a moment before, and now stood, shocked into silence by the sight of April's nudity.

April smiled, causing Eric to shiver.

"I want a divorce," April said simply. "And *she* wants the house back, our house. It was never really yours."

"Fucking whores," Eric whispered hoarsely.

"You're a bastard," April said happily. "We all know that, even little Cassie knows it, don't you, Cass? You've been wondering who I've been fucking, and now you know. Feel better, Eric?"

April held the open door in her hand and looked at Eric and Cassandra, pity on her face.

"Believe me when I say you don't want to fight this, Eric. You don't want to fight us. I'm sure, if she'll have you, that you and Cassandra will be very happy together. Until you fuck it up, that is."

April slammed the door to the game room, to *his* room in *his* house. But she was right, it had never been his house.

Eric Shay fell to his knees and puked Jack Daniel's on the Oriental carpet.

STILL LIFE WITH PECKERWOOD

by Anya Martin and Philip Nutman

Once a month my dearest friend comes to visit. Tonight I sense his presence, though I cannot see him. Due to circumstances beyond our timeless abilities, his magnificence is shielded from the eternal gaze of my eyes. And yet, I always know he is there, my constant companion, *the Moon*, even on nights like this one, shrouded in clouds of darkest pitch. Sky as black as the feathers of my bête noire—my once, or so I thought, friend—*that poet's* raven.

I know he is out there, for I have counted the days since his last passing and know it is time for him to visit me again.

My compatriot, the Moon. Full as a wheel of cheese, yet pearly white like the perfect secret of an oyster, the fine, melancholy luster of his rays far preferable to my mood than the burnished gold of the Sun, whose damnable brilliance would dry me out, crack my oily skin. The Sun whose blinding rays have streamed unmercifully through the window beside me for hours, drenching the far wall of the room and fading Her image if not Her memory.

Emilia, whose skin once gleamed like fine alabaster with cheeks of the most subtle pink and now lies dull and chalky like too many layers of powder trying desperately to de-age an older woman's face. Emilia, whose piercing green eyes once bewitched this poet's heart. Emilia, whose tresses cascaded like a thousand scarlet rivulets upon such dainty shoulders. Emilia's waist, so tiny my fingers and palms touched each other when I held it. Such lovely shoulders. Tiny fingers, tiny feet, a sweet trill of a giggle—like a little girl.

Sometimes, They would remember to close the curtains to shield her. Or so would some of Them for a time. Recently, though, They have been younger ones, more forgetful. Although They did buy a special set of curtains for the strange woman, the hideous, mangled thing that resembles a child's experiment with triangles. And for the ghastly, tasteless one that looks like somebody spilled their dinner and never rang for the maid. But mostly They just place the ones They say are special on my side or in the more shadowy corners beside the bookcase on the far wall to my left.

At first, it was just family until the Grandson started to collect. He and his wife talked of moving me, too, putting me away in the attic once, but his younger son, Harry, said he liked my expression—*it was spooky*—and the skull I bear in my fingers. Old "oooh-ooh." he dubbed it and would come by and ask it questions as if it were a fortune-teller who could predict Christmas presents and the victorious team in boys' sports tournaments. When my benefactor grew into a man, the collection grew stranger, and his wife wanted to take me down—*that grim-faced old geezer*—but he remains steadfast and will not allow her. The familiar faces have almost all now disappeared—*upward, I suppose*—until it is just me, Her, and the marble bust of Admiral Nelson, to whom Harry's wife claims to be related.

Pity, I often wonder if I would have liked the attic. At least it would have afforded me a different view. One hundred and fifty years of staring at the same sights is more time than any man, even a poet, desires to muse alone with only his thoughts, Her fading eyes, and a side-glance view of that scoundrel's acclaimed literary volume on the mahogany coffee table to keep him company. For it is Emilia whose curse was responsible for making me more than an image, and the canvas across the room is merely that. It does make me periodically giddy to think that Her loveliness is now mere bones and dust. And it was Edgar who was responsible for reducing me, Milford Nathaniel Peckerwood, into no more than an image on the wall of some distant relative's gallery.

And so I ponder, weak and weary of the endless tedium, as the old grandfather clock in the hall strikes midnight once again. And then, the silence, the perfect silence, the damnable sound of nothing descends again. I wait for the small dong of twelve-fifteen. If someone forgets to douse the hall lantern, I can watch the hands of the clock progress through the small oval window in the gallery door, my only "eye" into the outside world. On cloudless nights, I can track the time in the expansion and contraction of the moonbeams on the floor and onto Her. Tonight I am denied even that solace. Another night in the never-ending expanse of eternity drags on. It was to be a Crow. *Crow, more.* Cannot anyone see the improvement in the cadence? Remember my poem was published one month before his. It was so thoughtful of that celebrated poet to take the time to correspond with a fine Alabama lawyer whose true passion lay in the art of crafting words into melodic verses. Why does everyone believe that lying, pompous . . .

One o'clock, chimes the clock. Hickory dickory dock. Fee diddle dee dee. I thought of her first, my Emilie Lee, whom I loved as a child and would grow to love me, whom I would bury rather than seeing her love another, but who instead buried me alive.

Tap.

Something has hit the glass on the window, I suppose. An acorn, perhaps dropped by an overeager squirrel. One of my games is to ponder the origin of all the night noises.

Silence again.

I miss the boy. He is not half as much fun all grown up, a musician They said he was, but the sound that erupts from beneath the house where he is said to practice does not sound like any music I had heard, just noise fit to shatter the eardrum. I had wanted to tell the boy so many things, like the skull was an old Indian skull dug up by a friend, a wealthy landowner, in north Georgia in the old Cherokee territory. He presented it to me because he thought my manner was somewhat morbid, but it even made Emilia laugh. Her father had the right idea to marry her to a wealthy lawyer rather than that brash young lieutenant from Charleston who had no money in his family and more looks than any type of talent and intelligence.

Tap. Tap. Tap.

The sound was not loud but repeated itself in a quick sequence. It could not be that damnable raven again. *Go away.*

Tap. Tap. Tap.

Leave this old man alone. Is it not enough that your master received the glory for your creation instead of the true poetic genius?

Tap. Tap.

The sound ceased as suddenly as it had begun, and I feel a stupid, senile old man. Of course, there is no raven. I have seen stranger things, like a woman's evil heart imprisoning love in the stagnant confines of a canvas, but the sheer audacity of me to believe he whose name endures would be at all concerned with tormenting another poet completely forgotten. No, that would be too much of a compliment. He is in the ground, as are all my old friends and enemies, languishing in the sweet eternal peace that only I am denied.

A sharp creak pulls outward suddenly, and a single beam of

light hits the floor. The Moon returns, and floods up from the floor onto Her face brighter than daylight onto Her green eyes.

I do not want to gaze at those eyes anymore. I prefer the darkness after all. It hides the memories. If I could only close my eyes and sleep. If I could only die. If I could only cease this miserable existence and progress to another place, be it Heaven or Hell. I would prefer to dwell with the Lord in His kindgom of light, but I no longer care—just to quit the painting!

It is at that moment that I realize I am mistaken. The light is not my old friend Moon but a torch of some kind. It glides from one end of the room to the other, careful to avoid the glass of the door's oval eye and back onto the bookcase. And then it revolves onto me. For a moment I am blinded, and then it glides onward to the other side of the window, and I see two thin figures completely covered in queer tight-fitting black garb. One is a woman, I can tell by the unseemly revelation of the contours of her body against the torch held by the other, a man with a chest so brawny that it indicates physical activity of some sort.

He guides the torch while she opens the drapes covering the ugly woman and removes the frame from the wall, loosens the painting with gloved hand, and gently—with, again, only the slightest tap— lowers the frame to the floor. Then she takes the torch as he begins to loosen the canvas from the boards to which it is adhered with what appears to be a sharp-toothed instrument not unresembling the mouth of a serpent. The wood is laid beside the frame, canvas quickly but carefully rolled, and placed in a large duffel bag.

Then the torch scans the messy one, and again the ritual begins. Frame off the wall, picture removed, canvas gently disengaged from its wooden inner frame, meticulously rolled and stashed into the bag. And the thrill of freedom rushes over me like a gale wind. The thrill of a trip to someplace else. Anyplace else. I have heard Them speaking of a new world out there, a world full of wondrous machines called "cars" that take you from here to New York City in one hour. And things called "airplanes" with magnificent wings that transport one to California in a few hours more and occasionally crash, but usually just make your ears "pop" due to a circumstance called "turbulence." And plays that one can see without actors being present called "movies"; They are always speaking of "which movie did you see last night" or in the place called the Mall, where you can also shop or eat at a Scottish restaurant which also serves French-fried fare. Will I see any of these wonders? I would be happy just to walk in the park and smell the fresh scent of spring azaleas and daffodils in the crisp night air under my old friend the Moon. I have been dubbed a cynic by my dear Emilia and others, but I have always felt a soft spot for the unwavering beauty of that most graceful orb.

They are now rolling up a blue dog I have never seen before because he was on the same wall as I but beyond the window. And then the man lowers another painting and points it in my direction as he removes the boards—a nude woman with skin as pale as Emilia's sprawled like a Sabine temptress across a sapphire love seat. I cannot tell the color of her eyes because the torchlight is still too dim, but they appear gay and inviting and I remember when Emilia's were such, on a spring day under the dogwood behind the back terrace of my Southern home, Villa Persephone, named after the tragic, beautiful Greek goddess who agreed to marry Hades. Emilia, who at first was such a kind and generous wife, bringing me tea under the tree when I was so engrossed in the creative process as to not desire any break in my thoughts. Quiet evenings of cards in the drawing room or clutching my arm at the Opera, Her slim form bristling with excitement at the wondrous range of heavenly voices. Knitting as I read from Coleridge or Longfellow or my own works. If only he had really been killed in Texas fighting the damnable Mexicans and not, wonder of wonders, come home to steal Her heart away from me.

I first spied them kissing under that same dogwood tree when they thought I was taking my habitual afternoon nap. It was but a brief kiss at first, the blond lieutenant pressing lips to Hers and She drawing away, knowing it was wrong. And then the transformation, he starting to leave like a gentleman would and She, the whore, pulling him back and pressing Her lips long and hard against his.

I knew that Fanny dabbled in some form of magicks. She and my manservant, Taylor, were my only slaves, but other city slaves would come knocking on the back door and I would watch her measure out crushed herbs and roots to heal blisters, bring luck, or attract a lover. It was part of some queer, dark religion they brought over with them from Africa. Some of them may be God-fearing Christians, but I had long suspected that Fanny had some other religion on the side. I was never afraid of the Black Arts. Indeed, they fascinated me, the simplicity of casting a spell and manipulating the will of God to my own whim.

I burned the potion Fanny gave me along with a few strands of his hair, and within a day, he grew ill, very ill with scarlet fever. Of course, She ran to his bedside—"just a friend," She said—but within two weeks he was dead, and She was again only my Emilia.

Everything returned to its normal routine. Cards and knitting, me reading to Her a new novel by an English gentleman named Dickens. I tried to ignore the sad look that now stained Her lovely eyes. And then She told me She wanted to paint me, and I would sit for hours in the drawing room clasping the old Indian skull as She labored. A perfect likeness was what She had said She wanted to create. And then when the last brush stroke was complete, She pulled me over finally to look at it. Imagine my surprise when I saw that the man in the painting She had labored upon so long and meticulously had no face. It was then that Her eyes began to change and I first began truly to see Her as the vile creature began to cackle with laughter, chanting in an arcane language I could not understand. As I went for Her throat—the screech of Her voice so grating and horrible to my ears—I found myself dragged instead away from Her and into the portrait.

She hung me over the fireplace to watch as my lifeless body was proclaimed dead by the coroner. My will had clearly stated that I wished to be buried under the front steps (to prevent Her from ever bringing another suitor across them), but She gleefully told me that She had had the church declare that last wish ungodly and I had been buried in the town cemetery instead. Mute for eternity, I could only listen and watch as She never remarried but brought Her countless lovers into the drawing room to let me watch them seduce Her and then carry Her in their arms upstairs. My only solace was to see Her grow old and cracked until no lovers would come anymore. Until the day when the men in black suits and women in black dresses arrived to declare that She had finally died, alone.

I was packed up, along with Her picture and other sundry possessions, and shipped by train to my Yankee nephew's mansion in New England, where I have dwelt ever since.

My memories are interrupted as I notice that my two night visitors are not rolling up any more paintings. They are perusing the bookcase with an intense sense of purpose. She pulls out one book, and he shakes his head. Then she points at the coffee table, and he nods. The torchlight hits the cover: *The Complete and Unabridged Poems of Edgar Allan Poe*. It is the first edition that has haunted me for over a century. They pause as she hands the book to her accomplice, and then he hands her the torch and begins to peruse the pages carefully, lovingly.

I want to scream, "No, the real poet is here." I want to point them to the thin, forgotten volume in the far corner of the bottom shelf, to the poems that he stole from me so shamelessly. For him to say that he sent me his works in friendly correspondence, and I was the thief! My cadence is so much more lush, only the deaf ear could truly believe otherwise.

But, of course, I sit silent, only staring at them, a lifeless work of art, a likeness of a long-forgotten relative. No value for a thief. They will leave me. The walls are empty now, except for me and Her and Admiral Nelson. They will leave me alone with Her and the dour-faced English naval hero who is too heavy to be lifted by fewer than two men.

"Come on, Stan, we've got to hurry," the woman whispers, the first words passed between them. "You can gush over it later when we're safe in Cancún."

"Sorry, Carla," the man whispers back. "It's just you know how much I've wanted to get hold of this, how much money it's going to get us. Good ol' Edgar!"

He pulls a thin, slippery cover out of the bag, carefully drapes the book, and eases it inside the side pocket so as not to damage the rolled paintings.

"Okay, let's go," Carla whispers.

They start to crawl out the window, but then suddenly Stan steps back inside. His eyes dart around the room, the light with them, as if he thinks he has forgotten something. Unexpectedly, they lock on me.

"Wait a minute," Stan whispers. "We forgot about him."

"We've got to get out of here," Carla urges, sounding worried.

"No, this is that guy who says Poe plagiarized his work," Stan adds softly. "Remember that guy I told you about? What was his name, Pecker-something. Yeah, I almost forgot that his picture was here, too. Poor old fucker, must've eaten him up, that Poe first edition across the room from him on the coffee table."

"Stan, we've been lucky this long," Carla goes on, her voice rising ever so slightly. "Let's go."

"No, I want to take him along." Stan's voice drops as if in warning to her. "As a memento of the last great heist. Poe's volume will bring us a fortune, along with the Picasso, the Renoir, the little Jasper Johns, but no one's gonna miss this guy. I kinda feel sorry for him. I think we owe it to him, babe."

"All right," Carla whispers impatiently, stepping back into the room. "But make it quick."

With that, he lifts me off the wall and removes me from the frame, turning my back toward her for the first time since the last move. It tickles when he removes the nails from the board. He cannot use the serpent teeth because my nails are older, heavier, unlike the odd metal prongs used to connect the younger paintings. Then, with a sudden tingle, I am rolled up and clutched in his hand, and he carries me out the window.

My vision turns to pitch, but I can smell the fresh night air, a scent I could not forget. At least I am not in the bag. I do not have to rub shoulders with that damnable tome. This thief does remember me. *Somebody remembers me.* And now I am to rest in the place of honor in his home. What difference does it make that it is a home bought with wealth obtained by the sale of stolen possessions? I will be remembered and appreciated.

From the motion, I infer that these thieves—my liberators, my public—run a short distance from the house. How I wish to see my old, dear friend Moon and to gaze at the facade of the place of my incarceration! Stan, however, keeps me rolled and holds my portrait with reverence, for which I am grateful. I hope their abode will be a magnificent place and that they will hang me somewhere with a splendid view. *Ah, to be remembered!* I, a poet, cannot find words superlative enough to describe the sense of elation I feel.

They slow then, as I sought those elusive words, and the sound of a door opening distracts me from my jubilant reverie. Stan's gentle hands lay me carefully on a leather surface, and I am aware that the duffle bag is placed beside me. Darkness lessens somewhat as my canvas unrolls a trifle, allowing my ever-open eyes to detect the alabaster luminescence of my constant companion of many years, now peeking out from the clouds.

"We've done it, Carla! This is it! Man, I can't fuckin' believe those stupid bastards were only using that antiquated alarm system."

"We're not out of the woods yet, hon," Carla replies. "And don't forget to change clothes."

"Jeez! You're right. Where would I be without you, babe?"

"Wasting away in Riker's, probably."

"Sure as shit, sweet pea."

The sounds of fabric slipping from young, adventurous bodies follow their exchange, and I decide I like this couple, despite the fact that young Stan has the manners and vocabulary of a guttersnipe, and yet has taste enough to take an interest in me. Miss Carla, I sense, loves her brash, larcenous beau fiercely, and the knowledge makes me yearn for my long-lost youth.

"You ready?" asks Stan.

"Just a sec. Okay."

"Love you, babe."

The sound of a kiss follows, then a click, a whir, and the roar of some infernal machine. We are obviously in one of those horseless carriages they call "cars," and I wish I could see more. In fact, I am quite giddy—and, perhaps, a tad fearful—at the thought of being transported in a machine. But then we are off and the sensation is pleasantly surprising.

"You know how much that Picasso's worth?"

"Half a million," Carla replies.

"One-point-five, baby. One-point-five."

Silence descends then, and I wonder what painting they are referring to. Surely not that hideous triangular woman? One could hardly call *that* art.

My liberators continue to guide our travels in quiet for a little while, and any trepidation I had fades like the colors of Her portrait. The sensation is most pleasing and lulls me into a reverie. Words which had eluded me earlier now flow forth unbidden. If only I could write them down!

Then, as I am measuring the beat of a line, refining to the precise dictates of iambic pentameter, Miss Carla's sudden urgent tone derails my inspired train of thought.

"Slow down, Stan, you're going too fast."

"More likely to attract attention at this time of night if I stick to the limit like some drunk pretending to be sober."

"Slow down! I think I saw something blue up ahead," she stresses.

"You're imagining things."

"No. There—in the median, hiding in the bushes."

"Fuck. Well spotted. Probably just the SD doing their job. Old joe cop's snacking on a doughnut, waiting to slap down a DUI." Stan laughs.

Our motion slows steadily, and I wonder what they are talking about, the nuances of their slang escaping me.

"Damn, he pulled out," Carla snaps. "He's following us."

"No, he isn't. It's just a coincidence. If he was, he'd have those blues going."

"Slow down."

"Honey, I'm going five under the limit."

Then a sudden, high-pitched banshee wail assails my ancient ears, and the horseless carriage lurches forward.

"Shit!"

"Oh, hell," Carla cries. "Maybe they're only checking for insurance."

"I don't think so! Damn! There must have been a secondary alarm."

A sudden, frantic spurt of power tosses my rolled form backward, thrusting me up against the duffel bag as a terrible roar descends from somewhere in front.

"Try and catch me, you dirty rat!" Stan laughs.

The roaring increases, the devilish wail retreats somewhat, and a peculiar affliction assaults my stomach. Then it dawns on me—I am feeling sick, a sensation I had long forgotten.

"Slow down! The road bends ahead!" Carla, ever the voice of reason, shouts.

"I can't! We've gotta lose him!"

"Stan! No!"

"Hold on, baby!"

"Look out! He's over the line!"

Nothing could prepare me for the frantic motion which hurled me over and over as my nighttime escape from Her dead eyes turns into a rolling barrel ride, a terrible, unearthly bellowing like a Spanish bull slain by a toreador roaring around us. A most dreadful crashing, smashing cacophony explodes and my new friends and I are flung violently to one side. But the torment continues as Miss Carla screams and Stan cries out in terror. Sailors at the mercy of a cruel sea are we, tossed and turned and—

Then I am free, flying through the night air.

NO! I want to cry. No! No!

My portrait glides slowly, with such unexpected gentleness in contrast to the terrifying violence, and as I float to the soft embrace of a grassy embankment, my canvas unrolls, allowing me to see what has happened.

Stan's horseless carriage is a gnarled mess of metal and broken glass lying upon its side. And there, not more than a stone's throw away, is another of those infernal contraptions. It, too, looks like it has been smote by the hammer of Thor, the God of Thunder. Behind the wreckage, a third vehicle approaches, seemingly the source of the harpy's screech, a fact confirmed when it comes to a stop and the noise ceases. Only the satanic red and bright blue of its lanterns persists, painting the dark countryside with rhythmic splashes of primary colors. Then poor Miss Carla begins to scream, and from my vantage point on the embankment I see why.

Tongues of fire lick at the back and belly of the metal beast.

"Run! Get out!" I shout in my eternal silence. "Save yourselves, my friends!"

A tall man in some kind of military uniform I do not recognize steps from the vehicle of flashing lights and runs toward the rapidly spreading conflagration. Then an explosion, the likes of which I had never imagined, splits the sky asunder more violently than any lightning storm I had witnessed as a young man in Florida. The sound deafens this poet's ears and is followed by a hot wind of dragon's breath which snatches me from my grassy resting place.

Up, up I go, rolling, then tumbling down, down toward the road. But no, it is not to be. A spring breeze decides at that moment to chase the fiery wind, and on I go, borne aloft by invisible arms. As I float over the other vehicle I see a young man, bloodied and beaten, struggle to free himself from the smashed carriage. Then he is gone as the blessed breeze snatches me away from the tragic scene.

Oh, my poor friends! Dear Stan of the profane mouth, poor Miss Carla. How right you were. And now my freedom is empty, for I shall never hang on the wall of your home and watch two lives in the making. Once again, I feel the truth of the pronouncement "the wages of sin are death."

The breeze exhausts itself and I flutter down to hook onto a bush.

I am cold and wet despite the sun's steadily warming rays, for it rained before dawn, a deluge of biblical proportions. Some of my oil has run and I feel most queer. My left eye, I fear, has drooped a little and now my perspective on the radiant countryside is askew. It promises to be a fiercely hot day, for it is not yet noon. Will it hurt as I dry, Her brush strokes flaking as the elements undo Her artful work?

Yes, I will soon be free and pray the Good Lord will take me with open arms into His place. I will endure the pain, for certainly that will come as the weather consumes me, and in fact, I welcome it. After one hundred and fifty years of numbing confinement, it is wonderful to feel something. At least I have the scent of blooming flowers and the hedgerow song of birds to stimulate the higher senses.

I will be free, but who will mourn for me?

Dedicated to the memory of Dr. Thomas Holley Chivers, "the Lost Poet of Georgia," who did, in fact, accuse Poe of plagiarism and, later in life, according to local legend, requested to be buried beneath the doorstep of his home, Villa Allegra, so that his lovely wife would never remarry.

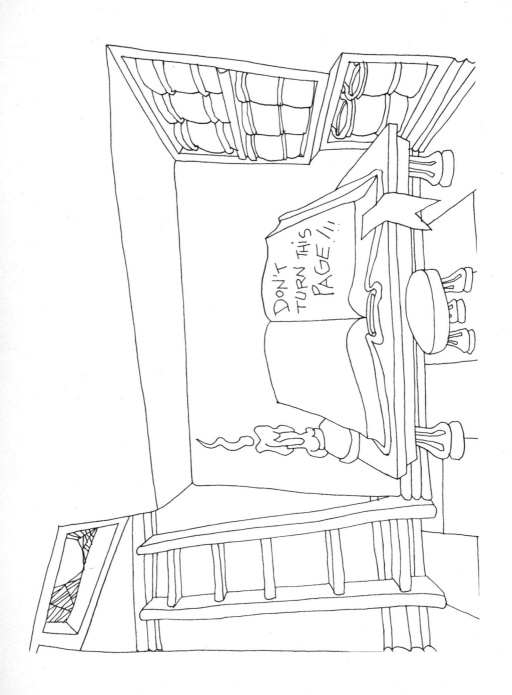

REUNION
by Mike Lee

From my perch on the thirteenth floor of the Hyatt Hotel, I had an exceptional view of Town Lake and downtown Austin. The sky was clear, a few puffy clouds out near the western horizon. The breeze was warm and inviting, and I could smell the budding flowers planted on the edge of the balcony.

I looked out at the lake. It was before rush hour, so traffic was slow, the movements correspondingly lethargic. I spotted a pair of canoeists paddling under the Congress Avenue Bridge, probably to get a closer look at the home of one of the largest bat habitats in North America. A solitary jogger kept a slow pace on the dirt trail on the far shore, passing a family setting up a picnic on the embankment above him, the mother spreading a floral sheet out beside their parked Volvo station wagon as the father unloaded the goodies. Their three kids had run to the shore, and I could see their mother gesturing for them to return while smoothing down the fabric. The lake was notorious for its water moccasins, though I doubted she knew about that. I leaned over the flower bed and looked directly below to see the diners at the outdoor café.

It was the height of the late lunch rush, which in this part of the country would stretch for hours, occasionally running into dinner. This was typical for a Wednesday in the middle of a Texas spring afternoon, especially in Austin. Most of the people down here didn't place too much emphasis on strenuous work or timeliness. Indeed, the first aspect of my lifestyle I'd had to drop after I left Austin was the propensity to operate on European time, an attribute I was all too willing to give up since I was thrown into a situation where I lived and died on making deadlines. However, from espying the humming activity of hungry diners and harried waiters, I felt a twinge of regret, this disturbing feeling I always had when I lived here that I was on the outside of all the fun everyone else was having.

I stepped back and lit another Camel. I thought that perhaps coming back wasn't such a good idea after all. If I kept obsessing about this, I was going to drive myself crazy.

I went to the telephone and called Eddie to let him know I was in town. An effeminate male voice answered and informed me that Eddie was out. I told the guy my room number and asked that Eddie call when he got in. When I got off I wondered when that would be. Reminded of the diners celebrating the Texas siesta downstairs, I assumed that it might not be for a while.

I opened my overnight bag and unloaded its contents: toiletries in the bathroom, the books I had brought with me on the bed stand, the CDs and Walkman on the bed.

This trip truly began several months back after I called around the Austin-area schools for their annuals from the late seventies as part of my research for my next novel. The yearbooks were a good place to start. Not only did I get a sick kick out of looking at the faces of the rubes I grew up with, I also received inspiration just from looking at the rows of photographs. I always looked for something special—nothing I could really put a finger on per se, just an expression, or lack thereof, that I would take note of and attempt to draw a characterization from. It was also the best way to set an accurate time frame. Styles, visual manifestations of social stratification, and various details of the high school and college experience always find their way into triggering a rush of memories. It was a more accurate approach than looking through magazines; they only reflected individual opinions, not the accurate picture of the past that these slick records of teenage angst and triumph recorded.

I began to receive several of them in the mail. Some replied to my sincere inquiries, others did not, but after a month I had most of the books I had originally requested. At the beginning of my research I was disappointed, especially with the annuals from my old high school. A lot within those pages brought back only bad memories, memories I had made redundant with my last book.

Soon, I realized that this approach was going to be a waste of my time. I was out of ideas for the moment, feeling like the proverbial drowning puppy.

I was thinking I should've known better until I received a 1976 yearbook from my junior high and finally came upon something that startled me. The girl's photograph was on the same page as mine, two rows above. Her piercing eyes gazed out at me from the slightly off-focused photograph framed among the rows on the page. I guessed that the eerie quality of the reproduction was due to poor printing, but this only added a more disturbing gloss to her wounded smile.

I flipped back to the cover. O'Henry Junior High was the feeder school to Austin High, yet I didn't remember ever crossing paths with this girl at either place. I assumed she had moved before then; Austin is a college town with a lot of transient families. Most likely she moved out of the district, which made me feel a little depressed. The girl looked like someone I would have wanted to hang out with during my days of teenage hell. Like nearly everyone back then, she probably would not have given me the time of day.

I stared down at her picture. Her hair was dark and curly, falling past her shoulders with the bangs sloppily cut at her eyebrows. The girl's soft, round face called attention to her pale complexion, accentuated by the overexposed one-size-fits-all kind of lighting school photographers are notorious for.

Her expression drew me toward her. Her smile was a thin drab incision cutting across her face, inscrutable yet betraying a knowledge that I could only guess at. It was rare for me to see a portrait so disturbingly out of context.

I looked through the book carefully to see if there were any additional pictures of this girl. After finding none, or any other references to her in the index, I wound up going back over the other books looking for additional photographs of the girl. As I suspected, she wasn't in any of the high-school books, not even in the junior-high one from the previous year. It was as if she came and went abruptly, a dark angel who swept through the eighth grade, made a few passing friends, possibly impressed a teacher or two, and moved on to an unknown fate, perhaps forgotten by everyone who came in contact with her. She was perfect to write about. No need for release forms in this situation.

I thought about the photograph's peculiar effect on me. It seemed to me as if there was something she wanted to say but was not able to. It was chilling, and I could only suspect the number of reasons why her intensity stuck out so. Later that night in New York, I had an experience that crystallized for me why I should return home and solve a particular mystery that heretofore I had given no thought to.

I walked back to the desk and opened my briefcase. I pulled out the annual and had begun to open it when the telephone rang again. It was Eddie, assuring me he would pick me up in a couple of hours. After I hung up, I picked up the book and opened it.

I stared at the girl's photograph. I didn't like the feeling it inspired in me. I pulled out my red spiral notebook and reviewed the notes I had taken over the last few months and slipped out several Xeroxes of articles I had requested from a connection at the Austin newspaper. The more I read, the worse I felt; I could sense a prickling on the back of my neck, and I had long ago given up on scratching to soothe it. As I studied the clippings and my cramped handwriting in the spiral, I was convinced I held the key, so to speak, to solving the mystery that has obsessed me since the moment I first saw the girl's picture. Although on the surface what I had planned was a long shot, I believed that this could be over in a matter of hours.

The sun had set by the time I met Eddie at the lobby elevators. He was with another old running buddy of mine, Johnny Quentin, who came up and slapped me on the shoulder.

"So I'm damned glad to see you after all these years!" he said, reaching for my hand.

"Hey, man, you remember I don't do soul handshakes," I replied.

Eddie stepped forward. "God, you're getting fat."

"Thanks a lot, you don't look so good yourself." His six-foot frame was acquiring a potbelly equal to mine, which was not surprising considering all three of us were hitting the high side of thirty and never met a workout we liked. Indeed, even though Johnny's lanky frame remained somewhat intact, he himself was looking worse for wear in the hair department. I wanted to mention that his hairline reminded me of a map of Napoleon's retreat from Moscow, but I figured saying it would spoil our reunion at too early a juncture.

"Yeah, we're gettin' old," I said, putting on my best Foghorn Leghorn voice to mask my gloom at having to be so rudely reminded of the creeping of age.

"Yep, no one left us such a goodly heritage," Eddie replied. "C'mon. Let's add to that there spare tire."

"As long as you're paying." In the old days Eddie had always sloughed off the check, usually to me, since I was the one who had steady employment. Now with a business, maybe he had learned some responsibility, if not manners.

"No, we're taking you over to the house," Johnny replied. "I have a ton of leftovers from a party last night. I figured that this is what you wanted."

"You're always a stand-up guy, I guess," I said, a little nervous.

The three of us had known each other since my sophomore year in high school. We had shared just about every experience three underachieving neurotics could have, good and bad. For instance, I was Johnny's best man at his wedding and his suffering roommate when he crashed at my apartment at the time of the divorce—which was caused by his wife having an affair with Eddie. Once, he beat the crap out of me when I wrecked his car and at another time he stopped speaking to me for a while after I fired him from a job. Despite all of this, we somehow managed to maintain a good relationship, while there were many who crossed our paths who ceased to speak to us for lesser sins. I guess our saving grace was that even through the worst we remained pathologically loyal to one another, for whatever that was worth. That was the main reason why I had called both of them up before I came to Austin. I trusted no one else.

"As you probably remember," Johnny explained when we arrived at the house, "the Carlton place was abandoned for several years until this New York developer bought it and began the renovation."

"I'm surprised no one ever tore the place down," I replied. "Damn, now I know why this house always gave me the creeps."

"In this town big money is a major factor in causing mass amnesia," Eddie cracked as he turned off the ignition.

"Don't you know it," said Johnny.

I opened the car door and as I stepped out I looked up at the house. The late-spring wind blew in from the north and I pulled my jacket tighter around me.

The Carlton house gave off little warmth or feeling of home, although I believed my sentiments were colored by the knowledge of its recent history. The building was constructed of solid oak and cedar, which explained its survival of decades of deterioration and abandonment, thus giving a rationale to repair the place. The restoration work on the house and surrounding yard was quite adequate, yet I had found nothing particularly striking or unique. It didn't help that the architecture was the common-variety late Victorian with certain regional flourishes. An enormous front porch skirted the entire front and large captain's windows that jutted out from the facade on the second and third floor were in keeping with the long hot Texas summers. The only extraordinary aspect of the house was a square, dark-tiled steeple-like tower with circular windows that rose above the third floor. If it was any house but this, I wouldn't have given it more than a passing glance if I drove by.

"I believe this is when Johnny is going to tell us that the house is haunted," Eddie cracked while Johnny unlocked the front door. I winced, but held my tongue.

"Not that I know of, really," Johnny replied. "Haven't had any trouble the entire time I've been here."

"But weren't there problems during the construction?" Eddie asked.

Johnny reached out to the panel of switches beside the door and flipped on the interior lights one at a time. "Just the usual you'd expect when various hucksters run out of money or are busted by the IRS. I haven't seen any ghosts of headless drug dealers traipsing down the staircase. Or, for that matter, any mysterious accidents, flying kitchen implements, blood gurgling out of toilets, or unusual swarms of insects gathering in odd corners—we do have roaches and the occasional mouse, however, though none of them have exhibited any of the traits associated with possessed beings or nearby UFO activity."

"Sounds like you've been reading up on the subject Johnny," I commented.

"I watch *The X-Files*."

I looked around the room. "This stuff doesn't look authentic by a long shot," I noted. The furnishings resembled a middle-brow interpretation of nineteenth-century interiors and I suspected most of it was purchased at Ethan Allen.

"Consider the source," Eddie said. "You can take them out of the trash. . . ."

"Let's go to the kitchen and pick out what we want warmed up," Johnny said, an edge in his voice. "I'm hungry."

"So, are you ready for tonight?" Eddie asked between mouthfuls of his microwaved roast beef.

"Uh, yeah." I wasn't paying much attention. I stared at my plate, thinking about how much I'd prefer being back with my family in New York. I was already considering giving up on doing this follow-up to the first book. As I cut another piece from my turkey steak I decided that I'd try my hand at science fiction instead.

"Are you going to tell us what the house has to do with your new book?" Johnny was trying to jump-start the conversation. He had already finished his meal and lit a cigarette, tossing the match into the remains of his creamed mashed potatoes. This succeeded in furthering the loss of my appetite and I pushed my plate toward the edge of the table.

"It depends," I replied. "I'm guessing that this is what the audience wants. But I wanted to get the three of us together tonight because I have a few questions to ask about the house."

I looked at Johnny. "Since you're running the place, I'm hoping that you can help me out concerning some information I've found out about it."

Johnny shrugged. "Sure. I'll try to help."

"Good." I reached for the bottle of vodka in front of me and poured another drink. Same old Johnny, I thought. He suffers from that Austin self-deception, confusing open indifference with decisiveness.

I asked Johnny, "I'm dumbfounded—they finally finished the restoration work?" The apparently unending reconstruction and renovation of the house was a standing joke with the locals.

"Oh yeah, a while back—six months ago. The Junior League bought it after *The New Yorker* went under and finished it up fairly quickly. I got hired through Maggie Wright, remember her?"

"Oh Christ." I was surprised to hear her name. "How did that white-trash princess get to be in the Junior League?" I also wondered if Johnny was sleeping with her.

Eddie interjected, "The usual ladder. She married a city councilman. Ain't no glass ceiling high enough when it comes to the marriage contract."

"Or divorce," I replied, shooting a zinger at both of them. I sipped my vodka and tonic. "So I like what they've done to the place."

"Sure," Johnny replied. "It is really amazing the work that was done to the entire structure. Really wonderful achievement, considering the circumstances."

"*Especially* considering the circumstances," added Eddie.

"I know," Johnny said. "With the crap involving the S and Ls and the land fraud that went along with it."

I chortled. "That ain't all, brother. Not nearly enough."

"Don't you know it," Eddie replied, not truly aware what I meant by my remark.

"I don't think so," I was incredulous. I assumed they hadn't an idea what I was talking about.

"Do you both know about Huggy Bear?" I asked.

Johnny scratched his chin. "Yeah, kind of. He was the creepy guy running the hippy cult that lived in this house. Went to the loony bin for murdering a rival."

"Yeah, everyone knows that part of the story," I said. "But over the years I did a little research on them. I think both of you will get a kick out of it."

This exercise was annoying them. Johnny groused, "We could have a conversation about more mundane subjects, but the two of you have got me hanging like a bastard."

I blinked and held out my palm. "Easy, easy. I'll tell the whole story."

Johnny gave a furtive glance toward the front door of the house. "Why don't we get on with this? I really hate this dancing-around-the-edges garbage."

Eddie looked at my drink. "You finished with that?"

"I'd like to enjoy it, considering who is paying." My behavior only served to make them more paranoid, so I figured that I might as well take advantage of whatever niceties I could get while I went out of my way to mess with their minds.

"Well, okay," I answered. I turned to Eddie. "When did you move to Austin?"

"In seventy-eight."

"Then that might explain why you might not've heard the full story, though I still can't believe you hadn't. Anyway, back in the mid-seventies the Carlton house was a hippy commune. Really nasty bunch of creeps. I used to avoid them like the plague, more so than the other freaks because, if I remember correctly, they were in some kind of cult."

"Like the power church down in south Austin?" Johnny nervously asked.

"Yeah, kind of sort of. Except these people were really out there. Or at least that's what the paper said."

Eddie bummed a smoke from Johnny and lit it off the end of

the one he stubbed out in the ashtray. I noticed his hands were shaking.

I continued, "So there was this dude living there. Huge guy—I think he played football at Austin High a few years before but got acid-damaged in a hurry. Went by the name Huggy Bear, but that was only for his looks."

Johnny rolled his eyes up. "God, if I remember correctly, he was a real mean bastard."

"Indeed he was. For all intents and purposes, he was the leader and the main reason we gave the block a wide berth."

"Wait a minute," Eddie said. From his expression I could tell it was starting to come back to him now. "I think I did hear something about this. Wasn't this a murder case? I once read about this crazy hippy who killed a hitchhiker on trial the summer I moved here."

"Uh-huh," I replied. "That was the other guy, the one who was supposedly in on it with Huggy Bear. But all the strange stuff had happened a couple of years before that. Stuff that never made it into the media."

For the next hour they sat spellbound as I related what I had learned about Huggy Bear and his merry band of Manson wannabes holed up in the then-crumbling Carlton house.

As well as spooking their neighbors with their bizarre occult practices, which included the usual mysterious disappearances of family pets and incessant playing of Tangerine Dream records, the hippies were long rumored to have been involved in manufacturing crystal meth for the local biker gangs. The hippies also paid protection to the cops, which explained why they seemed to be getting away with just about everything under the sun. It was the same old story, replayed in a dozen college towns back then, and it continues to this day with different players.

But as is always the case in these sad tales of cheap decadence and small-town avarice, there was a line to be crossed and Huggy Bear bulled over it with a tractor trailer.

I remember the story all too well. There was a sergeant on the force who let his greed carry him too far. He lost a ton of money in a dope deal that was busted by the Rangers down in Laredo. He supposedly was months behind on the house and car payments and probably the family Neiman-Marcus bill as well. The bum was so far gone he had only one alternative before the repo men came to strip his dream life away.

His way out was to nail the Carlton-House hippies to the wall, above all Huggy Bear, for an extra cool ten grand, which in 1976 money was a lot to working fools like you and me.

The cop believed he had the plan all figured out. As it was, it was a fortuitious time for him to shake down the hippies. The word on the street was that the greasy, smelly cretins at Carlton House had just finished a noxious batch of crank, enough to fry every machine head from Austin to Tyler and points Arkansas. The sleazy bastard enlisted the aid of two of his fellow officers as well as the leader of a rival biker gang based in south Austin. The deal was to hijack the shipment with a "raid" on the premises and hold the whole batch up for ransom and hand over half of it. The south Austin bikers would get the held half of crank as their share and the three cops would split the money they extorted from Huggy.

The sergeant assumed the hippies would have no choice. Whoever they were working with wasn't going to go after a bunch of dirty cops; instead they would take their righteous anger out on Huggy Bear.

What the sergeant didn't count on was Huggy Bear's insanity and misplaced sense of pride, two concepts historically confused in Texas.

The phony raid went off without a hitch. The hippies were in the process of loading their van when the cops held them up. While Huggy and several of his minions were sent off to cool their heels in the city drunk tank, the sergeant drove the load down to south Austin bikerland. The hippies were then released the next morning with a message: Come up with the ten grand or face the consequences of screwing the meanest bunch of white trash on two wheels in central Texas.

Just after sundown the sergeant received his reply from Huggy. Essentially the crazed hippy informed him to return the speed or he would mail the sergeant's darling daughter to him in pieces. To reinforce Huggy's sincere intention to have his crank returned posthaste, the biker involved in the job suddenly appeared dead in front of the police station sans eyes, tongue, and hands. Twisted around the biker's neck was proof they had the girl, the strap of her hand-tooled leather handbag with the stamped personalized initials clearly visible despite the bloodstains.

It was obvious that Huggy Bear had gone over the top. I couldn't help but wonder if it was hubris or the fact that he had sampled too much of his wares that led him to sign what turned out to be his own death warrant. Dumping a corpse on the doorstep of cop central was poor modus operandi in a small southern city.

The sergeant had a nervous breakdown and cried to the chief, who freaked out and immediately ordered a raid on the Carlton house. During the frenetic search, the police uncovered an Aquarian House of Usher. Through the pervading stink caused by the hippies' disregard for soap and backed-up toilets, they found several filthy and obviously abused children, a pair of teenage girls chained up in the attic, used as sex slaves for Huggy, a speed lab in the kitchen, and several bales of marijuana in the basement.

The worst they discovered was in the basement, where the stench was so powerful that a couple of the raiders tossed their cookies. One enterprising cop with a sinus problem was able to discover the source: a male corpse stuffed in garbage bags buried under stacks of newspapers and other debris. As it was learned later during the trial, he was an unfortunate who recently had made a poor life choice involving Huggy Bear's business operations.

The irony of the matter was that the sergeant's daughter wasn't even there. She turned up that night at home claiming that her bag was stolen out of her school locker that morning. One of the hippy kids they busted said she took it on orders from Huggy. The hippies claimed they never had the girl to begin with, which made the story all the more absurd.

The adults were carted off to jail and the kids dumped with Youth Services while the cops spent the next several days searching the grounds for more corpses. Aside from a pile of animal bones and the usual cartoon pseudo-satanist paraphernalia, they didn't come up with anything to add to their laundry list of charges. Huggy got slapped with murdering the biker and the basement critter but was judged loony and shipped to Rusk State Hospital. They managed to find one guy competent enough to take the fall, which was the case I remembered reading about. The remainder of the commune from hell either went down for various drug charges or disappeared. Nearly forgotten in all this was the sergeant and the two losers with him. All three pleaded down to felony possession of the crank shipment and vanished into the sunset after parole.

Johnny was stunned. "How come I didn't hear about any of this?"

"I learned the details from a former APD detective who now owns a country-and-western bar in lower Manhattan. Small world, no?"

"I guess that's what happens when human garbage attempts to do something reasonably high-tech," Eddie opined.

I stubbed out another cigarette. "Seems typical for these parts. That's more or less what the old cop told me."

After we cleared off the table and washed the dishes, Johnny led us on a tour through the house. When we entered the library, I felt a twinge in my stomach. My meal hadn't mixed well with the cigarettes and vodka tonics, and that creeping sensation I had been feeling all day returned.

Fortunately, the library's decor was an improvement over the tawdry hideousness of the rest of the main floor. Three walls were lined with floor-to-ceiling mahogany bookcases. I had wondered how the Junior Leaguers had decided to use an actual period shelving instead of Ikea; even so, it was a lucky accident. Although the stuffed chairs and burnished oak rolltop desk didn't match the bookcases, overall the room had a homier feel than the rest of the house.

I walked up to a shelf and stared at the books stacked there. I suspected they were the typical Goodwill by-the-yard garbage, purchased in order to make the room look like an authentic library. Otherwise everything seemed in order, except I had a troubling feeling where I stood. Instinctively, I pushed at the shelf, half expecting it to creak open, exposing a hidden passageway. The surface didn't give. If there was a secret door there, it had probably been boarded up during the renovation. However, I felt a chill, and I remembered something I had read during the course of my research.

"You looking for something?" Johnny asked incredulously.

I stepped back. "No, just curious at the titles you have here."

"You can take what you want. Nobody notices."

Later we walked up the staircase to the second-floor landing. As we passed each room Johnny opened the door and switched on the lights to show us tacky wallpaper and four-poster beds more appropriate for Graceland than a restored landmark.

"One of the amazing things about this house was that they didn't have to totally gut it," Johnny explained. "The interior walls and floors on the second and third floors are all original."

"I thought you said the cops ripped up the place," Eddie reminded me.

"Only the basement, as far as I know," I replied.

Johnny added, "Also, the crew got sloppy at the end of the job and just replastered and painted the upper floors. You'll notice it when you're in the attic."

"Typical half-ass Austin job." Eddie smirked.

Just as we reached the door to the narrow stairway that led to the attic, I had another attack that took the breath out of me.

I stopped and leaned against the wall, breathing hard.

"What's the matter, man?" Johnny inquired.

"Just getting old." When I caught my breath I decided to get to the point of why I was here.

"Did you guys go to junior high with a Rachel Kyle?"

Johnny and Eddie looked at each other quizzically. Eddie shrugged. "No, the name doesn't ring a bell. What did she look like?"

When I described her Eddie only nodded. Johnny scratched his neck. "To tell you the truth, I can't recall. I might recognize her if I went through my old yearbooks except they're over at my mom's house. Sorry."

"Fair enough. That's why I brought these books along," I replied, patting my black leather briefcase. I still felt weird, though I didn't quite know why.

"O'Henry was a big school," Johnny said.

"Yeah, it was pretty easy to fall through the cracks in that hellhole, just like Austin High," added Eddie. "Anyhow, she left before I moved here."

"I suppose so," I said. "I was only wondering."

"Is she somebody you met up in the big city?" Johnny inquired.

"Yeah. I guess so."

After I called my wife to let her know where I was, Johnny cleared off the coffee table to make room for the yearbooks I had brought.

The three of us stared down at the photograph. "Her picture still doesn't do anything for me," Johnny said. "What does she have to do with this story?"

"It's hard for me to explain," I replied. "But I'll take a stab at it."

Eddie stared at me. "Well, we're all dying to know."

I closed the book and leaned back in the couch. "I think she's buried somewhere in this house."

There was an uncomfortable silence in the room. Eddie tittered in his seat opposite me while Johnny coughed. After a few moments Johnny nodded his head and leaned over the table. He slid his fingers absently over the cover of the O'Henry yearbook and pulled it toward him.

"Where the hell did you get that stupid idea?" he said. "That's the craziest idea I've heard in years."

"I have my reasons," I replied, uncertain about whether or not I should tell them the rest of the story.

I decided to dispense with the strange and went straight for the car crash. "The old detective told me that this girl—Rachel Kyle—had vanished a month before the raid. From what he told me, I'm now convinced the hippies had something to do with her disappearance."

"What, Huggy had another slave girl that got missed in the search?" Johnny nodded with disbelief.

I lit a cigarette. "That might be the case."

Eddie got out of the chair and began to pace around the room. "Man, you're really freaking me out."

"I'm not making any of this up. The cop I talked to filled in the holes, so to speak. For instance, the police gave up awful quick on the search after they found the body in the basement. Also, the girl was a real problem child—a runaway—and wasn't reported missing until after the bust. With all that was going on at the time, Rachel Kyle got lost in the shuffle. It wasn't until I showed the old detective the yearbook that he remembered the case."

"I still don't really get it," Johnny said.

"Just trust me on this," I replied. "I want to take a look around the house."

Eddie leaned against a wall. "What makes you so damned sure of yourself?"

I got up and moved toward the door. "C'mon, I'll show you both what I mean."

After we stopped at a utility closet for an ax and a flashlight, we went downstairs toward the library. When we entered the room I again felt that prickling sensation rising up the back of my neck. I turned toward the bookcase that had attracted my attention before and stepped up to it.

I began to pull out the books. "Help me out here. I want to move this bookcase out."

After a moment's hesitation Johnny and Eddie stepped up and soon we had emptied the shelves. We pulled out the bookcase and dragged it to the side to expose the wall behind it. Although it had probably been painted months before, I could smell the fresh paint. What I found off-kilter was a crack that had formed lengthwise from the ceiling. As if by impulse, I placed my palm flat against the whitewashed surface. When my fingers touched the ridges of the perforation, I was enveloped by a realization that sent me reeling.

After I recovered my balance, I silently stared in horror at my outstretched hand, inches from the spot where I had just touched the crack.

I turned around, holding out my arm. "Give me the ax," I ordered Johnny. After he handed it over, I swung it against the wall with all the force I could muster.

Or *through,* because the ax crashed through the surface like papier-mâché, enveloping us in a cloud of dust. Although I was barely able to keep my grip, I was able to pull out the handle and hacked several more times at the hole I had made. I then placed the ax aside and peeled away the jagged pieces of plastered Sheetrock, making a hole large enough for us to look in. Johnny came up beside me and flicked on the flashlight.

"What the hell—" I felt Eddie's breath on my shoulder.

"Mother of God," Johnny gasped.

I had expected an empty room, or a small crawl space. Instead, in the glow of Johnny's flashlight we viewed an abandoned fireplace shaft. I estimated the shaft to be only three feet wide, running from the roof down to the first floor. When Johnny raised the flashlight we saw a ragged piece of clothesline hanging from a beam above.

Johnny lowered the light toward the floor of the shaft. We gasped in unison when we saw on the ground below us scattered bits of clothing, including a wooden clog and what was later identified as a shredded pair of blue jeans. Unmistakable amid the debris was a skull, its empty eyes filled with cobwebs.

Suddenly we were sent falling to the ground by a burst of cold air that blew in from below. Its force rattled the windows and knocked a lamp onto the floor.

After it passed, Eddie sat up and stared at the gaping wound in the wall. He asked, "How did you know?"

I cleared my throat. "Two simple reasons. One, the house should have had a fireplace and didn't, and two, I felt a draft coming from behind the bookcase," I replied.

Eddie nudged me. "No, I mean about the girl."

I paused. "I was only following up on my instincts," I replied, again avoiding telling the whole story.

We called the police and they spent the next morning recovering the bones from the shaft. Johnny came up with a good explanation as they took our statements: we were looking for hidden hippy treasure, whatever that meant, but Eddie and I went along with it—and so did the police. I didn't blame them—they really screwed up the last time.

I decided it would have been best to get the hell out of town and I took a flight back to New York that night. I arrived at my apartment at one in the morning, in time to see my wife breast-feeding our baby. She understood that I was very disturbed about my trip and thankfully let the subject slide. She kissed me good night after we put the infant in her crib and returned to bed. I went to my desk and carefully typed up the notes I had scribbled furiously in my spiral during the flight home.

It struck me that I was a coward for not telling anyone about how I *knew* what was behind the library wall at the Carlton house. However, if I dared explain, I'd stand accused of paranoia, or of having the overactive imagination of a skittish author in a desperate search for an adroit scenario to sell.

Both of these explanations were only easy justifications to pacify everyone's distress. In reality, there was much to be examined—all I wish I could conveniently ignore. The conclusions I drew from my thoughts were troublesome, particularly since I returned to the relative safety of homebound normalcy. In retrospect, while my discovery solved this mystery, it only opened more grotesque questions that may never be answered. For instance, the day after I returned to New York, I received a call from Eddie informing me that Huggy Bear was found dead in his room at Rusk—drowned in his toilet. I wasn't surprised; justice has a way of eventually working itself out down in Texas, thank God. How, I don't want to find out.

Yet what happened after I returned home was what disturbed me the most, and gave me reason to keep much of what I have experienced to myself. Simply put, when I looked down at my daughter lying in her crib that night I was able to discern significance in the way she stared at me with her dark green eyes.

I picked her up and whispered, "There you go, girl. I did what you asked."

She smiled, a twinkle of gratitude in her expression. And, as it was when I held her in my arms after I first saw the girl's photograph, I knew what she meant.

THE HEAD

by Melissa Mia Hall

William called Taylor Brent, the real-estate woman after the first flush. It had to be some sort of joke. What kind of toilet deodorizer came in blood red? It was supposed to be pine green or brilliant sea blue or even a satisfying no-color bleach bubbling with sanitary glee.

"You're kidding me, right?" He laughed in what he hoped was a vaguely seductive way. His latest divorce had left him unusually uncertain about his ability to attract available females. William had secretly wondered if he had bought the house because the price was right or because Taylor had been willing to go out with him to close the deal. "Red for Valentine's Day?"

"Red what?"

"Toilet water, you know, in the commode." The silence on the other end made him very nervous. He thought he detected a hushed snicker, then the sound of another call trying to get through.

"Um, William, I have to take this call. Listen, I'll get back to you. You've probably got plumbing problems. Rust, maybe?"

The line went dead. Great legs. Black hair. Skin like ivory snow. So maybe he'd never see her again. She was too pretty, taut, unbelievably successful for her age. Had to be still in her twenties. Maybe early thirties. Could still sell post-earthquake real estate in Los Angeles and San Francisco. Sold some to him, in fact, in post-fire, postflood Malibu. A great buy, really cheap. So he wanted to live on the edge for a while. He'd stopped practicing medicine, had made some incredibly great investments in the movie business and computer games. He'd wanted to live out a beach fantasy, to live by the sea, maybe learn how to surf. When he was a kid growing up in central Texas, the Beach Boys were his favorite group, not the Beatles or the Stones.

And, in the meanwhile, there was blood in the second-floor

toilet of his handsome new house. And it smelled funny. So maybe it was just a plumbing problem. Or maybe he was losing his mind.

William stared at his cordless phone. He snapped the antenna down and looked up the circular iron stairway. She had told him the last owner had poured an enormous amount of money into renovation. Imported tile, marble, elaborate designer fixtures. Stark black and white set off by silver accents. On impulse he had bought thick red towels. He had since decided to replace them with charcoal gray.

The house had three bathrooms, one upstairs and two downstairs. The water in all of the commodes except for the master bedroom's looked suitably normal. Maybe if he looked again, the commode water would be clear. It was possible his eyes had just fooled him again. They had been fooled before, especially by women who had impressed him with beauty that inevitably faded, either due to encroaching fat, age, or a sudden irreversible attack of bad taste. His past three wives had all gone to seed in this fashion.

The first wife, busty Brenda, his old college sweetheart (rah rah LSU), had gained twenty pounds or more during the two years they spent together. Big boobs were okay but forget the love handles and fanny pack—she probably was packing an extra fifty pounds by now. He hadn't seen her in ten years or more. She had remarried since their short, ill-advised marriage aborted during his residency in Houston. She'd paired up with some lout ex-football-player-turned-café-owner in New Orleans. He'd heard she'd had four kids after their own daughter Dana died so suddenly and tragically, of SIDS—sudden infant death syndrome. What they used to call "crib death." William sighed. He was sorry about that. But Brenda had somehow blamed him. Then she'd wanted another baby and he'd wanted out. She was just so clingy, needy, and fat. What a waste of a political science degree.

Meredith, his second wife, he'd met at a producer's birthday party in Brentwood. At the time he'd been impressed by her golden California tan, blond-streaked hair, willowy figure, and bodacious acting talent. She'd been in two blockbuster features and had been a rising star. Then they got married and she wanted a baby. A terrible idea, that. He had finally gotten her to drop it. Her career started wimping out because she began spending entirely too much time baking in the sun and began to get horribly boring. By the time they'd divorced, she had skin like a crocodile, looked like she was fifty, and the poor thing was only what—thirty-five—and had taken dieting to a new low and ended up anorexic, in and out of rehab clinics he was still paying the bills for. What a waste of a once talented actress, now unable to get any parts except those of washed-up alcoholics or country-club matrons!

Then, last but not least of the fading beauties was his third wife, Lizanne, the hideous girl-child, ex–MTV V-J, and Paris model he had recently shaken loose. Her looks had been ruined by a descent into self-righteous feminist posturing. She had chopped off her luxuriant auburn mane, dropping her cutting-edge fashion genius for a back-to-basics blahness that was both depressing and grim. Save the rain forest, save the animals, and picket, picket, picket. What a waste of a modeling career!

He punched the realtor's phone number again.

"Hello?"

"Taylor, I want you to come over and see this."

"William? I said I'd get back to you—"

He was standing in the bathroom again. Looking at the blood in the toilet. "I think it's a deal breaker."

"Excuse me? You own that house now. It's too late to back out."

He looked into the mirror at the head. At the horrible circles under the eyes, at the maggots crawling out of the corner of the mouth.

The phone fell from his grasp and tumbled to the floor. It made a hollow noise, a breaking sound, then he heard a meaningless buzz that meant Taylor wasn't listening.

A water bug crawled over his handmade leather loafer. The size of it impressed him. He tried to crush it with his toe, but it scuttled away, crawled into a crack near the shower stall.

He hated showers, especially this one. The door was supposed to be unbreakable. The crack he'd noticed this morning had gotten suddenly wider. Taylor hadn't pointed that out. He had a right to complain.

Hot in here. William turned to look at the wall switch. The heater was on. He couldn't remember turning it on, but maybe he thought he'd flicked the light switch. That could be fixed. He turned off the heat as sweat dripped down the back of his collar. He wiped his neck and then stared incredulously at the blood on his hand. How had he cut himself? He took his shirt off and looked for bloodstains. There were none. His hand was now clean. Had he imagined it?

Another water bug scuttled across the floor and hesitated in front of him. William quickly smashed it with his foot, congratulating himself this time on his excellent aim. He picked it up with a piece of toilet paper and pitched it into the commode, eyeing the suddenly clear water with disdain.

Impossible! He flushed and watched the water go down and return noisily in fits of frothy red. Better. He wasn't making this up. No way. It looked suddenly familiar. A woman's head arose from the macabre bowl like a mermaid's, hair streaked with blood but face breathtakingly beautiful. Her chin tilted upward and her blank eyes seemed etched with icy cobwebs. Laura? He hadn't thought about Laura in a very long time. He was never married to her. They broke up after that mess in Galveston, a hundred years ago.

Behind him the nearly transparent door to the shower stall suddenly opened. William heard the sound with a clutching to his gut, a rushing horrible fear that someone with a knife had been hiding there, invisible but real. He looked into the mirror above the washbasin and saw a woman's naked torso missing a head.

"William, I need you." The voice came from the commode.

The hair on William's neck rose. He felt like a cartoon in one of those EC comics he loved when he was a kid. He visualized a balloon with unspeakable sounds like "eech—yow! #!* Eeek-OHMY—G-G—" issuing above his head. The humor of the situation had not escaped him. Some woman's joke. His bravado returned, his old sense of his devil-may-care attractiveness. He could always get the girl. He always had a date to the prom. He could always get laid. His life wasn't over. Some girl was crazy over him and she had a wicked sense of humor. The torso had to have a head. His eyes were just fooling him.

"And you are?" he said with more bravado than he actually felt.

Before his eyes the torso disintegrated. He looked around wildly, hoping that someone would appear and explain what had happened. He searched the bathroom frantically for proof of the practical joke. All he could find was a pool of blood on the floor.

Despite this alarming turn of events, William felt oddly relieved. There was an explanation for everything. The bathroom was, quite simply, haunted.

The tightness in his shoulders relaxed. William took a deep breath and smiled at the hideous face in the mirror now featuring long bleeding scratches on its cheeks and, really, only a superficial resemblance to William himself.

He hit redial. "Taylor, get over here now. I don't care what you're doing. You owe me!" He cut the connection off and exited the bathroom in full sweat. His Obsession for Men mixed with the scent of terror clinging to him like a dirty bathrobe, William took the stairs in record time.

It took a while to get his breath. He stood in his immaculate living room and stared at his expensive artworks and leather sofa. The last tenant had had impeccable taste. He'd left the sofa and one of the paintings, a watery rendition of a very depressed young lady who had either slit her wrists or poured maple syrup over them. It was hard to figure out which.

Thankfully, an hour later, as William sat on the edge of the cold sofa, the door buzzed. He let Taylor in with an enormous loopy smile on his lips. "I'm so glad to see you!"

Taylor brushed the dark hair from her forehead with her sunglasses. "So what's the crisis? Are you hurt—what?" A little breathlessly, Taylor went past him, checking the house suspiciously. "Was there a break-in—did you have an accident?" She looked at him again, pausing in the middle of the living room. She bore more than a striking resemblance to his old girlfriend Laura. Odd that he'd never noticed before.

William was embarrassed. "The toilet, uh—the bathroom, I need to know what the story is. I mean, you didn't tell me about the history of this place. Was there a murder there—here? I mean, I think it's haunted."

Taylor sort of giggled into her hand. "Yeah, right. William, have you been sleeping okay? Do you think maybe you ought to, you know, see someone? If you're having problems, like seeing things, that indicates to me that you might need some, uh, counseling."

She walked to the kitchen, William following her like a pet poodle. He wanted her to pet him. For the first time in his life since his childhood, since maybe when Dana died, William was scared.

"Got any Evian?" She pulled open the fridge. "Jeez, look at all the booze in here. When was the last time you ate any healthy food, William?"

"Let's go out to eat."

"I really can't spare the time. I've got to go check out this place in the Hollywood Hills some actor trashed, see what it's going to take to put it out on the market." She undid the cap on an Evian. "You sure scared the pants off of me."

William took that as an invitation. Old programs are hard to erase. "Is that right? Let me see—" He pushed her against the fridge and put his hand up her red skirt. No panties, just a tiny slip!

She screamed. "Pervert—" The water spilled on William's unzipped pants and wilted his pride.

"Sorry—I just get so lonely."

"Try the personal ads or call one of those sex numbers. Seriously, William, aren't you getting a little old for the playboy routine? I mean it's not like you look like Robert Redford or anything. Maybe I can fix you up with my mother."

She didn't bother to wipe up the water. After smoothing her skirt and checking her lipstick, she headed for the door.

William ran after her. "Was there a murder or a ghost, something you didn't tell me about in this house?"

"Sure, but what house doesn't have a sad story connected to it?"

"And?" He eagerly followed her to the door. She stood in a patch of foggy sunlight, her face a dark, unreadable blob.

"Her name was Louise or Laura—yeah, Laura something. She fell in love with this guy her father didn't approve of. They lived here—the guy and the girl—for a while and she got pregnant and she lost the kid in the bathroom, you know, a miscarriage, and then she died. And the murder? The father killed himself after killing the boyfriend. Really grisly. Maybe incestuous complications. Rumor had it, it was the father's kid, not the boyfriend's, and the boyfriend found out and there was this big fight and all. Truly terrible."

William sucked his breath in and held it for a second. The release of his breath seemed to empty out his whole soul. The fear was all that was left. "Is that it?"

The laugh sounded devilish. "No. The next tenant killed himself over the death of his wife and the next one killed herself over the death of her pet beagle."

"You're kidding me."

Taylor turned toward her Porsche. "Yeah, I am. The whole story is a lie. Nobody ever died here that I know of. William, I think the whole bathroom stuff is a hallucination. I mean, who gives a shit?"

William followed her out to the car. "Taylor—what are you saying—the first story is a lie—there really were no murders here?"

Taylor adjusted her sunglasses. "Maybe psychic murders or broken hearts, but no bloodletting that I've ever heard of." She sighed. "I could fix you up with my mom. She's only forty-eight."

"Cool." William took the phone number from Taylor's white and graceful hand. His shoulders sagged. Back to square one.

Could he stand dating someone his own age? Wouldn't that be a step down in his evolution as a bachelor? William just didn't want to be alone anymore. Maybe a mature woman would help him with his problem. If he could see someone who would understand and be compassionate, nonjudgmental, someone who had been there, done that—it was worth a try.

Lilli Brent looked really good for her age. She toyed with her grilled salmon salad and said something so softly he couldn't quite catch it. Her legs tantalized him, hem lengths shorter than her daughter's. Pale blond hair. Tight abs. Gorgeous breasts. Had to work out at least five days a week. Seductive eyes, long lashes, and only a vague circle under each, kind of like Susan Sarandon's.

William knew she didn't really want to be there at the café. She probably wanted to be at his home, in his arms, kissing passionately. There was, after all, a passion between them, a small fire that could be coaxed into a feverish bonfire. He sighed. One could dream. Taylor's mom looked like a cross between Loni Anderson and Brigitte Bardot (at thirty).

"I don't know what you're talking about. A haunted bathroom? That's absolutely ridiculous."

He couldn't figure it out. His luck with women had been running out for some time. It was just hard to admit it to himself.

She checked the time, took a call from her cellular phone, then smiled at him with what he suspected was more than a hint of pure derision.

"So, William, what do you want to do with this bathroom thing? I think you could call in a parapsychologist or maybe a shrink and do something about it. Put your mind at rest. Have you been getting enough sleep? Insomnia can be a killer, you know." Her phone buzzed again. "Excuse me—" She rattled on and on about a dentist in Beverly Hills while William ate his swordfish.

She had no interest in him whatsoever. She'd even had the nerve to mention his receding hairline and to suggest a place that specialized in male pattern baldness. Maybe it was because he wasn't active enough socially and hadn't been to any of the important L.A. parties lately. Maybe it was time to start doctoring again. Except, to be honest, that malpractice suit in Texas had kind of put a stop to that. It was hard to be rich, bored, and so unfulfilled.

Finally, during dessert she put the phone away and apologized. "I really know just how rude it is to talk during a meal with such a nice man, but my life is like a roller coaster. You see, I've fallen in love with my dentist. We're getting married. I didn't want to just blurt it out, but Taylor doesn't know yet. We just decided yesterday as he finished my latest crown."

"Oh." William licked the mousse off his spoon. He dreaded going home. Maybe it was time to find a new house. True, he'd only been at the current new one for six weeks, but maybe he wasn't cut out for California.

The threat of earthquakes, riots, fires, floods had bothered him for some time. At first he had enjoyed all of the excitement. After the second divorce, from the perennially troubled actress, he'd needed distractions, so he settled here. But after his disastrous marriage to Lizanne, he had also needed to be reminded that he was, after all, a survivor and nothing fate could dish out could beat him.

He recalled the January ninety-four earthquake. He had not been anywhere near Northridge. He had been asleep in the Brentwood house he'd leased for a short time. "This is it," he'd cried, pushing the naked starlet he was with out of bed. He'd picked up Natalie something-or-other the night before at some bar. She kept saying, "Are we gonna die, baby—are we gonna die?"—driving him nuts. Never saw her again. He probably should have, just to see if the house she shared with her mom in Sherman Oaks had been damaged. But it was best not to get involved with bimbos. The poor kid hadn't even attended college, had "acted" in a couple of low-budget horror flicks. Only thing Nat was good for was standing around naked and screaming. He could hardly remember what her face looked like, but he could still remember her buttocks; so firm, so round. He had moved from Brentwood shortly thereafter.

The cleaning service he hired to get the place in shape for the new realtor cleaned the bathroom thoroughly. He had not listed it with Taylor's company. Shame kept him from calling her. He didn't want to hear her laugh at him again.

William's hallucination or ghost or whatever appeared to have taken up permanent residence. William couldn't bear to be in the bathroom for more than a minute or so. Whenever he looked in the commode, there was blood. Whenever he looked into the shower stall, the sad woman called out to him and vanished.

A pain suddenly hit him as he inspected the gleaming toilet. Gas. He needed to go. No time to run downstairs.

He pulled his pants down and proceeded to groan. His stomach ached and he broke out in a sweat. Hurry! He wouldn't look down, mustn't look down. Just get it over with, he prayed.

He heard a soft gurgling moan. The distinct possibility of teeth sinking into the soft flesh of his buttocks made him tremble with fear and haste. He finished his business and jumped up, flushing the commode briskly without checking the color of the water or his stool.

"William—"

He zipped his pants and refused to turn around to see the ghost woman in the shower stall.

"William—"

The voice came from inside the commode.

A fat water bug ran across his toe.

The head rose again from inside the commode. An irresistible Medusa. Glistening snakes writhed on top of her hair and slid down to the floor. William did a dance to avoid them, all the while telling himself they were not real. His fear could not make him turn away. The woman's head spun around and became a man's head. A gargoyle, a monster, but it bore a distinctly familiar rakish air. A William touch, a dimple, a sneer.

"Flush it down the commode, old buddy, old friend. Pretend it didn't happen, pretend I don't exist."

The voice crackled like static electricity.

William resolved to move out immediately. He knew there was nothing wrong with him. It was this house, this bathroom. William was a good man. He never did anything deliberately wrong or cruel. The problems with women couldn't all be due to him. Women just changed too quickly, mutated like something dosed with weird radiation. At first they were so beautiful, deliciously tempting, like gift boxes all wrapped with ribbon and lace, glittering with tinsel and secrets. But after all the wrapping was discarded, William kept finding empty boxes. Women were all empty boxes. Some had soft tissue paper in them that would slip from his hands. Others had coarse paper in them that he had to wad and discard in the nearest trash can. Still others had shredded confetti in them that got all over the carpet and had to be vacuumed up. But every woman he'd gotten involved with had nothing inside of any worth. The trappings disappeared, leaving only ugly brown cardboard boxes that had to be recycled.

Discarding women after opening their boxes and being disappointed seemed the best choice. He could always find a new one. Maybe he was a perfectionist. Maybe he was cruel, but he didn't deserve this hallucination or this ghost, whatever it was. Usually the women appeared just as dissatisfied with him as he was with them by the time divorce proceedings were concluded.

The new house in Seattle was near the water, but not as close to the water as the Malibu house had been. Funny how living by the ocean was soothing. You didn't have to swim to appreciate the sound of crashing waves.

William bought a diet clinic and enjoyed dropping in from time to time to see what success his partner, Tyrone, was having with his overweight clients. Their program combined vitamin supplements, exercise, a sound diet plan, and some drug therapy; it seemed to be going well.

But William was still single, lonely, and depressed. He seemed to have lost his touch with women. It seemed as if he radiated bad karma or something.

There were three bathrooms at the new house. They were totally ghost free, extremely normal, and safe to enter. Until he had lived there for three months.

Then it all began again. In all three bathrooms. A ghost woman cried in each bathroom, water bugs, snakes, blood, and Lovecraftian heads (all with a strange resemblance to William on a very bad hair day) gazed down upon him from mirrors and commodes. William began to believe he was being punished for some heinous crime.

He began to believe it was because of Dana, the lost baby. Because of what happened such a long time ago. When he was so young. Maybe he had been cruel to divorce Brenda just because he didn't want children. After Dana's premature death he hadn't wanted to try again. Nothing could replace that sweet little thing, so innocent and fragile. A little angel that had flown away too soon. The crib had been his mother's. Brenda still had it, had seen nothing wrong with keeping it, and she'd probably used it for her other children. It seemed morbid to him. He should've burned it, given it away to the Salvation Army. It wasn't the crib's fault. She had just passed away one morning looking at her soft animal mobile that played Brahms's lullaby. It was Brenda's fault, if blame could be attributed to anyone. She should've watched the child more carefully, been more aware that her breathing was too shallow. It was a woman's duty to be vigilant. If she'd just been more vigilant. If he had—

William wiped away his tears. The rain in Seattle could be overwhelming. He sipped his coffee laced with brandy and sniffed. He could move again, but he was afraid any house would include a bathroom haunted by women in showers and heads in toilets and mirrors. Blood.

It wasn't his fault she died, nor was it Brenda's.

On impulse one day he called her, just to see if she was happy. She was. Her voice had been so distant. "Is that you, William? Gee, I thought you had died."

Maybe he had.

He called his second wife a month later, on yet another rainy cool day. Meredith had remarried, a screenwriter she called Pogo. She had given birth a few months earlier to twins, a boy and a girl they'd named Ian and Amanda. She was also set to star in the next Spielberg movie. Meredith didn't sound as distant as Brenda; her joy kept breaking into the conversation. She didn't blame him for their disappointing marriage.

"We just weren't right for each other. I kept wanting you to fill a void only I could fill. No wonder I was always starving. I kept thinking I was never thin enough—good enough for anything. And you know—I am—I am good. And William—I can eat a whole meal now. I have to. I must stay healthy for my kids.

"Pogo is so good with the babies. He never complains—well, maybe a little about poopy diapers—but let's face it, so do I! I know you never wanted kids, William, and I'm not angry anymore because you didn't. I've come to accept that there are some people who aren't meant to have children. But I've also realized that no one has the right to choose for you."

William cried after they disconnected. He was jealous and happy for her at the same time. Meredith now seemed to have been one box that had more than throwaway tissue paper in it. He wished for more than a moment to have her back again so he could see what was at the bottom of her box.

A month later he called Lizanne. She was not glad to hear from him.

"Who gives a flying fuck about your damn problems, Will—I mean who? Leave me alone. Get a life—I'm getting this phone number changed tomorrow—"

Silence.

William sighed. That night he visited each bathroom. He washed his face with steaming blood from the hot faucet and rinsed with icy water from the cold side that stung his cheeks and left gashes. He lit a candle in each shower stall so each ghost lady could have some warmth. He kissed each Gorgon's head as each rose to warn him of his impending doom.

"Remember the crime. . . ." each whispered as William stripped naked and stared at the scars on his legs, where long ago a young woman had stabbed him in a fit of grief.

A girl named Laura.

He wasn't married to her.

She was just a girl he had sex with and lived with for a time in Galveston before he married Brenda.

How she had grabbed her abdomen. How she had cried.

The toilet water rinsing off the blood. The commode flushing.

Laura hanging her head over the bowl. "It's gone, it's gone. What are we going to do?"

He hadn't remembered it for a long time.

"You flushed it down the commode. Oh, William—I need you—I need you—make it stop hurting."

The phone began ringing.

"Hello, you've reached William's voice mail, please leave a message after the beep and he'll get back with you."

"William, this is Laura. You might not remember me, but we have to talk. I need to tell you what it's like to be dead inside."

William's head was silent. It floated in the commode like a piece of raw meat studded with water-chestnut eyes.

He already knew. For years he had pretended he did not know what happened that night in Laura's bathroom. He'd opened a box that did not belong to him, had not liked what he found, so he killed it and flushed it down the commode. She had begged him not to, small, albeit a bit flabby in the stomach, Laura of the big blue eyes and soft, sexy laugh. The music student, scholar, fan of Debussy and Ravel. Dreamer. On a scholarship. Poetry lover. Fan of dogs and James Taylor, too. Liked chess and Monopoly only when you let her win.

His body started trembling. How he had ranted and raved about his life being sacred and inviolate. He had argued with her for days. She was so stubborn. Then he remembered how he had drugged and battered her into submission. How he'd threatened her with his lucky scalpel if she didn't agree that the baby was unnecessary and not welcome.

And now he did know what it was like to be dead inside. The memory had opened his own box and it was empty.

"Don't take it away from me—" she had begged him, but he was bigger, stronger, smarter, and going to be a surgeon. "You don't need a child. And I *won't* have a child," he'd said as she lost consciousness.

William opened the medicine cabinet above the lavatory and withdrew the scalpel he didn't have to use that long-ago night. He really used to call it his lucky scalpel, a reminder of how he had cut the cord to his younger medicine days. Now it was a souvenir of how everything began going wrong. He needed it now, for himself. The cut went deep. The head started laughing, then cried and was silent.

Everyone deserved to make their own choices. Laura didn't have one because he took it away from her.

And now he did not. Have a choice.

When he flushed the commode, the blood vanished, the ghost women sang, and the water bugs and snakes dissolved into a gold mist laced with butterfly wings.

Taylor's mother must've known Laura somehow, although the story Taylor told about the Malibu house had been grossly inaccurate—it was in Galveston that the murder occurred. And there was only one man involved and he didn't kill himself, just a fetus.

"It's been a long time, but I haven't forgotten you."

Lilli Brent appeared in the doorway and pulled off her blond wig to reveal short brown hair laced with white. Her beautiful face was streaked with tears and suddenly strikingly familiar.

"Oh Laura, my poor dear Laura—will you give me another chance? I'm different now; I've changed—" the head begged. "You had another baby—you had Taylor. Can't you forgive me, please?"

Laura dropped the scalpel, wiped clean of his blood, gently into the water. "I forgive you," she said, and flushed the toilet.

William rejoiced. The sacrifice had been accepted. She will now call 911 for help. He would not have to bleed to death.

"Laura—" he whispered with desperate longing.

Suddenly the apparition vanished as quickly as it had come.

He would have to save himself. He gripped the edge of the toilet bowl and summoned all the strength he had left to get on his knees. It was then that the little head with the tiny teeth chomped down on his hand and William fainted dead away. Maybe she had forgiven him, but he had not forgiven himself.

It had been a boy. William's free hand reached frantically for the flushing handle. "Let go of me—I said, let go—I'm sorry, okay? I was wrong, okay—please?"

The pain dissolved. William fell backward against the tile, blinking weakly at the bathroom ceiling. He grabbed a bath towel and held it tightly against the gash. The blood began clotting.

He would have to live.

The phone began ringing.

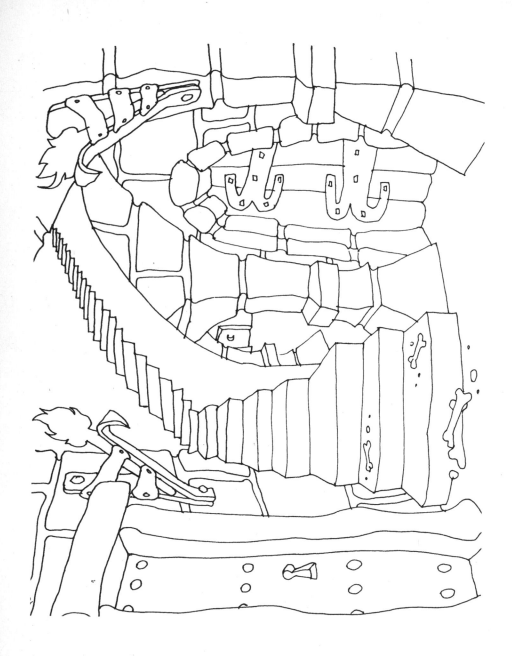

THE RATZ IN THE HALLS

by Gregory Nicoll

As the last scene of his life unspooled like broken film from a spinning metal reel, Stretch wondered how different it all might have ended if only he hadn't gone back alone to fetch the guitar amp. The torch on the wall was burning only dimly now, its faint gasoline smell giving way to the dank, penetrating musk of the dirty basement corridor. The air was viciously cold, and Stretch tugged with desperation at the chrome zipper of his jacket, its slide rasping against blood-soaked leather.

If only he hadn't gone back alone for that amp . . .

Up until then, everything had been cool.

They'd all met at sunset by the warehouse, and for once everybody actually showed up on time—even Laurie and Chris. He'd even turned the volume up high on his beeper, preparing for one of their inevitable sorry-but-we're-gonna-be-late-again calls. He was delighted to discover that tonight this precaution was unnecessary.

Hey, Stretch thought, sometimes you just live right. . . .

Since all of the band's stuff was already stowed neatly in their Chevy Suburban when they got there, the only thing he and Zann had to do was pack the cameras and the lighting gear into the remaining space before they set out for the location. The load-out was done in no time, and they were all on their way. Stretch led the others in his Volkswagen, his arm hanging out the window to gesture warnings of various hazards once they left the main road and rolled across open fields.

Night had fallen by the time they arrived, but the moon was almost full and it sure didn't take movie lights to make the deserted mansion look as eerie as the set of a Boris Karloff late show. Everyone was impressed by the scary old place, and three times Stretch had to repeat the story about how his pal Kelly had found this spook house while he was out on his motocross bike.

"Kelly was your friend who got killed, right?" asked Laurie, with her typical mixture of bluntness and compassion. "He was the one in that motorbike wreck you were telling us about, wasn't he?"

Stretch nodded. "Uh, yeah. In fact, this video is gonna be dedicated to Kelly." His voice became lower. "Kelly was a helluva guy. Did Chris tell you that my phone number is 555-FILM? Well, I got the idea from Kelly—his home phone was 555-BIKE."

Laurie smiled. "Mac told me you wanted the band to write a song called '555-BIKE'!"

"Yeah, that was one idea I had," Stretch said quietly, "but then I figured out I could do a tribute to him of my own—by shooting your video out here, at this cool place he found, and I could dedicate the whole project to him. Chris has already got the titles keyed in for me on his computer."

"Cool," said Laurie as she unclicked the latches on her guitar case. She hefted out a sleek blond-wood Fender electric bass, an instrument as slender and as filled with potential as Laurie herself. Her long blond hair hung down as straight as the bass's four strings. "Whenever you're doing something artistic," she said, "it always means so much more if you have a special person in mind when you're doing it."

Chris stepped over and wrapped his powerful arms around her, the black leather of his Brando jacket creaking as they embraced. "So do you think about *me* when you write your music, Laurie?" he asked.

"Of course I do," she whispered, kissing him softly on his cheek. "Don't you think about *me* when you load a reel of film into your Bolex?"

Chris grunted and squeezed her more tightly.

Stretch nudged Chris's shoulder and pointed at the camera cases. "I hate to break up a romance, but how about you think of Laurie *while you set up the cameras,* okay?"

Chris took the hint and got right to work. Zann had already fired up the little generator and had hung a series of electric lights leading down the basement steps. Now she was clearing trash from under the staircase, stuffing it into a huge plastic bag. Laurie and the rest of the band—Mac, Katy, and Ann—were busy bumping their instrument cases down the long stone staircase. Alternately they cursed at the major bitch this task had become and did bad impressions of Bela Lugosi in *Dracula* as they realized how much the cellar of this old place resembled a set from a 1930s Universal Pictures monster rally.

The basement was musty and cold, with a faint smell of something vaguely dirty and unpleasant. It was a relief when Zann finally opened a can of gasoline and began soaking the end of a torch with it, because the piercing scent of the fuel covered up everything else. When she finally lit it, the explosion of light and warmth drew gasps of joy from the entire group.

Then, as the torchlight settled into a rhythmic flicker, the hall took on a strangely menacing aspect. The crew fell silent. Mac had just finished tuning his guitar, and he jokingly played a melody from *Swan Lake*. Nobody laughed.

"This place is *creepy*," Katy declared, holding on to her microphone like it was a billy club.

Ann nervously tapped her drumsticks together. "Really, *really* creepy."

"There's something *in the air* here," whispered Laurie. "Spirits . . . "

"But that's what we're here for," Stretch reminded them, "the *atmosphere!* This is gonna be the spookiest music video ever made." He looked over at the staircase and smiled. "Zann, I love what you've done with those bones over there."

Zann shrugged. "I found those under the staircase. I guess they're from a dog or a deer that died here. It looks like rats chewed on them."

"Rats?" snapped Katy. "There are *rats* in this place?"

Mac smiled. "Of course. We're the Ratz."

"This isn't funny. I don't like being around any rodents."

"Then why," quipped Mac, "did you join a rock-and-roll band?"

Stretch loudly cleared his throat. "Look, everybody, the sooner we get started, the sooner we can leave and head back to the warehouse for the wrap party."

Slowly, the magic began to happen. Stretch only referred briefly to his storyboards, preferring to run on pure instinct as he directed the shooting. Chris was always one step ahead of him with the camera setup, syncing his steadicam moves precisely with Stretch's concepts. Zann darted in and out of the shot, doctoring this wall or that with just the right squirt of aerosol "spiderweb," glycerine "perspiration," or "fog" from the rattling beesmoker.

The band got into the groove right away, and to Stretch's

amazement, nobody complained about the minimum of three takes he insisted on for each shot. "One for me," he'd say, "one for Kelly . . . and one for Eastman Kodak." Over and over throughout the evening, the Ratz hammered out their song "The Collect Call of Cthulhu" from the new *Exham Priory* CD, each time pumping it with just as much enthusiasm as they had the first time. Katy flitted from door to door along the dark cellar corridor, whirling in place to sing each verse framed by a different stone archway. Mac improvised a Karloffian shuffle down the staircase, striking a power chord on his bloodred Gibson SG guitar as he staggered at each step. Laurie leaned against the wall under the metal torch holder and let the flame glow like a crown of fire on her hair as she flailed away on her bass. Ann pounded the drums so hard that Zann suggested they all wear hard hats for fear the whole building would collapse on top of them.

Stretch's only regret was that his pal Kelly had not lived to see this. Kelly had loved it when Stretch was there to watch him win at motocross; and conducting a successful video shoot was as close as Stretch would ever come to achieving that kind of glory. And without Kelly, he never would have found this cool place to make the little video that was going so incredibly well.

It was half-past midnight when Stretch finally let out a long sigh and announced, "That's a cut, that's a print, that's a wrap—and, ladies and gentlemen, *that's a video.*"

The gang's cheers echoed up and down the staircase, and along the lengths of the basement's long dark hallway.

However, loading out all the gear afterward was, unexpectedly, a major chore. Stretch's careful plan had not taken into account how much more difficult it was going to be to haul everything *up* from the basement than it was simply to roll-bump-toss it all down there in the first place. By the time almost all the stuff was dragged up to the waiting Suburban, nobody had the energy or the imagination to repack it carefully. Once the bulk of it was stuffed in there, the big Chevy's rear doors would barely close.

"Hey, Stretch," said Zann, "there's still one amplifier left down there. You're gonna have to take it in your VW."

Stretch wiped his forehead. He was sweating, from all the lifting and hauling, even in the night chill. He took one look inside the Suburban and realized that the musicians and the filmmakers were getting extremely eager to unwind at the wrap party. And, bless their hearts, they had all been so patient up till now that he didn't want to push them any further.

"I'll go back for the amp," he volunteered. "You guys wanna go on ahead without me?"

Their explosive *"YES!"* nearly popped the Suburban's windows from the frames.

Stretch gestured for them to drive off. "I'll be right along behind you guys, just as soon as I get that last piece of gear."

"And don't forget to put out that torch, too!" Zann called as she climbed into the front seat. She yanked the door shut and pointed forward. Mac gunned the engine and popped the big vehicle's transmission into gear.

Stretch gave them a thumbs-up and a farewell wave.

The long white Chevy Suburban pulled away, its taillights spreading a delta of glowing amber light on the ground. Stretch watched as it retraced the path across the open field, its lights growing smaller as they faded into the darkness, until at last they winked out like the last tiny ember at the end of a burned match.

He was alone now.

The night swirled coldly around him.

Zann had taken down all the electric lights; they and the little generator that had powered them were all safely aboard the retreating Suburban. It was dark outside here by the front steps of the old mansion. Stretch could barely make out the distant shape of his own car a few yards away. Except for the glow of the moon, the only illumination was the distant ghostly flicker of torchlight in the foyer. It danced up the staircase from deep in the basement, casting its glow from the open basement door, just inside the main hall.

Stretch took a deep breath of the chilly night air and went back inside. He started down the rough stone basement stairs, the soles of his boots making an awful scraping sound with each step. He wondered briefly why he hadn't noticed that noise while they were down here filming. Surely Chris and Zann and all the others must have made just as much noise with their boots. . . .

There was no handrail on either side of the staircase, so he braced himself against the wall to the right as he descended, using his hand spread flat against the dirty stone. At its highest point the staircase was almost twenty feet off the cellar floor. A drop from the left side would end with a most unpleasant connection against the solid stone surface below.

Halfway down the staircase, illuminated in a pool of flickering torchlight, was the amplifier. It was a small one, a battered Fender Squire that belonged to Mac. It was black, and the band name RATZ was stencil-lettered across its top and sides with white paint.

As Stretch reached down to get a grip on the amp, he heard a small, distant sound. Something moved deep inside the basement, rustling and skittering. He paused and listened carefully, but over the beating of his own heart and the throb of the blood in his ears, he could now hear nothing but the faint hissing of the burning torch. He took another deep breath, and then he bent down once more to hoist the amplifier.

The amp was hard and smooth in his bare hands, and although it was somewhat heavier than he had expected, Stretch managed to pick it right up and stand straight. He glanced at the burning torch and regretted that he had no convenient way of blowing it out or switching it off. He had already begun to dread the idea of making a second trip back down into this dark, deserted hellhole just to retrieve that torch. He wondered if it might be all right just to leave it there to burn out on its own.

But what if it set the place on fire? So what? The house was abandoned anyway, right?

No, he thought, there might be a forest fire or something. I've got to take that torch down and put it out, just as soon as this amp is safely aboard the veedub. . . .

He started up the steps, his boot heels crunching hard on the stones.

Something brushed against his right leg.

He kicked out with his right foot—and then wobbled with his heavy burden as he found himself dangerously off balance. He swung himself back to the left, and while still staggering under the weight of the amp, he felt something whip savagely against his left knee. It was smooth and slender but huge, like the tail of a giant rat.

Stretch let out a startled cry as he lost his balance. Somehow he managed to bring the amplifier straight down onto one of the stones steps with a resounding hollow CLUNG!—but he was not so lucky in controlling his own fall. Stretch felt himself rolling off the edge of the staircase. He clawed frantically for a grip and felt layers of skin peel painfully off the tips of his fingers as they rasped along the stones. At last he dangled from the top of the steps and, with a grunt of resignation, felt himself fall free.

As his body struck the cellar floor the explosion of pain in his right kneecap nearly made him pass out. He reached up desperately for anything to seize, and his hand batted against something slender and whiplike. Stretch let out a startled cry as he realized that *this* was the thing that had tripped him up, the object his imagination had transformed into the tail of a giant rat.

It was the electric cord of the amplifier.

He lay there for several minutes, blinking back the tears of pain and cursing his own stupidity. How could he have been so dumb, he asked himself, so completely careless? And how was he gonna get himself out of here? His right knee had taken the full force of the fall, and he felt certain that he wouldn't be able to walk again until he'd had some major surgery done on it.

Maybe, he thought, if I can pull myself back up to my feet, I can limp out to the car and . . .

But how to get back to his feet? He looked at the dangling amplifier cord. He watched as it swayed back and forth in the faint torchlight like a pendulum. Maybe, if he could get a grip on it . . .

Stretch reached out and caught the swaying black cord with his right hand. It was thick, made of rubber or plastic or something smooth and really stiff, and it had a heavy-duty three-prong plug on its end. He gripped it securely and began to pull. From up above on the staircase came a faint scraping sound, which stopped abruptly as Stretch continued to pull.

The plan seemed to be working. By gradually increasing his hold on the amplifier cord, Stretch started to raise himself up from the floor. His left leg straightened as he rose, taking on more of the weight of his body, and—

The electric cord abruptly went slack.

Stretch shot one terrified glance upward, just in time to see the Fender Squire tilt over the edge of the staircase and begin its violent descent toward him.

He was cut off in mid-scream by the sledgehammer blow of the amp as it smashed what remained of his leg.

Stretch revived sometime later to the sound of something moving near him in the dark. It was cold, and his legs and hands were caked with blood. He glanced up at the torchlight and noticed that it had faded considerably now.

How long did Zann say that thing would burn for? He dimly recalled that she'd replaced the torch with a fresh one at some point during the shoot, but he had no idea how long ago that had been. Glancing down the darkened corridor of the basement hall, he noticed what appeared to be several tiny points of light moving toward him. With a shock, he realized what they were.

Eyes.

The corridor had come alive with rats. *Rats!* The same rats that had gnawed bare the animal bones Zann found under the staircase . . .

Stretch let out a shriek as something moved on his hip.

Chirp-cheep, came its little electronic sound.

The tiny, faraway noise of his beeper going off seemed as out of place here as a marching brass band playing the theme from *Rocky,* but it had an immediate effect on the rats. They scattered, apparently spooked by the unfamiliar sonics.

Although he was still crumpled on the cold, dirty stone floor, Stretch managed to swivel his hips carefully and turn himself so he could see the digital display on top of the beeper. It showed the warehouse's phone number.

Great, he thought. They all got back to the warehouse and tapped the keg, and now that they're all probably way more than half-drunk, somebody finally got around to wondering where the hell I am. . . . Probably Chris or Mac . . .

He shuddered as he saw his damaged leg. The falling amp had damn near finished him off. His right foot now looked like a broken strawberry Pop-Tart.

If only he hadn't gone back alone for that amp . . .

Damn, he thought, no point torturing myself over it any further. At least I'm feelin' no pain. . . .

It was true. Something had cut off the sensation in his leg—a slipped disk, a pinched nerve—and at least he was spared the searing agony of feeling a major portion of his anatomy squashed like a cockroach under a boot. He wondered briefly if his cock would still work, and if he was looking at permanent below-the-waist paralysis.

Well, he thought, if I wind up cooling my heels in a wheelchair, at least I'll get all the best parking spaces. . . .

A few minutes later the rats returned.

It wasn't the sight of their glowing eyes, or even the faint skittering of their claws on the stone floor, that tipped Stretch off to their approach. This time, it was their stink.

Stretch thought perhaps that his sense of smell had become more acute, as if to make up for the loss of feeling in his lower body. The foul musk of the cellar was unbearable, and even the moss and lichen on the stone walls seemed to give off intense odors of their own. But the approach of the rats was just as alarming to his nostrils as it was to his eyes and his ears. They *stank*.

Perhaps it was the rats' dirty rumpled fur, liberally peppered with tiny crawling black parasites, or the awful carrion contagion of their breath. Maybe it was the fetid muck on their tiny clawed feet and their long pink wormlike tails. Whatever it was, the rancid smell coming from them nearly made Stretch hurl.

They moved closer, twelve of them—no, maybe as many as twenty—skittering up the corridor.

Stretch reached for his beeper. If only, he thought, if only a call would come through, *right* now . . .

Then he smiled. Of course, there was a way he could make the beeper go off without the benefit of an incoming call. It always chirped once when he shut it off and then on again.

He reached down, found the tiny smooth plastic knob of the on/off switch, and snapped it back and forth.

Chirp-cheep, went the beeper.

The rats turned and scattered.

Stretch triumphantly snapped the nob again and again: *Chirp-cheep, chirp-cheep, chirp-cheep, chirp-cheep.*

The rats were gone, lost from view somewhere in the distant darkness of the basement hall.

The beeper chimed shrilly. Another call was coming in.

Stretch looked down at the digital display and recognized Laurie's phone number. For a moment he was surprised that she remembered his number, but it quickly occurred to him that this might be Chris calling from Laurie's place. Besides, how hard was it to remember a phone number like 555-FILM? He had the late, great Kelly to thank for inspiring that.

Good ol' Kelly, the original Mr. For-a-Good-Time-Call-555-BIKE.

So—Laurie, or Chris, or Chris *and* Laurie were worried about him. Maybe Chris would drive back out here. Maybe—

Oh shit, he thought.

The digital display on the beeper was flickering weakly now, and the tiny red light beside it suddenly lit up: LOW BATT.

Great, he thought. Just great. The batteries are fixing to give out on the only thing that's keeping me from being eaten alive.

He smelled them again, the rats—the hungry, persistent rats. He took a deep breath and poised his thumb on the on/off switch.

Up above, the flame of the burning torch flickered like a strobe light, and then, with a final farewell hiss, it winked out.

Stretch could not see the rats at all now, for the basement was completely, absolutely dark. But he could hear them. And he could smell them.

God, could he smell them.

He waited until he felt the first brush of their awful fur against his arm before he began snapping the nob: *Chirp-cheep, chirp-cheep, chirp-cheep.*

The tail of one of them whipped against his cheek, but they dispersed like smoke in a gust of wind. Stretch snapped the nob again as they vanished, but the beeper's batteries were at last completely gone. There was no further electronic response from the tiny plastic device. It was dead.

And soon, thought Stretch, I'll be dead, too.

Damn. If only I hadn't gone back for that amp. If only I hadn't come up with the idea to shoot this video out here in the middle of godforsaken nowhere. I coulda been safe at home. . . .

Why the hell does anyone take crazy risks like this anyway? Why does anyone live like this, or ride a motorcycle like Kelly did, or—

"A ship in harbor is safe," whispered a voice behind him, "but that's not what ships are for."

Stretch felt like he'd been stabbed through the heart with an icicle. "What the—*who?*"

But he knew who it was. His voice caught in his throat. "Kelly?"

"I've been here the whole time, guy. You did great. I'm proud of you. You've got nothing to regret."

"Kelly? Kelly, how—I mean—*why,* why are you back?"

There was no response, no sound of any kind in the basement hall.

"Kelly? *Kelly?*"

There was no light at all in the basement hall. Stretch felt as though his eyes were duct-taped shut, or else plucked out entirely.

"Kelly. . . "

There was no smell in the basement hall. Stretch realized that his nostrils had failed just as the sensations of his lower body had.

Chirp-cheep.

Completely numbed from the hair on his head to the tips of his toenails, Stretch glanced down at the dead beeper. Its digital displayed glowed with the number of an incoming call.

The caller's number was *555-BIKE.*

Chris tapped the ash off the end of his cigarette and looked up at the monitor screen. The air in the tiny editing studio was heavy with smoke, the scent of cold metal hardware, and the smell of warm wiring and transistors. Chris shook his head as he gestured at the screen. "It's brilliant, isn't it?"

Laurie smiled and brushed a strand of her long blond hair from her face. "It's incredible, Chris, just incredible. I don't think the band has ever looked so good."

Chris depressed the rewind button and the image on the big screen stuttered into high-speed backward motion. Tiny tracking lines flickered across the image. Guitar strings vibrated hard, then went stone still as the musician's fingers flew up to seize them briefly before whipping away as if the strings were hot to the touch.

"I'm still trying to figure out this part right here," said Chris. "The sequence where Katy is singing as she walks from door to door down the hallway."

"I still can't believe she did that," said Laurie. "She was such a scaredy-cat about the rats down there, but once you started rolling that shot and Stretch gave her the cue, she just headed right on down there and did it with no problem. She was great. I was gonna say something about it at the time, but I thought she'd snap out of it. It was like she had a guardian angel watching over her."

Chris brought the spinning tape to a stop and carefully cued up the corridor shot. "Maybe she did. Catch this action here." He pointed at the upper left corner of the monitor screen.

The scene played just as it had played a hundred times before, through days of previewing the raw footage, through transferring the film to digital video, and through a week of intense editing. Katy stood in the corridor with her dark hair and heavy makeup, looking like a miniature Elvira. As she sang, walked, sang, and walked farther, eerie shadows played on the walls behind her.

"There," said Chris, pressing the pause button. "Right *there.*"

Laurie squinted and leaned closer to the screen. "You mean this gray-and-white thing right here?"

Chris nodded. "What does it look like to you?"

Laurie's forehead creased. "Well . . . sorta like . . . I don't know. . . . Maybe, uh . . . two guys on a motorcycle?"

The cigarette fell from Chris's lips. He flicked it off his lap and stomped it flat on the studio floor. "*Two* guys? It looked like just *one* to me."

Laurie's hands traced the odd monochrome image at the upper left edge of the screen. There was a tiny crackle of static electricity as her fingertips met the glass. "No, it really looks like two. See? Here's the guy riding it up front. He has a helmet on and his hands are on the handlebars. And then *this*, this right here, it's a second guy who's riding right behind him and—"

Laurie's breath caught in her throat. Her face went pale.

"What is it?" asked Chris. He put his arm around her and squeezed her close against him. The smell of his leather jacket mingled with the warm cotton fuzz of her sweater.

"Laurie, talk to me. What's wrong?"

She lowered her eyes from the screen and shook her head. "Nothing's wrong, Chris." She leaned against his cheek, the stubble of his beard rough but somehow comforting against the smooth skin of her own face. "Nothing's wrong at all," she said quietly. "In fact, everything's right. It's just like it oughta be."

Chris hugged Laurie again and then leaned toward the screen.

"It's Kelly," said Laurie. "Kelly's the one with the helmet. The guy riding with him is—Stretch."

Chris squinted through his eyeglasses. He let out his breath slowly. "Heavy," he whispered. "That's heavy."

"You *are* gonna leave it in there, aren't you?" she asked.

Chris nodded quickly. "Oh yeah. In fact . . . " He pressed several buttons on the digital editing deck, and the video's brief credits sequence appeared on another screen. Gothic script scrolled briskly by. When the final line appeared, Chris paused the computer and made a minor edit.

Laurie smiled. "That's perfect."

The last credit now read: *Dedicated to the Memory of Kelly—and Stretch.*

Chris wrapped his right arm around Laurie. She encircled his waist with her left. As they hugged, Chris reached over with his free hand and switched off the equipment.

The computer's screen winked off instantly, the CPU's internal fan spinning slowly to a stop.

The overhead speakers crackled as the last jolt of electricity surged through them.

The image on the video monitor stuttered as the power was cut. Though the screen went dark, it glowed for a few seconds with a strange ambient light all its own. Nowhere was this light brighter than in the upper left corner, where a distorted, wheeled shape beamed with a peculiar brightness that lingered long after Chris and Laurie had stepped out of the editing studio, long after they had locked it up, and long after they strolled out into the starry night to love and to live for as long as fate would allow them.

As they turned the corner at the end of the block and headed toward Laurie's place, a motorcycle roared past them up the street, carrying two dark figures.

They smiled as it passed, and held each other tight.

AN EYE FOR AN EYE
by Norman Partridge

Wanda's eyesight was bad. She wore these clunky glasses with Catwoman frames and lenses thicker than a Fatburger, but they didn't prevent her from having extended conversations with department-store mannequins every once in a while. Anything a foot and a half past her nose might as well have been located on the planet Pluto as far as she was concerned, so it wasn't surprising that it took a dead black cat with a pair of bewitched glass eyes to show us the way to the house where Hollywood died.

The cat belonged to Madame Estrella, a geriatric fortune-teller who did readings for the low-rent crowd out by the beach. Ten bucks across her leathery palm and she'd tell you anything you wanted to hear. Not that she was all con and crapola, you understand. She could make some serious connections with the truth when she wanted to. The crone had some power, all right. Power rooted in ages past. Crystal-ball kind of stuff.

The old bat sure didn't have much to show for it, though, living as she did in a cramped stucco bungalow that hadn't been painted since the days of Rudolph Valentino. Liked the bottle a little too much, she did. Even so, her mojo could do some serious workin' when she put her mind to it, believe you me.

I mean, I saw well enough with my own two eyes what she did with the dead cat, and I've got 20/20 vision. It breaks down like this—the first time I saw the damn thing, it was *stuffed,* and I don't mean to say our feline friend had pigged out on Friskies. Uh-uh. This little pussy was a taxidermist's dream—gutted and stitched—just like Roy Rogers's famous horse, Trigger.

And that wasn't the only thing the dead cat had in common with Trigger. The kitty had been in the movies, too. Hissed at Karloff and Lugosi in *The Black Cat,* way back in 1934. When the little furball finally turned paws up and headed for that big litter box in the sky in the early forties, its trainer had it stuffed and sold the corpse to a collector—along with a copy of the kitty's contract with Universal Studios as authentication, of course. And then *that* fellow ended up beachside without a pension, at which point he traded the carcass to Estrella for some charms that were supposed to help him put the whammy on a curse.

Whatever she gave him didn't do much good, because a curse straight from the dark heart of Hollywood is a tough nut to crack. At least that's the way I figure it, looking back. But I'll get to that in a minute.

First up, our feline friend. In particular, said kitty's relationship with the powers of one aged fortune-teller. Like I said, I saw the cat—stuffed and mounted—the first time Wanda brought me to Madame Estrella's little stucco palace. It's like this—we're sneaking into the house, tripping through shadows because it's way too late and all the lights are out and Wanda's twice as blind in the dark as she is in the light. My eyes are quick to adjust, though, and just when I'm getting the lay of the land I come face-to-face with the furry terror that once stalked Boris and Bela. Damn thing is crouched on a bookshelf, at eye level, its lips twisted into an eternal snarl, and the moonlight spilling though the living-room window catches its glass eyes just right, and I'm thinking I see dark red pits inside those glowing green orbs, and I gasp just like some stupid ten-year-old, stumbling into Wanda while I'm at it.

Of course, a couple seconds tick off in the direction of eternity and I haven't been clawed to death, at which time I notice that the seemingly ferocious furball is about as mobile as Plymouth Rock. Wanda pokes her nose in the cat's face and realizes what has happened. She starts laughing at me, and I can't really hold that against her, even now. Then she whispers the story in my ear, cluing me in on the dead *gato's* career in Hollyweird.

"Damn," I said (and enthusiastically, because the cash register in my head was instantly *ding-ding-ding*ing). "If that story of yours checks out, this mangy kitty could bring us some serious *scratch.* Believe it or not, movie nuts will drop some major change for stuff like this. Even weird stuff. In fact, the *weirder* the *better.*"

"I don't know for a fact that the story is true, but it's direct from Madame's lips, and my sixth sense tells me that the old fossil believes it." Wanda winked at me from behind those Coke-bottle specs of hers. "Madame also says that her friend knows about a house that's filled with stuff that's way past *mondo* on the weirdness scale. He calls it *the house where Hollywood died.*"

"Oh yeah?" I said.

"Yeah." Wanda nodded.

"So where can we find Madame's friend? And how do we know he's on the level?"

"First question—I don't know; the guy hasn't been around in a couple of weeks. Second question—the great Madame swears that the story checks out."

"And what makes Her Magnificence so sure about that?"

"She's seen the place in her crystal ball, dummy."

"No shit?" says I, and none too quietly, because at that point my enthusiasm had really gone on the boil, crystal ball or no.

"No shit *whatsoever*," says Wanda, putting a finger to my lips. "But quiet down. We don't want to wake Madame. She can get kind of testy, believe me."

Quiet down I did, because I believed the stories Wanda had told me about the old fortune-teller's powers. After all, I'd seen Wanda do a spooky thing or two in the month I'd known her, so crystal balls were definitely entering my own personal realm of possibility.

Still, I pretty much forgot about Wanda's warning once we'd made it to the safety of her bedroom. We weren't too quiet then. Wanda didn't help any, of course. She'd purr like a kitten, and then she'd growl, and I'd laugh . . . and finally we got all that purring and growling and laughing out of our systems and fell asleep. But even then the money was never far from my thoughts, or my dreams. Too bad Wanda's warning about Madame didn't stick with me the same way.

Because the next morning when we woke up tangled in Wanda's sheets, the damn cat was right there in the middle of everything. It had traded in the Plymouth Rock act for something a tad more mobile, hissing and clawing for all it was worth while Madame Estrella cackled at us from the bedroom doorway.

It was then that I recalled Wanda's comment about Madame being *testy. Testy*, my ass. If a little bedspring symphony could cause the old biddy to raise a cat from the dead and send it scratching and clawing at the bedspring musicians who had offended her, I'd hate to see what she would have done if someone really got on her bad side. I'm gonna have scars, if I live that long. As for Madame—

I certainly didn't put up much resistance—I screamed bloody murder and tried to pull the covers over my head, but the kitty from hell shredded both blanket and sheet like two-ply toilet paper. Wanda was the one who sprang into action. She fumbled for her glasses and balanced them on her nose. Her eyes went all cold behind those thick lenses, and a couple of words in some weird foreign language boiled over her tongue, and suddenly the cat flew across the room and slammed into the wall.

Wanda blinked and Madame Estrella made like the cat. She jerked straight out of her shoes and shot backward, her bony skull cracking plaster as she hit the wall in the hallway, her dentures rattling.

Such abuse would have chilled me out, mere mortal that I am, but not Madame Estrella. The old bat managed to continue cackling like she had one of those novelty-store Bag o' Laughs hidden under her turban, like the whole thing was the best joke in the world. Even from a good ten-foot distance I could catch the mingled miasma of vodka and Polident on her breath.

"Good morning, dearies," was all she said.

"Grandma," Wanda said, her voice even and sure. "Sometimes I could just *kill* you."

Wanda didn't mean it, though.

Because when push came to shove, I was the one who ended up killing Madame Estrella.

Wanda wanted it that way, of course. Blood being thicker than water, and all like that. And though the end came pretty *viciously,* it wasn't like the whole thing was particularly *calculated.* Not in a *premeditated* way, anyway. I mean, we wouldn't have killed Wanda's granny unless we really *had* to, and we certainly didn't mean for things to get so *messy.*

Fact is, we tried to be really nice about it. After I was properly introduced, I went out and bought Madame a fifth of vodka. The good stuff—that expensive Russian kind. I bought her a pastrami sandwich, too. And a big bag of Cheetos.

"Breakfast of champions" was what Madame Estrella called it. She devoured the Cheetos and slammed down half the vodka, posthaste. Then she went to work on the sandwich, and we went to work on her.

"Wanda was telling me about the cat," I began.

Madame nodded, swallowed.

"She says it was a movie star," I said.

"*Ungh,*" came Madame's reply as she gobbled another healthy bite of pastrami sandwich.

"Wanda says you got it from a guy who's cursed or something?"

A thin rope of pastrami hung from Madame's mouth; she slurped it down like a raw red worm. "Cursed?" She grinned greasily, sparing me an appraising squint. "Is that what my Wanda told you?"

"Yeah," I said. "She said something about the guy being

cursed, and that he traded you the dead cat so you'd work up a charm or something." At that moment the not-so-dead cat brushed up against my leg and my spine went cold, but I pressed on. "Wanda said that this guy had other stuff, too. Or if he didn't actually *have* it, he knew where to *find* it. Hollywood stuff."

"*Rare* and *valuable* stuff," Wanda said. "Isn't that right, Grandma?"

"Now, you two don't go messing with *that*. My friend Mr. Arkoff is *cursed*. He *sees* things. The *ghosts* of Hollywood. The ghosts of *monsters*."

The last sentence came to us in a conspiratorial whisper, along with a shower of partially masticated bread crumbs.

We were quiet for a moment, and then Wanda pushed the crystal ball across the table so that it sat squarely before her grandmother. "Why don't you show us what he sees?" she suggested, her tone completely innocent. "I think Russell needs some convincing."

"Oh no," I put in. "I saw the cat. Anything your grandma says, I'll believe—"

Wanda cut me off with a sharp cough at that point, and I realized that I'd said the wrong thing. I tried to patch it up, saying, "But I'd sure be interested to see how a crystal ball works, Madame Estrella. If you don't mind, that is."

Madame grinned slyly, pushing the ball toward Wanda. "Why don't *you* demonstrate, my dear?"

Wanda tittered like a shy girl at a cotillion, adjusting her glasses. "Oh, Grandma. You know I don't have the sight the way you do."

"Bad genes, I'm afraid." Madame shook her aged head. "That father of yours, he was no good. *Blind as a bat,* to boot."

Wanda moped.

I sighed.

Madame took one last hit off the vodka bottle, then pulled the crystal ball her way, exhaling expansively. "All *right,* if you're both going to be so *childish* about it."

The old woman's hands were little more than arthritic claws, but they proved amazingly supple as they cut strange patterns in the air. For a moment her fingers settled over the glass globe. Smoke seemed to fill the crystal, clearing only when a few words crossed Madame's tongue, words that sounded surprisingly similar to the incantation Wanda had uttered in the bedroom.

A dull halo of light encircled the crystal. The picture that formed in the glass was hazy, like a poorly tuned television, but I could make it out. A shoddy room, similar to the place I rented down by the beach. There was a sagging couch in one corner, and a couple of figures sitting there.

The Frankenstein monster and Kharis the Mummy.

I didn't say a word, but my jaw literally dropped open. And then the perspective changed, as if a camera were doing a pan of the apartment. I glimpsed an open door . . . a bathroom . . .

. . . something big and green in the tub.

"The Creature from the Black Lagoon!" No sooner did the words cross my lips than the perspective changed again. I saw a window. Slivered venetian blinds. And beyond, in the distance, I could make out a signpost—

It didn't say THE TWILIGHT ZONE.

No. BUD'S GAS was what it said.

"Jesus!" I said, turning to Wanda. "It's the gas station across from my apartment! This guy Arkoff lives in my building!"

If Madame Estrella's eyes had been knives, Wanda would have been slashed to a bloody mess. "You little bitch!" the old woman screeched. "Just forget about it! You're not going to do it! And this dope of a boyfriend of yours isn't going to help you! You don't have the *sight,* Wanda! You weren't meant to have it!" Her arthritic hands floated before her, fingers twisting like rotten twigs. "Don't move an inch, either of you!"

Wanda moved, though. So did I, mostly because I wasn't crazy about being referred to as "this dope of a boyfriend of yours." Madame kept talking, but her voice had changed, and the words that spilled from her lips were spoken in that strange, unrecognizable tongue.

The old crone's eyes were surprisingly clear and bright, and they burned me to the core. I stumbled backward, but Wanda grabbed me. Held me tight. Whispered that everything would be all right.

It wasn't, though. I blacked out for a second, Wanda's voice a cold river of blood flowing in my head, a cold river that carried words in that strange foreign tongue.

I came to an instant later, and I was scared.

So scared that I was whimpering.

And that wasn't the worst of it. I was down on the floor, on all fours. My mouth was full of fangs. Madame teetered above me, laughing that Bag o' Laughs laugh of hers, and then she turned her attention to Wanda, saying, "Two legs or four, a coward is still a coward, dearie."

Her words scorched my ears. And suddenly I could feel Wanda there, right inside my head, and just as suddenly I wasn't scared anymore. I was mad—or Wanda was mad—I couldn't decide which, because both of us were in there.

One thing was for certain—a growl rose in my throat, and Madame's laughter died in hers. In an instant her eyes were brimming with fear.

She wasn't afraid for herself, though. No. She whirled surprisingly fast and snatched up the crystal ball. "Mr. Arkoff!" she screeched. "Listen to me! They're coming for you! They'll kill you! You've got to run! Hide! You've got to—"

That was when I sprang.

Madame tossed the crystal ball at me.

Missed.

My jaws gaped wide.

A few nasty syllables spilled over Madame's lips.

I tore open the old biddy's throat before the syllables could turn into words, and the words into an incantation that might do me harm.

Her throat was a tender and surprisingly tasty treat. I tasted pastrami marinated with a splash of vodka. I tasted Cheetos, too.

But what really made the meal was the taste of blood.

Wanda stood above me, wiping flecks of blood off her glasses. "You make a pretty good Doberman," she said. "I'd hate to be the one to clean up after you, though."

I was on the kitchen floor, leaning against a cabinet, not quite sure how I'd gotten there. All I knew was that there wasn't much left of Madame, my belly was full, and my muscles felt like they'd been twisted into knots that would defy David Copperfield.

The remnants of the crystal ball covered the floor like so many uncut diamonds. I immediately thought of Mr. Arkoff and his Hollywood booty, and I favored Wanda with a worried stare. "Do you think the old codger heard Madame's warning?"

"I don't know." Wanda finished cleaning her glasses and slid them on. She stepped over Madame's corpse, simultaneously treating me to an eager smile.

I got up off the floor, groaning. "So what do we do?"

"Why, we get our avaricious asses in gear, Russell," she said. "That's what we do."

From what we'd seen in the crystal ball, I figured that Mr. Arkoff's apartment had to be directly above my own. Checking the nameplates on the mailboxes near the lone staircase confirmed my suspicions. So, with bat-eyed Wanda holding my hand for support and the dead kitty bringing up the rear, I hurriedly climbed the staircase to the third floor, and Apartment 305.

Immediately, I knew that we were too late, because Mr. Arkoff's front door was unlocked.

Even so it was a little scary entering the place, because I remembered my visions of Frankenstein's monster, and Kharis the Mummy, and the Creature. But no one was sitting on the couch near the window, and the bathtub was empty. Still, I needed an explanation, so I mentioned it to Wanda, knowing the whole thing sounded crazy.

"It *is* crazy," she said, waving one hand at the apartment walls, which were crowded with movie posters and stills.

"Remember, the images we saw in the crystal ball came to us through Arkoff's eyes, and Arkoff believes that he is *cursed*, haunted by Hollywood's past. What we saw were his own private *ghosts*. His *delusions*."

It seemed a reasonable explanation. Wanda seemed sure of it, and at the time it satisfied me. Together, we turned our attention to searching the apartment.

Arkoff had left in a hurry. That much was obvious. A few drawers hung open in the dresser near his bed, and the cramped bedroom closet had been rifled as well.

I dropped heavily onto the bed, suddenly exhausted. The cat followed—pouncing quite gracefully, considering that it was dead—and settled on my belly.

"No telling where the guy has gone," I said. "Too bad the crystal ball got busted."

"The crystal wouldn't do us any good," Wanda corrected, tapping her thick glasses with one finger. "I don't have the sight, remember? And you ate dear old Grandma."

"Don't remind me," I said, my belly suddenly churning under the weight of the undead feline. I gave the cat a little push and suggested it settle elsewhere. "So what do we do now?"

Wanda paced for a couple minutes, thinking it over. "I think we've got to rely on the greed factor," she said finally.

"The greed factor?"

"Yeah." She took a deep breath. "I figure it this way—Mr. Arkoff heard Grandma's warning. Now, we know he took that warning seriously, because he's not here. So he's convinced that someone is after him, and he's got to have a pretty good idea why."

"The memorabilia?" I suggested. "The stuff he's got hidden away?"

"Right as rain, Sherlock." Wanda grinned. "Now, our friend Mr. Arkoff is scared, but he's also greedy. He's a hoarder. He hasn't sold off his treasure trove. Just look at this apartment—it's packed with stills and posters. The guy would rather live like a pauper than part with his collection. Leaving this stuff behind is probably killing him."

"So . . . what?"

"He *wants* that Hollywood stuff he's got hidden away. He wants it all for himself. That's his *real* curse. And I'm willing to bet that no matter how frightened he is, he's not going to leave town without it."

"Yeah," I said. "I can go along with that. But without Grandma and her crystal ball, how do we figure out where the stuff is hidden?"

Wanda bent down and scooped the cat off the bed. It purred huskily, a sound that made me think of sand and sawdust, and its glass eyes twinkled exactly like two miniature crystal balls.

"Grandma brought our feline friend back to life," Wanda explained, scratching the kitty under its chin.

I smiled, catching on. "And Mr. Arkoff brought the little fleabag to Grandma's, direct from the place where Hollywood died."

Wanda nodded, setting the cat on the floor and ruffling its fur. "Can you show us the way home, puss?" she asked. "You can do that, can't you?"

Just like the door to Mr. Arkoff's apartment, the front door of the house where Hollywood died was unlocked. Unfortunately, the door to the particular room we were interested in wasn't.

I've seen some doors in my time, believe me. But I'd never seen a door like this one, not in five years of serious B&E. Three brass knobs on the damn thing. Plus a lock for each knob, every one a burglar's nightmare. Someone's paranoia was running at a fever pitch, all right. But that little infobite warmed my mercenary heart, because it meant that we'd come to the right place.

"Can you open it?" Wanda asked.

I grinned and reached for my picklock. ASAP, I checked that action, because I was tired, and my powers of concentration were pulsing at near-Neanderthal ebb, and I was just about out of patience. We'd been three hours finding the place, following the cat hither and yon, and as far as I could tell we were directly in the middle of nowhere. Strictly Borgo Pass territory, if you remember your *Dracula*.

So I did the dirty with the worn heel of my boot.

The brass plates around the doorknobs buckled when my kick landed.

The molding splintered.

And the door swung open, open-sesame sweet.

The room was real attractive, if early conspicuous consumption happened to be your preferred cup of decorative motif.

There was a television in one corner, complete with rabbit ears that a particularly inventive family of spiders was using for a trapeze, judging by the cobwebs. Some weird kind of objet d'art TV in the middle of the room, blank screen gleaming like a cyclopean eye. And in the corner, the *pièce de résistance*—stacked high and haphazardly in the Leaning Tower of Pisa manner, gleaming like a JD's ransom of stolen hubcaps—an inviting collection of film canisters. *Frankenstein, The Mummy, Dracula, The Wolfman, Creature from the Black Lagoon*—all the Universal classics.

And everywhere, memorabilia. Posters, stills, costumes, masks, stop-motion miniatures, original screenplays.

Everything but the mysterious Mr. Arkoff.

"You think we missed him?" Wanda asked.

"I don't know. Maybe we got here first."

"Yeah," she said. "Maybe you're right. Let's look around."

Wanda checked out the film canisters. I turned to a projector that sat in one corner of the room. The machine, like the television rabbit ears, was festooned with cobwebs. I slashed through them with one hand, and a black widow tumbled through the air like one of the Flying Walendas on a very bad day.

With grace of which the human machine was incapable, the spider hit the floor and skittered for cover. It disappeared under the objet d'art TV, and I took a closer look at the projector. "Check this out," I said to Wanda. "This projector doesn't have a lens."

"You're very observant." It was a man's voice, and it came from the doorway.

I whirled. Mr. Arkoff was a small man with a very big gun and a very thick pair of glasses.

The right lens was large and practically square, but the left lens was round, and smaller.

Exactly like the lens of a movie projector.

*   *   *

"They're *my* ghosts," Mr. Arkoff said, gun leveled at me as he entered the room. "You're not going to steal them from me. If you take them away, *I'll die*. That's the curse."

"Ghosts?" I said, backing off. "I don't know what you're talking about, pal. I came here looking for something I can sell. I admit that. But *ghosts* . . . I don't believe in anything that I can't see."

I didn't really mean that last part, because I'd seen plenty of stuff in the past six hours that pushed the weirdness envelope pretty hard . . . and I believed every bit of it. All I wanted to do was buy some time. I glanced at Wanda, expecting her to do something, the way she had when the dead cat attacked us. But she just stood there, watching.

"My ghosts never actually lived, of course," Mr. Arkoff explained, motioning to the menacing figures that graced the movie posters hanging on the walls. "But they were real, in their own way." He tapped the round lens in his glasses. "And they all traveled through this piece of glass, and they all left something behind in it. I don't know why, or how. But when I look through this lens, I can see them . . . and *they* can see me. I wish I'd never put these glasses on . . . but I did, the first time I visited this room so many years ago. And if I ever take them off . . . why, the ghosts of Hollywood will *get* me. . . ."

The whole thing was William Castle weird—*13 Ghosts* to be exact, if you remember your fifties creature features, which I'm sure Mr. Arkoff did. Still, I wanted to tell him that I didn't care about his glasses, that I only cared about the masks, the posters, the stuff that sent visions of easy money tangoing through my cerebrum.

But I couldn't say a word. See, that cold river of blood was running in my head again, that cold river that carried words in that strange foreign tongue.

They were Wanda's words. She was in my head again, just as she'd been when she made me attack her grandmother. Any second now, I expected to turn into a Doberman and chow down on Mr. Arkoff.

Only that didn't happen. Wanda didn't change me into anything remotely frightening. Instead, she made me take one gigantic but merely mortal step forward. And she made me say, "Give me the glasses, Mr. Arkoff."

Arkoff didn't hesitate. Not that he gave me the glasses. The pistol bucked in his hand, and a slug trenched my cheek and tore through my right earlobe. I wanted to scream, but Wanda pushed me forward. I slammed into Arkoff as the gun went off again. The bullet missed me, smashing into the projector with a brittle *clang*, and then we were fighting over the gun, Arkoff spinning away from me, and as he moved I slapped one hand across his face.

Or, I should say, Wanda made me do it.

Arkoff's glasses slipped over his nose. They dropped, almost gently, to the floor.

Wanda snatched them up before I could make another move. Suddenly she wasn't in my head anymore, and again I went for Arkoff's gun, smashing his hand against the door frame.

The little man grunted. The gun clattered to the floor, and I kicked it into the hallway.

I turned to Wanda. She started at me, and I saw her eyes clearly, as I'd never seen them before. They were colder than they'd ever been, especially the one framed by the round lens that had come from the movie projector.

Wanda pushed Arkoff's glasses high on her nose. "Grandma was right," she said. "I never had the sight. I always had to rely on other things—like manipulation. Old tricks. Turning men into dogs, and dogs into men." She glanced at me, and I shivered. "But now I'm seeing things pretty clearly. I'm seeing another world. It's beautiful, Russell. Everything is black-and-white."

"Wanda," I said. "Don't—"

She laughed. "I don't think I'll be needing you anymore, Russell," she said. "I've found some new friends who are a whole lot less squeamish than you."

That was when Mr. Arkoff screamed. I whirled just as he was dragged from the room, into the shadowy hallway.

I didn't see a thing, but I could hear well enough. A werewolf howl eclipsed Arkoff's screams, and then came the sound of powerful jaws splitting human bones. Next, as the victim grew quiet, came the whisper of decayed bandages dragging over the stairway, the heavy thump of a monster's oversized boots in the hallway, and the cold, peculiarly Transylvanian laughter of a vampire.

"No," I said. "They're not *real*. They're only *movies!*"

"Don't worry," Wanda said. "You won't see a thing. Not without the glasses. You'll never see them coming."

I glanced at her, and then at the doorway. An ominous silence lurked in the shadow-choked corridor. Maybe I could make it. The gun was out there somewhere. I doubted that bullets could harm the ghosts of Hollywood, but Wanda was a different story—

"Those are nasty thoughts, Russell."

I glared at her. "Get out of my head!"

Wanda's reply was an amused grin.

And then she wasn't grinning anymore, because—just like she said—she could see things clearly now.

And she saw the dead cat coming, saw clearly the gleam in its eyes as it sprang at her. Maybe she saw her own reflection in those green glass globes, or maybe she saw Madame Estrella. I don't know. I only know that the cat latched onto her head, a fury of scratching claws and ripping fangs, and Wanda went down screaming, and Mr. Arkoff's glasses were swatted from her face.

They hit the floor, the lenses covered with blood.

I stepped on them as hard as I could, praying that curses were not simple creations of the imagination.

The lenses shattered under my boot.

And that was when I ran.

It's quiet here, under the boardwalk. Dark, too. If Wanda is alive— which I doubt—I don't think she'll ever come looking for me. Not without those glasses.

The dead cat found me, though. I woke up one morning and there it was, snuggled up next to me, purring its sand-and-sawdust purr.

We make a good team, down here in the darkness. The cat is pretty good at snaring rats. And when the fog rolls in, covering the beach in a cottony shroud, we hit the Dumpsters up on the board-walk and eat like a couple of kings.

We're careful, though. I'm sure that those ghosts are out there somewhere, even if they can't be seen.

I listen for them, in the dark, in the fog.

I listen for the melancholy wail of a werewolf's howl . . . and the thunder of heavy boots ringing on the boardwalk as a monster walks the night . . . the unmistakable sound of a mummy's uneven tread, muffled by bandages fashioned near the Nile (or in the wardrobe department at Universal Studios, I'm not sure which). . . .

The sound of a vampire's cape whispering over the sand . . . and the tireless kick of the Creature's webbed feet as he makes his way through cold Pacific tides . . .

You can hear ghosts, I'm sure, if you listen carefully.

I'm not sure if you can ever outrun them, though.

But I plan to try.

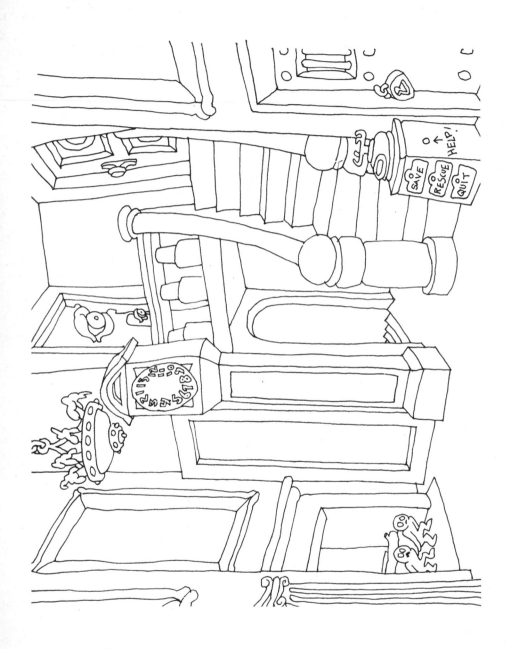

CURTAINS FOR NAT CRUMLEY
by T. E. D. Klein

He heard the creak of ancient floorboards, the scurrying of rats, and the squeak of hand-forged hinges as a massive oak door was slammed shut. From somewhere below came the crackle of flames and the clanking of metal on rock. Footfalls echoed from a monstrous stone staircase and reverberated through the gloomy halls.

Which was odd, on the face of it, since he was living in a studio apartment.

All journeys, it is said, start with a single step. This one had started when Nathan "Nat" Crumley stepped unsteadily out of his bathtub, wearing nothing but a frown.

It was October in the city, and just beginning to grow dark. Crumley, raised on the principle of a clean mind in a clean body and still a believer in the latter, had been taking a long, luxuriant shower.

It was an unusual time for a shower, a time when most of his neighbors in the building had either just returned from work, had settled down to dinner, or had already parked themselves in front of the TV; but Nat Crumley knew from nearly thirty years' experience that it was the best time to bathe. The building was an old one, just seven stories high, and the water heater in the basement was in frequent need of repair; if you waited until bedtime, or chose to shower in the morning when tenants in the other apartments were preparing for work, you might well find yourself without hot water.

But he had a more important reason for showering now. He was planning to drop over to the Social Center this evening—its full name, the West Side Seniors' Resource Center, sounded too depressingly geriatric—and he wanted to look his best, especially because a curvaceous blond widow named Estelle Gitlitz might be there, playing canasta with her friends.

He had seen Estelle just last night, for a pair of mocha decafs at one of the many small coffee bars that had sprung up in the neighborhood. It had taken him months to work up the courage to ask her out. Their date had not gone well—Estelle had not seemed entertained by his reminiscences of thirty years in the collection department of a local printing plant, where he'd methodically arranged payment schedules for small impoverished publishers who would otherwise have faced legal action—and after half an hour she had excused herself and left; she hadn't even asked him to walk her home. But maybe she would call. He hoped she would.

Or maybe she'd be at the Social Center tonight. It was the only place he had for meeting women lately, now that he'd stopped working; it was damned near the only place he could afford. There'd been women at the office that he'd flirted with, some he had dated, and two he'd even slept with, briefly. But all that was behind him; he hadn't set foot in the office for nearly a year. Ever since he'd accepted early retirement, electing to live frugally on his pension and his buyout money (for he was still too young for Social Security, thank God), he had looked to the Center for female companionship.

Running a hand over his chin, as he stood there in the tub with the water coursing down his sparse hair, bony shoulders, and legs that might normally be called spindly (except that spindles are more graceful and sturdy), Crumley realized that he needed a shave. He was meticulous about being clean-shaven and well-groomed—so meticulous that he tended to spend more time preparing for a date than on the date itself. In fact, he was meticulous in all things, maybe too much so; he'd been told more than once that he was not an easy man to live with. He was quick to find fault with other people's work, behavior, and appearance, though equally quick to apologize. He was prone to tiny, unexpected bursts of rage—unexpected even to him—though never directed at anything other than typewriters, toasters, and other inanimate objects. His wife had divorced him decades ago, after just three years of marriage; his grown-up daughter had moved across the country and telephoned only on holidays.

He reached for the razor, a throwaway plastic thing, in its customary place on a corner of the flat rim of the tub. It wasn't there.

For one confused moment he was startled, then frightened, then actually furious at the loss—he was, above all else, a creature of habit—but suddenly he remembered: he had put it away yesterday in the medicine cabinet. He had hoped, at the time, that Estelle might possibly come over, after their coffee date, for some late-night TV and maybe something more; just in case, he'd spent an hour cleaning the apartment. It had not been an unpleasant task; he liked cleaning up, and he believed that he liked playing host, rare though it was that he had guests. It had turned out, this time, that he'd cleaned up for no one but himself.

The tub in which he was showering took up one wall, end to end, of the tiny windowless bathroom. The medicine cabinet, concealed behind a large hinged mirror, was attached to the same wall as the showerhead, with the bathroom sink projecting just below it. Because of the sink's bulk and its closeness to the bathtub, one was all but prevented from stepping in or out of the tub at that end. Invariably, therefore, Crumley would open the shower curtain from the opposite end, farthest from the spray of water. The curtain itself was of faded cream-colored plastic with vertical yellow stripes, like the bars of an old-fashioned jail cell; he left it spread wide and unwrinkled even when he wasn't showering, in an effort to keep mildew at bay. He was conscientious about things like that.

This October evening, with a touch of cold in the air, Crumley broke with habit; he needed the razor, and wasn't about to step dripping from the tub to retrieve it. Directing the flow of water so that it wouldn't spray on the floor, he opened the curtain from the showerhead side, the side that normally remained closed. All too aware that half of all household accidents happen in bathrooms, he grasped the end of the round metal curtain rod with one hand where it was attached by screws to the wall, then placed a foot cautiously onto the edge of the tub. With his other foot still inside the tub, up to its ankle in warm water, he stretched precariously toward the medicine cabinet with his free hand and slowly swung its mirrored door toward him. Reaching beneath it, he groped blindly along the cabinet's bottom shelf, fingers searching for the razor among bottles of tranquilizers and vitamin pills.

It occurred to him, as he gazed idly into the mirror, that this was an unusual position to find himself in. Indeed, he had probably not assumed this particular position, foot planted firmly on this particular spot, facing the mirror at this particular angle, in all the thirty years he'd lived in the apartment.

He paused for a moment, puzzled. Something didn't look

quite right. There was something odd about the reflection in the mirror.

As he always did except in the chilliest weather, he had left the bathroom door half open; otherwise the airless little room became too steamy, and the dampness was bad for the paint. Even now, the mirror was slightly fogged, but he could still see himself in it. Behind him he could see the open doorway and, beyond it, the hall, most of it dark now because of the advancing night and, in contrast to the brightly lit bathroom, all the darker; he was not the sort of man to waste electricity by leaving lights burning in other rooms.

Directly outside the doorway, however, a portion of the hall was illuminated by the light spilling from the bathroom. And in this parallelogram of light, the hall looked . . . different.

While his fingers resumed their search for the razor, he studied the view in the mirror. Seen from this unfamiliar angle, the hall looked somehow wider. In truth it was barely wide enough for even a skinny man like Nat Crumley to walk through without brushing against the sides, especially since he'd fitted a small shallow bookcase against one of the walls. Now, outside the doorway, the hall appeared almost cavernous; and where once the bookshelves had displayed a ragged collection of cartoon books, crossword puzzle books, and other cheap paperbacks, now the shelves had taken on a more substantial look—at least the narrow section that was visible—and seemed to support more substantial-looking books of uniform size and uniform dark binding; or so they appeared, however indistinctly, in the mirror.

And it was the mirror, no doubt, that was the source of this illusion. His brain clung to that certainty, even as his eyes noticed something else. Above the bookshelves, in the circumscribed area of light, he could make out the bottom corner of a painting that had been hanging in the hall for the past thirty years. It was a painting he knew well, one that he'd completed as a boy of twelve, a paint-by-numbers picture of ducks sitting placidly in a pond. It was the first such painting he'd ever gotten right; he knew every furry cattail, every cloud. He remembered how, in his awkward fingers, his paintbrush had strayed outside the lines on several earlier attempts—a picture of sailboats, one of the Alps, another of Old Mexico—and how he'd torn up the paintings in a rage.

Yet tonight, unless his eyes were deceiving him, the painting looked larger than he'd remembered. And though most of the scene lay in shadow, it appeared to him as if the little duck pond had been replaced by something darker, and that the crabbed, meticulous style of his youth had given way to one looser, cruder, and more disordered.

Had the painting, the books, really changed? No, it simply did not compute. "There ain't no such animal," he heard himself say, unconsciously quoting what the New Jersey farmer had said upon seeing a camel for the first time.

Yielding, nonetheless, to a certain curiosity, he was about to look over his shoulder to examine the doorway directly—a maneuver that, in his present position, would have meant twisting his head and upper body to an uncomfortable degree while keeping his feet planted where they were—but at that moment his fingers encountered the plastic handle of the razor. Reflexively he shut the medicine-cabinet door and withdrew back into the shower, closing the curtain again.

As he lathered his face and stood shaving—ordinary bath soap, he believed, was as good as shaving cream and far more economical—he tried to make sense of what he'd seen. He'd been the victim of an optical illusion, a trick of the shadows, a freak of perspective; of this he was sure. Blame it on the unfamiliar angle of the mirror, or on the steam from the shower that, even now, was rising in clouds around him.

The other possibility, of course, was that, just beyond the shower curtain, something very weird had just happened. It was a possibility so far removed from his normal experience that he hardly knew how to get a grip on it.

Finished shaving, Crumley placed the razor back in its usual spot on the rim of the tub. He reached once again for the soap, but a tiny worm of uncertainty now gnawed at him: What if, out there, the world had somehow changed? What if he was, in effect, an unwilling traveler, lost and far from home?

It was a childish fear, and not a terribly real one, but he couldn't resist, just for a moment, sliding back the shower curtain from the opposite end, the end farthest from the faucets. Gripping the towel rack and leaning outward, hair dripping onto the bathroom rug, he peered through the steam at the medicine-cabinet mirror—and, to his relief, was able to make out the dark familiar hallway, a cozy place of crossword puzzle books and paddling ducks.

He closed the curtain and stepped back beneath the shower, his mind once more at ease, but already playing with a new idea. What if that bigger hallway, with its darker books and cruder art, was just as real as the one he knew lay outside the door; but what if it could only be glimpsed from the other end of the tub?

It would be a little thing, he realized, the smallest of inconsistencies—and yet momentous. You stuck your head out of one end of the shower and you were one place; you peered out of the other end and you were somewhere else. Somewhere very similar, maybe, but different enough to set the universe on its ear.

And that's just what it would do; that's all it would take to shred the laws of logic. A Cheerio rising slowly out of your cereal bowl was as monstrous an affront to the known universe as a flying saucer twice as big as Texas.

Idly he wondered, if such a thing were true, who'd be the most appropriate one to call. A friend? A physicist? The *Enquirer*? The police?

Impulsively he drew back the curtain from the end by the showerhead—letting in, as he did so, a wave of cold air—and stood looking out at the world. The mirror, by now, was too fogged to reveal anything, and the hall outside, from where he stood, was lost in shadow. Carefully he turned the showerhead to avoid wetting the floor; then, holding on to the sink to keep his balance, his back to the doorway, he stepped out of the tub and onto the bathroom rug.

Even before he had the chance to turn around, he heard the ringing of the telephone. It came from his bedroom, a few feet down the hall. For a second it occurred to him that perhaps the sound was a touch deeper than the sound his phone normally made; but then, he was so prone to losing his temper, smashing telephones, and having to buy new ones—all of them flimsy plastic affairs—that he was hard-pressed to remember exactly what the latest phone sounded like.

At the second ring, all thought fled. After the third, he knew, his current phone machine would answer (unless he'd smashed that one as well; he couldn't remember), at which point, many a caller—who knows, maybe even Estelle Gitlitz—might well hang up. Crumley had trained himself to get to the phone before that third ring.

Galvanized into action, he snatched a towel from the rack, and, with the shower still running, he hurried down the darkened hall into his bedroom. That this room—the main room in the apartment, comprising living room and dining room as well—seemed a few steps farther away than usual was not something he had much time to notice; nor did he so much as glance at the picture on the wall.

The bedroom was dark, but his hand found the phone as it commenced its third ring. He picked it up before the sound had died.

"Hello?"

From the other end came the rumble of traffic. Someone was calling from a pay phone on the street, or maybe from the subway.

"Hi," shouted a woman's voice, above the din. "This is Marcy Wykoff. We're running a little late."

"Who'd you say it was?" asked Crumley. He knew no Marcy Wykoff.

"I can barely hear you," she shouted. "Brad and I took a wrong turn up one of your winding country roads—"

"Are you sure you've got the right number?"

"—but it's okay, we're back on the highway now."

As if to prove the veracity of what she said, her words were drowned out by the thunder of what sounded like the Cannonball Express. By the time it had passed, to be replaced by a series of blasts on the sort of horn he associated with little English sports cars, the woman was saying:

"—following your map, so we should be there in half an hour, maybe forty-five minutes. Oops, Brad's honking, gotta go. Bye."

He stood there dripping in the darkness, the towel in one hand, the dead phone in the other. The floor felt cold beneath his feet; wasn't there supposed to be a rug here? The phone felt too heavy in his hand. In the sudden silence, he found himself gazing at the window across the room. The sun had set, and the first few stars were beginning to appear.

It was several seconds before he registered exactly what he was looking at. He was looking at the sky. The night sky. Complete with stars.

But the sky was not visible from this window—at least it hadn't been until this moment. Except for a narrow strip at the top, it was blocked by other buildings.

Now, however the only things blocking the sky were—he swallowed hard—trees.

Where the hell was he? Breathless with panic, he dropped the phone and looked wildly around the darkened room. His fingers found a switch; there was a quick scurrying sound, and the room was flooded with light, revealing ancient-looking paneled walls, a high ceiling, a foot-worn plank floor, shelves of books, a rumpled bed.

This was not his room.

The realization hit him with the force of a nightmare, one of those nightmares in which we find ourselves wandering naked through a classroom or a cocktail party. Suddenly feeling very vulnerable, he wrapped the towel around his pale midriff.

The first thing that occurred to him, though it made no sense at all, was that somehow, crazily, he had wandered into someone else's apartment in the same building, someone who wasn't home right now; that he had taken a shower in someone else's bathroom; and that he must get back to his own apartment at all costs.

What do you do when you step out of the shower and find yourself in someone else's home? You step back in the shower. It was crazy, all right—as senseless as a horse or a child running back into a burning building—but at the moment, its fairy-tale logic appealed to him. I'll just dash back into the shower, he told himself. (The shower was still going; he could hear it down the hall.) Once I'm back under the hot water, I'll be safe. All this will be gone; all will be well again. . . .

He had replaced the phone (beside an answering machine that definitely wasn't his) and was about to sneak back into the hall to the bathroom when, above the sound of the water, he heard the slamming of a door—a heavier, more solid door than had ever existed in a studio apartment. The thud of footfalls and the scrape of metal echoed through the corridor.

The sound was unmistakable; panic seized his heart like a fist. Someone huge and clumsy was dragging something up a stone staircase.

Yes, staircase. There was no sense kidding himself: this was no apartment. He wasn't even in the city. He was in an unknown house, he didn't know where; and at this very moment, its occupant was coming up the stairs.

He stood in the doorway, trembling with indecision. He could step into the hall right now and greet whoever was approaching; he could acknowledge he was trespassing, admit that he was lost, and throw himself upon the other's mercy. Maybe that was what he ought to do. At least, that way, there was a chance that maybe they could talk this whole thing over. . . .

But maybe he didn't have to give himself up; maybe he could get away with it. Maybe he could hide right here in this room, wait for the right moment, and somehow escape—flee the house or slip back into the shower—without ever being discovered.

It was a gamble either way, presenting risks beyond calculation. He could step out into the hall and take the consequences, or he could hide right here and pray that maybe, just maybe, he'd get off scot-free.

The only problem with hiding was that, if he was caught—discovered here in someone else's bedroom, dressed only in a towel, and sopping wet—the consequences would be much, much worse.

The footsteps came closer. They sounded huge.

He hid.

As he squeezed himself behind the open bedroom door, he realized, with dismay, that he should have remembered to turn off the light. Anyone entering the darkened hall would notice it immediately.

But it was already too late to turn it off; that, too, would be noticed. And anyway, the switch itself was on the opposite wall; there was no way he could reach it and remain concealed.

Down the hall, the footsteps paused. Several seconds passed; then the silence was broken by what sounded like the opening of a door. The steps resumed, but softer now, and then seemed to recede, as if the occupant of the house had disappeared into another room. From somewhere came the muffled clank of metal.

Crumley waited, listening. Whoever was out there remained nearby, but busy with other things—at least for the moment. He felt chilled to the bone, standing here half-naked with a puddle of cold water growing at his feet; he was shivering, as much from cold as from fear. But maybe, if he hid here long enough and kept silent, the person out there would go away.

He stared out at his new surroundings, which struck him, in his present predicament, as dangerously, almost obscenely, well lit. From where he stood, he could see an edge of rumpled bed and a section of expensive-looking bookcase—less than half the room, but enough to know that its occupant was a very different sort of person than he was. He felt a flash of anger at the bed, and perhaps a touch of envy; he'd never left his bed unmade, even as a boy, and had always been sure to put hospital corners on the blankets.

He scanned the contents of the bookcase. Instead of the familiar shelf of well-thumbed self-help books, biographies, and medieval histories that occupied one wall in his own room, the volumes here, most of them in dust jackets, looked newer; and judging from what he was able to read on their spines, they appeared to concern themselves with just a single subject: crime and criminals.

Or rather, one criminal. He noted a few of the titles: *The Count Jugula Murders. The Jugula File. The Mind of Count Jugula* by Colin Wilson. *Down for the Count* by Ann Rule. *Jugula Exposed* by someone named Von Goeler.

Weird.

And even weirder: All in a row in the center of one shelf, resplendent in their glossy dust jackets, stood nine hardcover editions of something written by the man himself, *Confessions of a Serial Killer* by Count Jugula.

Why in the world would anyone want so many copies of the same book?

The bottom shelf, he suddenly noticed, held a mass of lurid red paperbacks bearing the very same title, piled horizontally. There must have been more than a dozen in all—more than enough for even the most avid collector. Why, Crumley wondered, would someone buy so many?

His eye was caught by light reflected from something mounted on the wall just beyond his head. He turned and saw that it was an inscribed photograph, carefully framed, of a plump Oriental woman; he recognized her, after a moment, as a newscaster he'd seen interviewing celebrities on network TV. Standing on tiptoe to cut down the glare, he read the inscription: *To Count Jugula— Thanks for a fascinating afternoon!*

It dawned on him what those multiple copies of *Confessions of a Serial Killer* were. Author's copies.

A clank of metal echoed up the hall, followed by the sound of footsteps. Crumley's eyes widened; the steps were growing louder. He heard the floorboards creak as the occupant of the house— someone large and heavy, from the sound of him—drew closer to where he was hiding.

The worst thing, he reasoned, with someone of that size, would be to jump out at him. . . . No, the worst thing would be to do nothing. He should step into the hall right now; he should identify himself. It would go worse for him if he was discovered in here.

But he was paralyzed; his legs would not move. He stood frozen to the spot, watching with horror as a small stream of water from the puddle at his feet advanced slowly beneath the bedroom door.

Just beyond it, at the open doorway, the footsteps paused. Crumley, straining to listen, thought he heard the sound of breathing. Breathing softly; perhaps intentionally so. Not the thin, piercing sound of one who breathes through his nose, but the deeper sound of breathing through the mouth. Two long breaths. Three.

Then, with a hollow scrape of metal, the steps moved slowly on, advancing farther up the hall toward the bathroom.

Until this moment, above all thoughts of escape, Crumley had clung to a half-mad hope of dashing back into the safety of the shower. Now, however, with the author of *Confessions of a Serial Killer* headed in the very same direction, all such notions fled. The trick, he saw now, would be to get out of the damned house without getting caught.

And this would be the perfect chance.

Slipping around the door, Crumley peered warily into the hall. Outlined in the light streaming from the open bathroom doorway stood a wide, square-shouldered figure, partially enveloped by clouds of steam rising into the darkness. One hand held what looked like a barrel or a garbage can. Facing the light, with his broad back turned to Crumley, the man appeared to be staring inside the little room, toward the shower.

Just as Crumley made his move, he noticed something else, something he wished he hadn't. On the wall opposite the bathroom hung the painting he'd glimpsed in the mirror. He could see it in its entirety now, illuminated by the bathroom light; and just as he'd feared, it depicted nothing resembling a duck pond. From what he could make out, the subject was more a sort of anatomical study—a human hand, large, burly, and imperfectly rendered, holding by the hair a woman's severed head.

But by this time he had crept into the hall and was tiptoeing swiftly in the other direction, toward the distant stairs, praying he was too light to make the floorboards creak—and if they did, that the shower would mask their sound.

Before he'd gone more than a few steps, the telephone rang in the bedroom.

It was as loud and jarring as an alarm bell. He stopped dead; the game was up. He was old and skinny and wearing nothing but a towel; there was no way he'd escape the hulking creature behind him. He turned to face his antagonist, trying to say in one heartfelt expression, *I'm harmless, please don't kill me!*

Down the hall, the man by the bathroom hadn't moved. He continued to stare into the steamy little room.

The phone rang a second time—and still the man didn't move.

Neither did Crumley, the doomed smile now frozen on his face.

Seconds later, from the bedroom, came an audible click, then a whirring, and then a voice, sinister and insinuating:

"*Grrrreeeetings* to you. Theess eess Count Jugula's . . . *D and D!*" The speaker let out a screech of maniacal laughter that sounded as phony as the accent. "I'm tied up right now—or maybe tying up *someone else*—but you should leave your name and number, and I'll be sure to get back to you. If you don't, I'll be sure to *get* you!"

Throughout the message, Crumley had stood rooted to the spot, and the man in the hall hadn't moved.

Now he did—away from Crumley. Farther down the hall. As if he hadn't heard.

Like the deaf.

Crumley watched as the other shuffled slowly into the darkness. Yet he didn't seize the chance to turn and run. He stood dazed as if poleaxed, trying to make sense of what had just happened.

Even as the machine in the bedroom emitted an electronic beep, followed by another voice—a woman's voice, requesting a brochure and leaving an address in Cleveland—Crumley didn't move. The woman's message was baffling, yet he was far more baffled by what had preceded it. It had left him stunned.

He'd gone through a lot of phone machines in his time. From cheesy and primitive to state-of-the-art; he knew how poorly they reproduced voices. But he recognized the voice he'd heard on this one, distorted though it was by the tape and the phony accent. It was his own.

In the shadows at the far end of the hall, he saw the hulking figure open another doorway, reach inside, flick on a light, and disappear into a room. It was clear that Crumley hadn't been noticed, and that the phone had gone unheard.

Pushing all questions from his mind and willing himself to move, Crumley whirled and hurried toward the stairway, where the smooth wooden floorboards abruptly gave way to the roughness of stone. Chilly as the wood had been beneath his bare feet, the stone felt even colder as he padded down the stairs. Behind him he could hear the echo of hollow metal as the other—a mere servant, it now seemed—emptied garbage cans.

By the time he'd reached the bottom step, he was still in a daze, but his spirits, paradoxically, had begun to lift. He found himself beneath a high vaulted ceiling in what was obviously the front room of the house. Directly ahead, down a short, shadowed passage, lay the entrance.

He gazed at his surroundings with a growing sense of wonder and relief, like a tourist who, having just survived an air crash, regards the airport's souvenir shop and luggage carousel with the same astonishment he might normally have reserved for the Eiffel

Tower or the Pyramids. His odyssey through the chambers of the house, from shower down to foyer, so nightmarish until just a few seconds ago, had now begun to take on the quality of a dream— and perhaps even a good one. He was starting to feel comfortable here.

Best of all, there was a spot here to warm his feet, before an imposing stone fireplace almost too grand for the room, where flames fizzed and crackled on freshly stacked logs that looked as if they'd last the rest of the evening. An antique candelabra flickered atmospherically overhead, while the two electric lamps that pro- vided most of the room's light stood discreetly in the corners. Crumley was especially impressed by the tall grandfather clock, the sort he'd always wanted to own but had never had the space or money for, and by a grim-looking door near the foot of the stairs, adorned with iron bars and an improbably giant padlock, designed to look like the entrance to a dungeon, but in fact, he decided, the doorway to a wine cellar, one that might well be worth a visit.

Now that he'd begun to get his bearings, he could see what this place actually was: an old stone house converted to an inn—in fact, it appeared, judging from the room and its furnishings, a sort of *theme* inn. There was even, by the door, a simple check-in counter, complete with oversize guest book and credit-card machine.

Determined to explore the house further—*the* house? he'd half begun to think of it as *his* house, for he sensed that the mystery was going to be solved in his favor—he wandered through another doorway into what appeared to be the main room. It was as deserted as the first, dimly lit, and dominated by an even larger fireplace, though at the moment it was bare. The only illumination came from a recessed light in the ceiling. Most of the floor was covered by a thin green carpet and, near the fireplace, by a slightly ratty bearskin rug; as he circled the room the rug felt good against his feet. Along one wall a bay window revealed the dark shapes of trees and what may have been a lawn. Beyond the trees, the night looked almost impenetrable.

In the shadows against the farther wall, behind a row of high wooden chairs, stood a small but well-stocked bar. He crossed to it and, still in his damp towel, hoisted himself into one of the seats. The air here smelled pleasantly of liquor. On the bar top, just within the perimeter of light, lay a stack of printed cocktail napkins bearing a cartoon of a grinning ghoul in a cape with a high peaked collar. He noticed, with mingled relief and disappointment, that the ghoul's face was so crude as to be unrecognizable; after the shock of hearing his voice on the tape, he'd half expected that the face would be a caricature of his own. The creature was welcoming guests into a forbidding-looking mansion, Cartoon Gothic in style, surrounded by a flock of cartoon bats. A sign in front read COUNT JUGULA'S DEAD & DREADFAST.

Appalled by the pun, he winced and looked away—and noticed, on the wall above the bar, a set of framed pictures; or rather, he could see now, framed articles. They were in shadow, however; he couldn't make out what they said. Snapping on a small clown-shaped bar lamp, he got down from the chair and walked behind the bar to examine them.

The largest of them, an entire page from one of the supermarket tabloids, caught his eye first—not because of its size, but because it bore a muddy black-and-white photo of Crumley himself, or of a man who looked just like him, dressed in an expensive tie and jacket and standing, it appeared, before some sort of public building. He was grinning broadly; Crumley, though troubled, was pleased to see how good he looked. The headline proclaimed, PAROLED KILLER ALL SMILES NOW—BUT THE FANGS STILL SHOW.

Above it, and already slightly yellowed, hung a small newspaper editorial ("Blood Money") expressing outrage that "thanks to the liberal court's so-called 'Count Jugula' decision," a mass murderer could now become rich while serving time in prison for his crimes. It accused the Count of "cashing in on his notoriety."

And he'd apparently cashed in well, judging from the *Money* magazine article next to it: AN AUTHOR INVESTS PRUDENTLY—FROM HIS PRISON CELL. Nearby hung a photo, captioned *Jugula Spills All,* that looked as if it came from a local pennysaver. It depicted the Count, or Crumley, flourishing a pen before an open volume at a book signing, presumably after his release.

The Count's picture appeared again, along with several others Crumley didn't recognize, on the cover of a true-crime monthly called *CrimeBeat.* The story, "Men Who Kill Women—and the Women Who Love Them," contained a display quote in large red type that sprang out from the page: THERE'S NEVER BEEN A MURDERER, NO MATTER HOW DEPRAVED, THAT DIDN'T HAVE HIS COTERIE OF FANS.

Beneath it hung an illustrated feature from a travel magazine (COUNT ON THIS INNKEEPER—FOR A VACATION OFF THE BEATEN TRACK), describing how, "mellowed and rehabilitated," the former convict now devoted himself to his so-called "D-and-D." He was, the article declared, "the most affable of hosts, his violence all behind him: 'I've gotten it out of my system,' he explains. 'I want to get on with my life.'" A photo showed him smiling genially as he greeted two female guests, while their bags were carried upstairs by the shambling creature Crumley had seen in the hall. "I like to call him Igor," the Count confided in the caption, "but his real name is Bruce!"

A final photo, a flattering full-face publicity shot, appeared to have been clipped from the TV section of a newspaper. The caption said it all: *Nathan "Count Jugula" Crumley tells the NBC audience that life outside prison has been good to him.*

He reached for the nearest bottle, opened it, and drank.

He drank a good-bye to Nat Crumley—good-bye to "Nat," hello to the Count—and a toast to his peculiar good fortune. For more than half a century he'd led a life of restraint and strict routine, holding his demons in check; and all the while another man, the man he might have been, had been out in the world accomplishing great things. Instead of reading books on self-realization, Jugula had acted.

Now, thanks to the tiniest of breaks in that routine, with a single unwitting step out of character, he was that man.

Or almost. He certainly didn't feel very liberated. He was still an angry soul, a finicky misfit who smashed his possessions and forced himself to paint within the lines. Not like the genial Count Jugula.

But then, the Count was different; he had, so he claimed, gotten it all out of his system. Crumley had not. Not yet.

He was going to have to think about that.

Meanwhile, he had new responsibilities: the house to maintain, a reputation to uphold, a world full of enemies to occupy and obsess him. And right now there was cleaning up to do; the shower was still running, and he was still damp. He would have to wipe up all the spots where he'd been dripping. Guests were on their way, that's what the woman had said. The Wykoffs, they were called. He would have to get things ready for them. Tightening the towel around his waist, he hurried upstairs to turn off the shower.

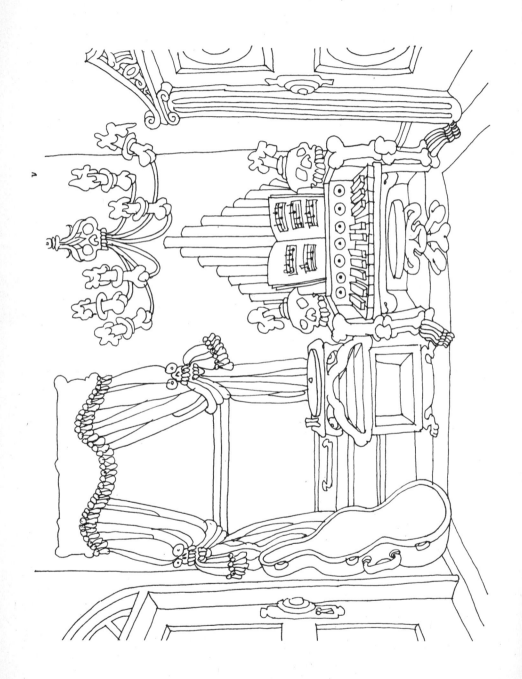

THE INVERTED VIOLIN

by Kathe Koja

In the house that was no house there were sixteen doors; Colin had counted them, one and two, turning each handle to bring the slow click like a key in the empty lock; key plates for locks on all the doors, shaped like dragons or stars or narrow faces, sharp metal faces with blind ovals for eyes.

The plate on the door to the music room was shaped like a violin.

Some of the doors—the pantry door, the library, the door of Colin's room—did not precisely fit the jambs: like puzzle pieces warped by rain or heat the doors must be pushed or tugged to fully close. Colin's mother said it was because the house was old, very old: "More than a hundred years," she told Colin, one musing hand on the newel post at the bottom of the stairs. "It's been modernized some, but most of the rooms were left pretty much the same—"

"A hundred years?" From above them on the stairs unseen, Meggie's voice: high and squeaky like a cartoon character's, a character on a show you never watch. "Is that older than you, Mommy?"

Colin's mother laughed, her smile meant to draw his: *isn't she cute?* but Colin turned away, turned to trudge up the stairs alone, to his room and its stubborn door. He did not think his sister was cute, a brother was what he wanted, a big brother like some of his friends had to take him places, the arcade, or movies; not a kindergarten sister, endless scatterer of doll parts and plastic animals from the pink bucket she wore like another limb—and his mother's glance reproving, hands on Meggie's shoulders, steering her away: "Stay out of your brother's room, Meg," but the glance for him as well, reminding him that he was ten, not five, and should be expected at least to tolerate if not understand: tolerate what? Meggie messing with his tapes or his computer, Meggie hiding underneath the bed, Meggie a bigger brat than ever since they came to this place and "She's upset," his mother told him, when Meggie had gone to bed. "She misses your dad, it's normal." A pause. "It would be normal for you to miss him, too."

Colin said nothing. Strange to think of Dad himself a stranger now, one of his trips that turned into forever; *now he's in Paris,* the next morning showing the letters, the fancy foreign stamps: Paris, and he would be coming for a visit sometime soon. "To see you, and your sister."

But not you, Colin said to himself; divorced people hate each other, right? He did not look at her, pouring juice, making coffee, there in the kitchen where they ate, preferring it to the dark of the dining room, eight big chairs with arms, like thrones, a tablecloth big as a tent; would they use that room if his father was here? Would he make them use it? Imagining his father, his mother eating in silence, even Meggie's mouth shut for once and "Why not now?" said Colin, looking not at his mother but out the window, at the yard that stretched far as a field: no fences, no way to know where their property ended and the world began. "Why can't he come now?"

"He'll come," her tired voice, "when he can. It's his job."

His job. A conductor, like someone who drove a bus, a train, *hey Mister Conductor here's my ticket!* but it was the other kind of conductor, Mr. Orchestra with his famous baton, flying all over the country when they needed him at home; *it's his job* to make music, to cause the divorce, send the three of them to this place, big empty house on a street that was no street, big stupid house and his mother the hired caretaker—*they need a break,* calm voice on the phone to his father, *just to decompress a little:* decompress, like astronauts in vacuum, travelers to places far away. When he was very small Colin had dreamed of being an astronaut, of floating in space; the violin changed all that, the violin and his father.

"He cares about you, Colin," his mother said. "You know that."

Colin said nothing. Out the window a glimpse of crows, flight to scatter dark across the lawn: one and two and six and twenty, round and black as notes on a staff.

It was the only room he had not explored, left untouched but for one cold glance during their first tour of the house: music stands and an upright piano, a guitar case, an old-fashioned record player with a complement of records, old classical records warped, his mother had said, sitting there like that for so long. Sun but not much warmth from the windows, casement windows facing north from which he could see a different slice of the same nothing view, the field yard stretched to nowhere.

"Look, Colin," his mother had said, "there's a violin."

Black case, silver clasps bright as dimes in the light: Colin said nothing, did not seem even to have heard so "Well, come on," his mother's sigh, "let's go see the rest of it." Down the hall with Meggie beside her, Meggie hanging on her arm like a baby; you could do that still, at five.

Touching the key plate on the door, a violin inverted; he had not noticed that it was upside down; his father would have noticed. *He's gifted*, the teacher had told them, Colin's father and mother both. *He could easily go on to play professionally.*

It's in the genes, said Colin's father, smile for Colin perched mute on the last tier of the risers, his face turned toward the window from which he could see the playground, the first early buds on the trees; he would like to be out there now, anywhere but in here. *Right, Colin?*

Silence.

Oh yes, his teacher had said, *he's really something.* Creak of the metal folding chair against the nonslip tile of the "music room," just a classroom really but with risers for the vocal class, some music stands, an inexpensive tape player on the corner desk; and Ms. March with her thin girlish face, round little glasses rimmed in blue and *Feel the music*, Ms. March always told them, *pay attention to what the music is making you feel.* Not like his father, who was always so worried about missed notes, flats and sharps and *Again*, as if it were a wall he was building, a wall between himself and the world, *do it again, Colin.* He was like that with his orchestra, too, Colin had seen him; who knew what the music made him feel? Maybe he didn't feel at all.

But now, Ms. March so earnest, hands folded between her knees, leaning far forward as if she were the kid and his parents were the teachers, *now Colin needs more than I can give. Now he needs—*

Oh, we can take it from here, Colin's father interrupting, brief smile to dwindle hers: *patronizing*, Colin's mother called it, walking out to the car, front seat, backseat like the dark side of the moon, *did you have to be so patronizing? Colin likes Ms. March, he's learned a lot in her class—*

Oh come on, this is baby stuff for a kid like him, he could play this

shit in his sleep. When school's over I'll arrange for a real tutor, some-
one who'll be able to—

No, Colin's voice low and dry, staring at his hands; cold hands, although the car was warm. *I don't want a tutor, I don't want to play the violin anymore.*

Nothing else said, silence in the car until they pulled into the driveway, his mother gone into the house, her house now and his father's gaze on him, eyes dark as his own: coldly, *Are you sure?*

Yes, as coldly, *I am:* and now nothing, no violin, no music, no father although since the divorce his presence already inconstant: no visit for weeks and then a weekend splurge, the movies, dinner, presents for Meggie—*Pinkie Ponies!* her cartoon squeal, cascade of pointy plastic, breathless with joy and greed—and: *Here,* an envelope proffered to Colin. *This is for you.* Their hands did not touch; Colin did not thank him, said nothing, left the envelope on the table untouched as the music-room door, unwanted as the newest letter read at breakfast, Colin's mother's careful edit, he could tell she was leaving things out: "'The tour is going exceptionally well. I expect to be able to . . . visit the kids as soon—soon. Give them my love. Tell Colin—'"

Her pause too long, she was not that good a liar and "Tell me what? Meggie, shut up!" as ponies pranced across the tablecloth, danced around the carton of milk. "Tell me what?"

"He just—he wants to know if you're practicing. The violin. Oh Colin, don't look that way, he doesn't mean—it's important to him, music, he wants it to be important to you too—"

In the end she gave in and let him read it, the whole letter there in his room, ignoring Meggie waiting with her bucket and "Come with us," his mother said; her tiredest voice, the voice that came after tears. "We're going out back for a walk."

No answer; again her invitation but when he still did not speak, sat behind silence like a door with a lock they left him with the letter from Paris, from Mr. Conductor who was full of stories about the success of his tour but not exactly sure when he was going to be able to squeeze in a visit: he would "try" to come later this summer, he would "do what I can" and "You're full of it," the whisper defiant, as if his father could somehow hear. "You're full of bullshit."

Tell Colin when I come I'm bringing him a violin, and that I expect him to be able to play it. If you still have that cheap fiddle he used at school make him practice on that, he needs the practice. He's probably forgotten everything by now.

"Bullshit," again in a whisper, feeling in his throat like pressing fingers, hot fingers closing off his breath and rising then as if impelled, Colin went to the window, the open window through which he could see his mother and Meggie, far off at the end of the yard, blurred figures moving in the golden morning heat and he wanted to throw the letter out the window, tear it up to make the pieces fly but instead left it there on the dresser beside the other envelope untouched, left it like a promise broken and in a kind of fury took up from beneath the bed his school violin: *cheap fiddle,* well that was bullshit, too, and he hadn't forgotten, practice or no practice, if he wanted to he could play something right—

—but the strings, he saw at once as he lifted the violin from its case, the strings were snapped and useless, as if he had turned the pegs too tight but he never did that, he knew better—and there half-hidden by the bedskirt's droop a tiny pink hair bow, half a minuscule pink comb: Meggie's toys, stuff for Pinkie Ponies and she must have been messing with his violin, there in his room where she didn't belong, must have turned the pegs until the strings let go. And then shoved it back beneath the bed and hoped he would never see; and why should he? when he had said more than once that he would never play it again?

Look Colin, there's a violin.

And so what if there was? Did that mean he was going to use it? *He could easily go on to play professionally:* and it *was* easy, had always been: learning how to use the bow or vibrate the strings, how to make the instrument do what he wanted it to do, feel what he meant it to feel, what he felt when he played. He had had a solo in the school recital, not long but intricate: looking up at its con-clusion to his mother's smile enormous, right up front with her camcorder and Meggie wriggling beside her, Meggie telling strangers *that's my brother playing, that's my brother!*

His father had not come to the recital.

He's probably forgotten everything by now.

The music room smelled not of dust but dryness, chamber in a lost museum, a place left clean against time. The music stands were very old, unlike the ones at school: silver flowers and treble clefs, thin legs spread like the frozen roots of a tree. The piano, he found, was somewhat out of tune but still mellow: "Chopsticks" and "Für Elise," "There Was an Old Lady," *he could play this shit in his sleep* and Colin shoved away from the bench, past the window and the stacks of ruined records, past the music stands and the black elegance of the violin case, its locks and hinges bright as if polished, recently polished by some sure and careful hand.

He's gifted.

I expect him to play it.

Fashioned of darkest wood—not painted but dark, like the shell of an ancient turtle, water at the bottom of a well—and larger, too, than the school violin, full-size, not three-quarter, with pegs as smooth and cold as stones and the bow as well strangely cold to his touch: from lying so long in the silence, the black velvet silence of the case.

He thought of his mother, and of Ms. March; he thought of the snapped strings on the school violin. He thought of his father spending money, a lot of money maybe on a new instrument, a gift he would bring on his "visit," which Colin could then casually reject: *No thanks,* with a smile, the smile his father had given Ms. March. *This one's better.*

Because it would be, he knew it; one look said so, one string plucked like the first sound made in all the world and *go on,* like a voice in his head, *go on* and in the case, nestled in an inner compartment he found the rosin, fresh as if new on the strings and the memory then of how it had felt to play in the recital—nervous, a little; and what else? happy? No, not happy exactly, sometimes the music was sad; but good. When he played—then or ever—he felt good.

It's in the genes.

Settling the violin in place, ready to play the practice tune Ms. March had taught them: *Up and down the strings I go/Quick and careful with my bow* but as he brought bow to strings he found a much different tune in mind, from a tape his father had given him, something, he thought, by Bach: *Learn this* although one listen had told Colin he could not play it, not now or even soon, it was full of things Ms. March had not taught them, things he did not yet know how to do

yet hear it, feel it tumble from him now, not flawless or even close but all the same (how?) he *had* it, had the feel of it here in this room without sun, pale light on the planes of the black violin and past even the surprise of the music it just felt *good* to play, he had missed without knowing the sweep of the bow, A and D and G and E like friends he had lost, left behind, turned away

and unbidden then the image of his father, arms folded, head to one side the way he liked to stand, as if he knew in advance what would happen but was just waiting for you to prove him right: and again the heat like pressure in Colin's eyes and throat, he did not cry, he had not cried since he was a little boy but

Listen, as if his father could truly hear him, Paris and nowhere, pure attention as the violin was pure sound: the bow in his hand, wrist and fingers and *Listen, Dad, listen to this*

as in the corner a presence, a feeling: like someone there and watching, more than one in the silence: *listen*

and see, half close your eyes to glimpse them, three of them, mother and—was it?—brother, like Colin but older, both present as shadows and behind them the dream-father more distinct: taller than the brother and smiling, he was definitely smiling at

Colin

as if he wanted to speak to him, his own name made a dream and *ghosts,* the thought less than a whisper, flicker in the mind's eye but he did not feel frightened, kept playing, the Bach again from the beginning, louder this time and see the smile from the dream-father, like Colin's father but not: almost the same on the outside, dark hair and eyes but the feeling from him so different, as if he would not care if Colin made mistakes, if sometimes he did not want to play or practice, if sometimes he wanted to cry because

Colin

was what mattered, what he wanted, how he felt and playing now as if the tune were his own, made from air and tears and the feel of his heart, beating and beating as if he had been running, pounding like hands on a door and

"Colin!"

much too loud, bow screech and dreadful the lurch from dream to see his mother in the doorway, one hand tight on the knob and "Colin," again, sharp and without a smile, "I've been calling you. We're back from our walk, lunch is ready."

The violin against his body, sheltered and close and "I'm not hungry," half turned away, facing the window and its empty light; was he crying? No. "No, I want to play," but "Lunch," his mother said and he followed, the tune companion, A and D and G and E as his mother made coffee, as Meggie dumped her milk, as he ate with swift economy then left as swiftly, before his mother could complain or call him back.

Not truly practice, though he called it that: "I have to," to his mother's frown, dry little lines in her forehead and "Colin," quiet, "you don't really—"

"He *said*. In the letter," and then gone, up the stairs and into the music room, silver stands and black velvet, playing through the songs he knew from school: "Junebug" and "Six Steps Up," "Falling Leaves," which was his recital solo but back like home to the Bach piece, near shy in his pleasure but each time it sounded better, practice makes perfect and somehow with each repetition— as if the music were the engine, the breathing heart—he saw more clearly the dream-family, ghost-family (which? did it matter? and his father's voice inside his head, sharp and scornful: *imaginary friends*) and clearest of all the dream-father listening, attentive to each motion, watching all that Colin did as if he could not see enough

and "Swimming," Meggie one-foot hopping, chanting at his door, "swimming, Mommy's taking us swimming—"

"I'm not going," said Colin, slow as if speaking from a dream; could Meggie see them? Could they see her? There in the corner, Meggie in the doorway, one foot and two and "You have to," made a song, a chant. "Mommy says you have to."

A long drive to the lake, water and wind, A and D and G and E and "You used to like swimming," his mother said, hand up to shade her eyes: looking at him, trying to see his face. "In fact you used to be really good at it."

Her voice a sound, water music and he thought of the dream-father walking, running across the sand, running into the lake and would he make a splash when he entered, would the water know he was there? What would it feel like to be that way? bodiless, weightless, as if in space, like music in the air.

And that night as he played, the Bach less than a whisper, the dream-father came alone: to stand transparent in the doorway, head nodding in rhythm, clapping hands soundless when the piece was through.

"What are you?" Colin said, lips barely moving.

That smile; near enough now to touch.

Don't you know?

"Letter from your dad, Colin," and careful the placement on his dresser, thin blue envelope, that messy slanting script and her pause conspicuous: *Aren't you going to read it?* but she didn't say that, only stood in the doorway, talking, talking as he waited for her to finish, to go so he could play; sometimes it seemed she and Meggie were the dream, loud through the house, talking to each other as if he weren't there: walks and backyard picnics, playing in the grass, they always asked him to come but even when he did it was never any fun, a waste of time because all he really wanted to do was go back inside and

"—be here till the end of August anyway I think we probably could, if you wanted to. Do you want to?"

and the other family, mother and brother now somehow missing, dissolved in the summer's heat but that was all right, was better really because as their substance waned the father seemed even stronger, more real than ever, mist made flesh and

"*Colin,*" and his mother all at once before him, somehow he had not seen her move. "Are you listening to me?"

His nod, once, twice past fleeting wonder, what would she say, do if he told her about the dream-father, the—what, ghost? but no ghosts he had ever heard of had ever been like this, not scary, not sad, better even than

his mother's hand on his shoulder now, a smile but tight, as if troubled and "You know it's good that you're practicing so hard, but now I think it's time to take a break. Even professionals need a break once in a while, your father says that they—"

"But I like to play," as if she were far away, wrong end of the telescope, floating in space. "The more I play the better I get."

"Colin," sitting down on the bed, heavy her weight against the springs, "I talked to your dad about all this, all the practicing, and he—we both think you ought to stop. At least for a while. It's all you do now, it's all you want to do, it's not good for anyone to be so—Anyway, your dad will be here in another week or two, and when he comes you can talk about it with him."

His gaze on hers past the flare inside, red the anger and something else, something deep and hot and dry: but no protest, nothing said because there was nothing to say, father or no father he would not stop playing and that was that.

That night in bed he lay sleepless, hot face turned away from the pillow, violin by the bed: and the dream-father came wordless to soothe him, to say by his presence that everything would be all right: *You can do what you want to,* the dream-father said, *you can do whatever you want.*

Cast white light of the swollen moon, shadow and silhouette and he slept then, in the arc of that smile, and woke to find that his mother had taken the violin.

Silence: in his room, in the house, in the long fields outside and he walked and walked, hour after hour, trudged to drop sullen on the spiky grass, furious past forgiveness, he would never forgive her now. Everywhere, he had looked everywhere and she trailing him with her explanations, excuses, *you can have it back when your father comes* but he would not listen, turned his face away, lay on the bed staring up at the ceiling until he could not stand the silence anymore: so up then and walking, himself a ghost trailed by the sound the grass made in his passing, the humid taste of the air and *now,* he thought, *now I'm really alone:* in the night, in the silence, alone without music, without the father that no one else could see.

Because without the violin he did not, could not come to Colin: stranded somehow in the music room, silver stands and old black records, once Colin thought he heard the out-of-tune piano but his mother had locked the door, keyhole glimpse to give him nothing, more nothing in days already so empty he could have screamed: empty silence like vacuum, *decompress* and "Please stop sulking," on the way to the airport, Meggie loud and unbearable in the front seat. "You haven't seen your father for four months, you can at least try to be a little bit pleasant."

And now this stranger, black suit, black bag, one-armed hug for Meggie who ran to him, backward slew of Ponies to make a path to Colin, Colin who stood and stared and *he's not real,* riding home in the backseat, *he's not real* in the house as his father (*which father*) turned to him and said, "So what's going on with you and all this practice, how come I could never get you to practice before?"

Silence; his father's gaze unsmiling and *She took it,* he could have said in his bitterness, *she hid it* but instead a kind of inspiration, the words from his mouth before he knew, words given him (how?) by his father, real father, dream-father and "I was playing that one," he said, "the one you showed me. From the tape—"

"The Bach?" with a frown as if disbelieving, "oh come on you're not playing *that,* you don't have the skill to—"

"I am too," but mildly. "Tell her to give it back, and I can show you."

"It's in the music room," his mother said; she had been listening, herself like a ghost in the doorway, insubstantial, out of reach and "You know you just got here," she said, but dully, as if she were very tired. "You just—"

"Show me," his father said, as if she wasn't there. "Come on."

One by one in ascension and *come on* in hopeful echo, from beyond the music-room door; the waves of silence receding, Colin could almost hear it, almost feel the bow in his hands and his mother arguing now with his father, words tight between her teeth and his own curt answer no answer at all but a demand: as usual, nothing had changed or ever would except that it had already, had changed forever and now would change some more, *come on* and there it lay, black case on the piano bench, black and silver and "Nice," as he took the case from Colin, the heat of Colin's grasp, "nice instrument." Dark gloss in the weak shine of the overhead, examining neck and strings and *hurry,* the thought a voice, *hurry hurry*

"The one I brought's better, but this one is still fairly—"

"I really wish you had talked to me about that, there are other things he needs more—"

hurry: come on

"We've been through this, I wrote you about it and if you had some kind of complaint you should have said something about it before I—"

and his hands were shaking, their voices discordant but he didn't care, didn't hear, could hear only the sound of the music he would make and there by the window the growing shimmer, white moon and the shape familiar, he could almost see, he had to play and "Go on," his father still glowering at his mother glowering back. "Go on, show me."

Hands out, smile sprung irresistible as at once the shape grew stronger, as Colin began at last to play: flawless, flawless his hands on the strings, the bow, back and forth in sure perfection and Colin's mother leaving then, gone in disgust from the doorway, gone as if she had never been and only the

three

of them there now: Colin warm, almost sweating with effort, eyes half-closed before black suit and folded arms, head to one side and watching, waiting for a mistake, a misstep, something

listen

his father now watching and listening, *hey Dad listen to this:* the spill and pour of the music, feeling in the room like pressure, the ancient music of vacuum and space

Colin's hands in motion, metronome pound of his heart and

a silhouette in hungry motion

the snap of a bowstring

I expect him to be able to play.

"Again," his father said, and smiled. "Colin, play it again."

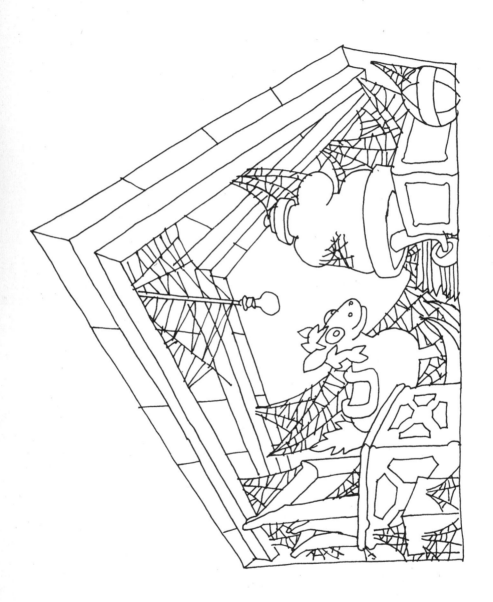

BUNDLING

by Lucy Taylor

DeAnna and her six-year-old daughter Shannon had just moved into the elegant old Nykamp house on Boulder's Mapleton Avenue when Shannon told her mother about the little girl living in the attic.

DeAnna was combing the tangles out of Shannon's hair, working out the snarls with careful concentration, but her mind was really a million miles away, thinking about her ex-husband David, about her new job as secretary to the assistant director at Dolen Sports, and about the bills that were piling up as inexorably as autumn leaves in a gale.

"Hmmm? What did you say?" she asked absently.

"The little girl who lives in the attic. Her name's Amy."

"Shannon, I believe we've talked about how naughty it is to tell fibs."

"No, Mom. There really is a little girl—she cries sometimes and—"

"Shannon, listen—" DeAnna could hear her voice vibrate with pent-up tension. It had been a lousy day. Her boss Mimi had found fault with every letter and report that DeAnna had transcribed. Mimi didn't want a secretary, thought DeAnna, she wanted a combination Doris Lessing and William Safire who could also take dictation and make coffee after shopping for the beans. Just thinking about it made her head bang like the inside of a bowling alley.

Shannon's recent antics weren't making things any easier, either. She'd reacted to her parents' divorce and, most recently, her father's arrest and incarceration, by becoming disruptive and belligerent in school. If Shannon didn't do better, her teacher had told DeAnna, she would have to be put in a special class for students with behavioral problems. Not to mention Mrs. Jernigan over on Pearl Street, who ran an after-school center for latchkey kids. Mrs. Jernigan had complained to DeAnna that Shannon was abusive to the other children, hitting and slapping them when she didn't get her way, and that she indulged in minor larcenies, pilfering candy and pogs and comic books from the other kids' lunch boxes and day packs.

Shannon Gates, the Terror of Day-Care, thought DeAnna, feeling her stomach knot up as tight as the tangles in her daughter's long hair.

"Look, Shannon, remember when you made up the story about being born in Europe and how your father was a famous race-car driver killed in a crash? Remember how I had to spank you when your teacher told me about that? You don't want to get spanked, do you?"

"But it's true!" yelled Shannon, and she whirled around, so fast that a clump of her dark chestnut hair pulled loose in the teeth of the comb. "I *did* see Amy. She lives up in the attic with all the fancy rugs!"

DeAnna sighed. She knew Shannon had been playing in the attic and felt guilty that she hadn't been up there yet to check it out. Attics could hold dangers, after all. Creepy-crawly, slithery things. And who knew what Grace Nykamp, from whom DeAnna was renting the house, or her brother George, the former owner, might have stashed away up there?

But DeAnna had been so busy and now this . . . the lies that Shannon kept telling. . . .

"All right," said DeAnna, snatching Shannon's hand, "let's go. · If there's a little girl living in the attic, I want to meet her."

They started up the stairs.

The first time Shannon had gone up into the attic, it was because she'd been angry at DeAnna and wanted to hide from her. DeAnna had lost her temper and slapped the child much harder than she meant to. And over such a little thing, DeAnna had thought later, a spilled glass of lemonade that could be mopped up off the linoleum in only a couple of minutes.

But in that one black moment the spill had seemed the final punctuation on a dozen other things that had gone wrong that day—the final divorce papers to be signed, the ticket for an expired registration handed out to her by a smirky cop with a dimple in his chin just like David's, then the snippy remark Mimi had made, "Oh, so glad you could make it back this afternoon, DeAnna, I know you have so many important matters to attend to besides *work*."

Too late, she'd heard the crack of the blow and Shannon's squeal, then the swift blossoming of a rosy handprint on her daughter's cheek.

Oh, dammit, Shannon, don't run away. I didn't mean to hurt you. Really I didn't. . . .

But Shannon had scooted from DeAnna's attempt at an embrace and dashed upstairs, sobbing. DeAnna had heard her feet on the attic stairs and thought about going after her, then decided not to. She didn't trust herself with Shannon these days. Her temper was explosive, unpredictable. Better if she calmed down before she went to talk to the child.

Except she was never calm these days, not really. She was just hanging on.

Shannon glared at her mother. "Amy doesn't come out for just anybody. She's scared."

"Well, let's try anyway."

As they went up the carpeted stairs with the magnificent polished mahogany banister and plum-colored, flocked wallpaper, DeAnna marveled yet again at her luck at getting a chance to house-sit here for the spring and summer. Grace Nykamp, whom DeAnna had met at a support group for women who were trying to quit smoking, had a six-month teaching job at the University of Denver and didn't feel up to making the two-hour commute every day from Boulder. She'd seemed so grateful to get DeAnna and Shannon to stay in the house and look after it that the rent she was asking was absurdly low.

"I just want to know the house is taken care of," Grace Nykamp had said. "My brother acquired so many nice things when he and his family lived there that I don't like to leave it unoccupied."

Despite her irritation at Shannon, DeAnna reminded herself that she had much to be grateful for. If it weren't for Grace Nykamp, she and Shannon would probably be holed up in an overpriced one-bedroom apartment somewhere in the boonies of Broomfield.

But then you didn't get a whole lot in the way of child support when your husband—correction, make that ex-husband as of two o'clock Tuesday—was doing five years for cocaine possession, she thought bitterly.

They reached the stairway to the attic. Feeling an inexplicable twinge of trepidation, DeAnna led the way.

She had expected an attic festooned with cobwebs and inundated with gloom. Instead, light poured in through two large dormer windows like skeins of bright yellow silk.

And along the walls and floor, what a treasure—heaps of brilliant Oriental carpets, complexly patterned and thickly fringed! All manner of lavish ornamentation, gorgeous stars and scrolls and swastikas, on rich saffron and scarlet and indigo fields. In one corner rested a heavy, vertical loom, as broad as a refrigerator and almost as tall. DeAnna assumed it was of a type still used by Middle Eastern women to weave rugs. Behind it, a dozen or more tightly rolled carpets were leaned up against the wall, where they resembled the trunks of riotously patterned trees, their complex designs spreading upward like a proliferation of crayon-colored kudzu.

DeAnna remembered now that Grace Nykamp had mentioned that her brother had owned an Oriental-rug business. Obviously he must have kept his extra stock up here, but why he would have left the rugs behind—and where he was now DeAnna didn't know.

"Amy, Amy, where are you? Shannon says you're here." She felt absurd, walking around the piles of carpets talking to an imaginary playmate.

"There," she said, turning to Shannon. "You see, there isn't any Amy. You made her up. You fibbed, didn't you?"

Shannon stuck out her lower lip in a pugnacious pout. "I told you," she said, "she's scared. She's hiding in the rugs so nobody will get her."

"Dammit, don't lie to me, Shannon."

"I'm not lying!" screamed Shannon, stamping her foot down on one of the carpets hard enough to raise a puff of dust.

"That's enough, young lady." DeAnna fought the urge to slap her. Spinning Shannon around by the shoulders, she started pushing her toward the door.

Something stirred. DeAnna looked behind her. The curtains at the dormer windows were trembling like a candle flame when air whispers across it. The fringe on the carpets stacked up behind the loom was swaying gently, like grass bending before a light breeze. And then the thinnest kiss of funneled air sleeked around DeAnna's legs, dank and wetly scented.

Perhaps there was a subtle draft coming in from downstairs, she thought. On the stairs, she glanced back. All movement now was stilled.

But something else intruded upon DeAnna's consciousness, minor but annoying. Shannon had been sneaking candy before suppertime again. She could smell it now, the faint fragrance of peppermint.

"Amy's lonely," said Shannon, looking up at DeAnna over her bowl of granola a few days later. "She wants me to come live with her."

DeAnna put down the classified section of the paper. Rumor around Dolen Sports was that half a dozen people were going to be let go by the end of the week. And if the principle of last hired, first fired applied, then DeAnna's job seemed particularly imperiled. She was studying the job possibilities—just in case—and finding the proliferation of minimum-wage, *what-cho-wanonya-burger* jobs depressing.

"Shannon, don't you mean that *you're* the one who's lonely? I know all this has been rough on you, the new house, new school, Daddy having to go away and not live with us anymore. It's hard for me, too, but we have to adjust and be thankful for—"

Shannon scowled and brought her fist with the spoon in it down so hard on the table that the cutlery did a clattery little jig. Coffee from DeAnna's cup sloshed over onto the newspaper. "Amy's not me. She's *her*. And she's lonely and sad and she doesn't want to be all by herself anymore!"

"That's it, I've had it," said DeAnna, throwing aside the sodden newspaper and leaping up from her chair. She grabbed Shannon by the shoulders and shook her hard, much harder than she meant to, but she was so damn frustrated, so angry, and . . . nothing was going right, *nothing,* and Shannon was being a spoiled brat, wasn't helping at all. . . .

What am I doing?

Shannon's face had gone very pale. Fat tears glided down her cheeks, leaving wet tracks like the glistening trails of slugs.

"All right, go on," said DeAnna. "Get ready for school. We'll talk about this when I pick you up from Mrs. Jernigan's tonight." She crumpled up the ruined paper. "And Shannon? No more sneaking sweets! You smell like a candy store."

But DeAnna never got around to talking to her daughter about her imaginary friend, because she had to finish proofing and correcting a sheaf of reports that had to be, absolutely *had* to be, on Mimi's desk by the next morning, and because, when DeAnna finally picked Shannon up at Mrs. Jernigan's, Shannon spent all evening glued to the TV set in the den. She didn't mention Amy anymore.

Until a few nights later.

DeAnna was feeling guilty about how little time she spent with her daughter these days—and how few children Shannon's age seemed to live in this affluent neighborhood of primarily well-to-do middle-aged couples whose children were too old to play with Shannon but too young to have produced grandchildren yet. Although it was already past her daughter's bedtime, she decided to make an exception and went upstairs to read Shannon a story.

Upon opening the door, DeAnna's first impression was that Shannon's bed was empty. She blinked, turned on the Power Ranger lamp by the door. Something was moving in the bed, thrashing slowly from side to side under the covers. Left, then right, like a very large cat playing catch-the-imaginary-mouse beneath the blanket.

"Shannon?"

Shannon poked her head up from beneath the covers. Her face was flushed, her hair tangled as though she'd been in a scuffle.

"What are you doing?"

"Bundling," said Shannon.

DeAnna was mystified. "What?"

"Bundling. Amy does it."

DeAnna felt her jaw muscles knot and start to twitch. "I thought we'd talked about this, Shannon. About how it's wrong to make up stories about imaginary people."

A single line, a crease of stubbornness and self-will just like her father's, bisected Shannon's forehead. "I'm not making Amy up. I saw her! She comes and talks to me! She wants me to stay with her!"

"There is no . . . " DeAnna's voice rose dangerously. She ordered herself to be calm. Shannon was lonely and making up imaginary playmates. Not all that unusual in children her age, nothing to get so irate about.

But it made DeAnna feel inadequate, this dependence of her daughter's on an imaginary friend. If DeAnna had more time to spend with her, more money for after-school activities like ballet lessons and piano and karate, not just long, dull hours hanging out at Mrs. Jernigan's, then Shannon would be better adjusted. She wouldn't feel compelled to fabricate.

"All right, look, I don't want to yell at you. I came up to read you a story. Would you like that?"

"Not a scary one. Amy doesn't like scary stories."

DeAnna bit her lip. She opened the book, picked out a story about dinosaur babies, and read it, even though it was obvious the little girl paid scant attention to the tale. DeAnna finally closed the book, cut off the light, and slipped out of the room.

The work Mimi had given her to take home tonight was going even more slowly than DeAnna had expected. Well after midnight, she was still hunched over the dining-room table, trying to organize the notes from Mimi's most recent sales meeting into some sort of coherent order. Her vision was getting blurry and the pain behind her temples suggested someone had fired a staple gun above her eyes.

She had just decided to call it a night, grab a few hours' sleep, and set the alarm clock for five the next morning when a muted thud sounded from upstairs.

DeAnna's head shot up. Her first thought was that the noise had come from Shannon's room, that maybe the child had fallen out of bed. Then she realized the sound had come from deeper in the house, from somewhere in the attic.

A burglar? The thought of someone shinnying up the elm tree next to the house and prying up one of the dormer windows to gain access, an idea that DeAnna would have found farfetched by light of day, now seemed a possibility.

Wondering if she should be dialing 911, DeAnna climbed the stairs. She checked first to make sure Shannon hadn't gotten out of bed and gone up into the attic, but the child appeared to be sleeping peacefully. No other noises came from up above. Yet DeAnna knew she had heard something land heavily on the attic floor.

It took DeAnna several nerve-fraying seconds to find the cord to the attic's overhead light and pull the switch. When she did, a pale ring of amber light illuminated the small room.

The many rugs leaned up against the wall stood like rows of brilliantly painted columns.

At first DeAnna observed nothing out of place. Then she realized that one of the larger carpets in the corner had toppled over like a felled tree and lay on the floor beside the loom.

She walked over and gave the carpet a nudge with her foot. Then a kick. The carpet was among the largest ones and must have covered at least sixty square feet when spread out flat. Even when she kicked full force, she could barely budge it. What, then, could have caused it to fall?

Gooseflesh peppered DeAnna's arms. She checked the other carpets, running a hand behind and underneath them, but felt only the smooth attic wall. The windows, when she checked them, were both locked. Even if they'd been open, it would have taken a hurricane-velocity wind to topple a tightly rolled carpet of that size.

As she stood speculating on the mystery DeAnna's nose was suddenly assailed by a dizzying odor, a sweet putrescence that made her head reel. A terrifying constriction seized her throat. For a moment she could draw no breath at all. She could feel the blood burning in her face and hear the ever-harsher thunder of her heart.

She stumbled toward the doorway, her lungs closing up at the sick-sweet mustiness that suggested the soiled warp and weft of a vomit-sodden rug.

On the stairs, she tripped and almost pitched forward before catching herself on the railing. Reaching the second floor, she sat down on the bottom step and drew in deep, slow breaths to quell her panic.

When she felt steady enough to walk, she went to her bedroom, found the pack of cigarettes she'd stashed away when she first decided to quit, and smoked half a dozen before she went to bed.

Two weeks before the Labor Day weekend, when DeAnna had planned to splurge and take Shannon to see the Royal Gorge in southern Colorado, Mimi's boss told DeAnna she was fired.

Nothing personal, Mr. Danforth pointed out. Budget considerations. Several others in the company were being sacked as well.

But for DeAnna it was the final blow in what seemed like a string of injustices. She went into the bathroom, cried until her makeup ran in sludgy runnels down her face, then said fuck it, took the afternoon off, and went home.

There, in a flurry of haste propelled by desperation, she set about composing a résumé. She sat at the desk in the cluttered study and rolled a sheet of paper through the typewriter to begin listing her prior jobs and qualifications.

Barely had she gotten past her name, address, and Social Security number, however, than the typewriter stopped printing. Opening up the carriage, she discovered that the ribbon cartridge had run out.

In the state of mind that she was in, the minor setback seemed like yet another cruel joke on the part of some malevolent universe that took pleasure in thwarting every effort on the part of a newly divorced, *very* newly unemployed mother. She put her head in her hands and counted to ten, smoked a cigarette and counted to twenty, fighting the urge to weep or to throw back her head and scream.

Instead she took a few deep breaths, regained what composure she could, and began a systematic search of the desk drawers for a new cartridge.

Neither Grace Nykamp nor her brother was exactly anal-retentive about neatness. The desk drawers were a jumble of crumpled papers, old tax reports and canceled checks, stationery, and letterhead. There were four spools of correcting tape that fit the typewriter but no ribbon cartridges.

DeAnna sighed and began rummaging through one of the bottom drawers. Near the back, she found a brown cardboard box of the type often used to store computer paper or other office supplies. Surely, she thought, this must be where Grace kept the typewriter ribbons.

Instead, when she pulled off the top of the box, she found a couple of boxes of slides, one marked Christmas '93, the other Christmas '94, and a photo album of the type where the photos are contained in clear plastic pouches and arranged vertically, overlapping each other.

DeAnna lifted out the album and thumbed through it. The pictures were of the typical family holiday variety: a man and woman who must have been Grace Nykamp's brother George and his wife Hélène posing in evening wear before a large, glittering tree, hanging up stockings, and opening gifts with a dark-haired little girl with skin that was at once pale, yet dusky.

So a little girl about Shannon's age *had* lived here at one time, thought DeAnna, mildly surprised. Although the house still contained numerous possessions that had clearly belonged to George and Hélène Nykamp, she had found not a single toy, no trace of a child's ever having lived here. Nor had Grace mentioned a niece when she was describing the house to DeAnna.

No matter, thought DeAnna, it was a coincidence that when the Nykamps had lived here, their daughter had been only a little younger than Shannon was now. Nothing more than that.

As DeAnna continued to peruse the album, a few photos that were stashed in an envelope near the back—apparently by someone who intended to put them in the album one day and then abandoned the project—fell out onto the floor. DeAnna gathered them up. In doing so, she noticed that someone had labeled the backs of the photos: George and Hélène getting ready for the museum fund-raiser; Aimée with her new dolls, age five; Aimée dressing up to be Gretel in the school play; Aimée saying her prayers before bed . . . Aimée this . . . Aimée that. . . .

Aimée?

Amy?

DeAnna's mind whirled.

Amy/Aimée . . . the names were similar, but Shannon would have had no knowledge of the second one, with its French spelling and pronunciation. To her, thought DeAnna, the name Aimée would have sounded like Amy.

Amy.

Slowly DeAnna tucked the album back in its box and put it away. Her hands felt as though she'd dipped them in ice water and then not dried them completely.

Amy.

DeAnna got out her address book, found Grace Nykamp's number, and dialed it. A recording told her the number was no longer in service, that the new number was unlisted. All DeAnna had now was Grace's address in north Denver. What the hell, she thought, I'm fired anyway. She decided to take the next afternoon off as well and visit Grace Nykamp.

"Promise me you won't go up into the attic anymore without me," DeAnna said.

Shannon looked up morosely from her breakfast. Her upper lip sported a milk mustache, and her tongue was bright red from eating strawberries with her cereal.

"You saw her," she said flatly. "You saw Amy."

"I thought we agreed, Shannon . . . no more fibs. I don't want you going up there because it's dirty . . . drafty . . . the last time I was up there, the air was so stale I could hardly breathe."

"It's because *she's* up there," Shannon said. "You know she is."

DeAnna felt her thin patience fraying. "Just do as I tell you if you don't want to get your bottom tanned. No more nonsense about Amy, do you hear?"

The child's features pinched tight with anger. "It's because you saw Amy and you won't admit it. She's sad and scared and she wants me with her. She's my friend. I don't have any friends and now you want to take my only friend away from me! You took Daddy away and now you want to take Amy away, too!"

"Dammit, Shannon, shut up!" DeAnna smacked her hard in the face.

Shannon spun sideways out of the chair and thumped down on her rear. For a moment she sat in stunned silence, then her mouth opened and the sobs began.

DeAnna's hand stung from the blow. She dropped to her knees and tried to pull Shannon to her, but the child recoiled as though confronting a monster and dashed up the hall.

Later, when DeAnna felt more in control, she went to comfort Shannon and get her ready for school. The child was not in her room. DeAnna found her in the attic, swaddled in one of the brightly colored carpets, so that only the top of her head showed.

Rolling back and forth, slowly, rhythmically, while she cried. Right, then left, then right again.

Bundling.

Grace Nykamp was a short, compact woman with a small, birdlike head, a saffron cast to her pale, faintly pockmarked skin, and dark hair scraped severely back off her forehead. On the few occasions that DeAnna had met her, she always wore a huge, oversized blouse or sweater, clearly meant to conceal breasts whose size was out of proportion to her otherwise petite frame. Today Grace appeared at the door of her apartment wearing black tights and a tentlike maroon shirt.

She looked up at DeAnna blankly for a moment before recognizing her.

"Mrs. Gates, I'm sorry, I wasn't expecting anyone." A look of alarm registered on her face. "Is there a problem? Did something happen to the house? You could have called me. . . ."

"I tried to," said DeAnna. "Your number's been changed."

"Oh, damn," said Grace, "I'm sorry. I had to have it changed again last week. There've been some annoying phone calls, waking me up at all hours of the night . . . terrible, hateful messages . . . it used to happen a few years ago, after . . . but I'm rambling, aren't I? Come in. Whatever it is, I'm sorry you had to drive all the way from Boulder to get in touch with me."

"It's all right," said DeAnna. "I took the afternoon off. And no, nothing's happened to the house. It's just that . . . I found these photos and . . . " DeAnna pulled the box with its album and slides out of her tote bag. "They were buried under a lot of junk in a desk drawer. I thought your brother and his wife might want them."

"You needn't have," said Grace Nykamp, her tone a degree or two below arctic. "My sister-in-law Hélène moved back to France four years ago. And my brother George is . . . dead."

"Oh," DeAnna said. "I'm sorry. I'd been hoping Shannon and the little girl—Aimée—could perhaps meet each other. Do your sister-in-law and Aimée ever come back to the States to visit? If she does, I'd like to have her over to play with Shannon."

For a moment Grace Nykamp's face was like a stopped clock, giving out nothing; then her cheeks folded inward like wadded, white tissues and she let out a small, choked sob.

"It was my brother, Aimée's father," Grace said when she could compose herself. "I didn't want to tell you what happened because I was afraid that if you knew its history, you wouldn't want to take the house. People can be so cruel . . . to this day . . . well, why do you think I had to have my phone number unlisted? I was getting ugly, hateful calls. People who think I should share my brother's guilt. As if I had any idea what was going on . . . as if I could have stopped him . . . "

"What happened?" said DeAnna, although she answered the question before Grace could. "Your brother, he killed her, didn't he?"

Grace nodded. "He killed Aimée. Then, when he realized what he'd done, he drove up Boulder Canyon and shot himself in his car. He was a moody, quiet man, but I never realized he could be so . . . cruel. He had his wife trained. She was afraid of him, told me later that she walked on eggshells whenever he was home. But Aimée, you can't break a child's spirit so easily and she was rambunctious, noisy. And so he used to punish her. . . ."

"How?" DeAnna asked.

"At first it was just the typical stuff—slaps, spankings, I saw bruises on her occasionally, but she always said it was from falling down. Then apparently a teacher reported him as a possible abuser and he changed tactics, decided he had to punish Aimée in a way that wouldn't leave marks.

"He didn't call it punishment," Grace said. "He called it 'restraining her.' When she'd get too loud or start crying or try to fight him, he'd do this thing to her . . . it was cruel . . . it was bizarre . . . he'd roll her up inside one of the rugs up in the attic and tie the ends shut for a few minutes until she quieted down. And then the last time . . . Hélène was away and . . . in his suicide note, he said Aimée had dropped a Lalique bowl full of peppermints and broken it . . . he rolled her up inside a rug and didn't let her out in time. . . . She suffocated."

"Dear God," murmured DeAnna.

"Hélène told me that he said our father had punished him the same way, although I was half-grown when George came along, so if Papa did such an awful thing, I never knew of it. He said it was called—"

"Bundling," said DeAnna.

Grace's eyes widened in surprise. "How did you—"

Deanna interrupted her, "I need to use your phone."

"In the hall."

She dialed Mrs. Jernigan's number. "I just wanted to make sure you keep Shannon there until I get her. Don't let her leave for any reason until I'm there."

There was a pause. Finally Mrs. Jernigan said, "I guess we've gotten our wires crossed, Mrs. Gates. Shannon never showed up here after school. I thought she was with you."

"Shannon!"

After trying without success to reach Shannon at the house, DeAnna made the drive back from Denver in forty minutes, speeding all the way. She told herself that even if Shannon were in the attic, there was nothing there to harm her. Just a room full of carpets and an old loom.

Just a room where a little girl had been smothered to death by her sadistic father.

She parked the car at a drunken angle in the driveway and ran into the house, calling her daughter's name.

No answer.

She ran upstairs, checked Shannon's room, then the attic.

No Shannon. No sound. DeAnna almost turned to go except . . . the loom had fallen down. The upright beams had landed across a carpet rolled up on the floor, sealing it off like a tube. And in the center of the carpet was a bulge that . . .

DeAnna rushed to lift the loom and open up the carpet. The brilliant florettes and arabesques unrolled to reveal Shannon's lifeless-looking form. She wasn't breathing. DeAnna opened the child's mouth and began giving her artificial respiration. Nothing.

She breathed more air into Shannon's lungs, waited.

Nothing.

"Oh God, Shannon, I'm sorry. I'm so sorry I didn't believe you. So sorry I yelled at you, hit you. . . . Oh, Shannon, I love you so much."

She was about to carry Shannon downstairs and call an ambulance when she felt a small gust of musty, fetid air, a dank breeze subtly tainted with sweetness. It curled against her cheek, and fluttered Shannon's hair.

DeAnna looked up.

A dark-haired little girl with skin the dusky hue of wilted roses stood a few feet away. She wore a simple flowered dress and a necklace of cheap plastic beads. Her gaze was filled with longing and immeasurable grief. She stared at Shannon.

"Aimée?" said DeAnna.

The child lifted her head.

"Aimée, let Shannon go. You don't need her here. You don't have to stay here anymore. You can go on. But please don't take Shannon with you. Please, Aimée, I love her."

The wraith child put both hands up as if to shield her face. For an instant DeAnna saw a string of rapid impressions—her handprint on Shannon's face, shaking Shannon, knocking her out of the kitchen chair—things that Aimée might have seen or sensed, that made her think Shannon was mistreated, that she wasn't loved.

"Oh God, no," DeAnna cried, and shut her eyes, tears streaming. "No, Aimée, you're wrong. I love Shannon. Please, I need her with me."

Aimée blinked long-lashed, close-set eyes. She seemed to shiver, her outline trembling with a soft vibration.

"You don't have to stay here in the attic, Aimee. You can go on."

Aimée's face paled and narrowed and her facsimile of flesh began to disassemble. Like a creature made from fraying threads, she thinned out and came unraveled.

DeAnna gathered Shannon up.

"Mom?"

Shannon opened her eyes, looked around. "Where's Amy? The carpet, I bundled up in it the way she showed me and then something fell down and hit the floor and I couldn't get out of the carpet. I couldn't breathe." She began to sob. "Are you mad? Are you gonna spank me?"

DeAnna wept and hugged her.

"It's all right, Shannon. I'm not mad at you. No matter what happens, I'll never hit you again. I promise you, I promise."

She said the words over and over as she looked over Shannon's head at the place where Aimée had disappeared. All that remained was a patch of dank and musty air and the faintest odor of peppermint.

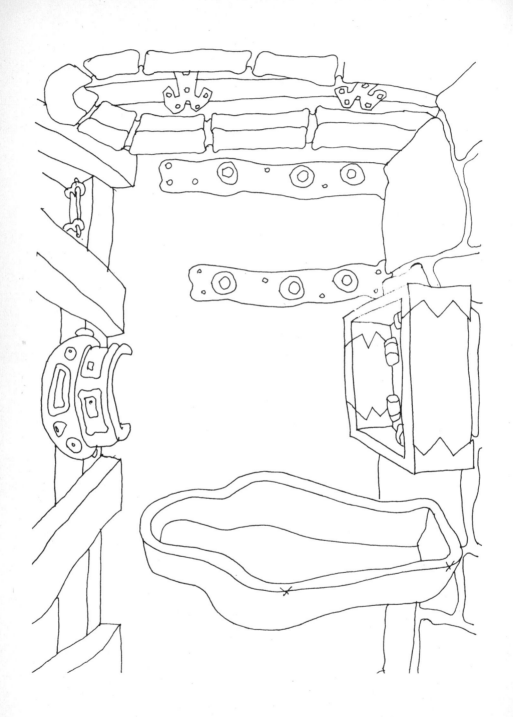

BONE TUNES

by Wayne Allen Sallee

I've lived down here all my twenty years. Or so it seems. Actually, I came down to the "wreck room," as Father has always called it, to play when I was younger. As my disease worsened I began to spend time here out of discipline. And by the time I had attained a reasonable threshold of pain, the next thing to do was lose my senses. So to speak.

First it was my eyes. Father unscrewed each and every lightbulb so that I might remain in the dark, for the most part. But there is one wall that catches sunlight through the window above the drainage vent. I do not know what direction that is. Father thinks it is best that I stay conditioned. Knowing things like directions would only serve to distract me when it was time to go to battle. He must be right. I've never lost a brawl since Father first entered me into the neighborhood competition in the summer of 1962.

I never knew anything about my mother, other than that she went completely mindless once I slithered out of her womb, my mutated shoulders and elbows tearing through her pelvic area. Father has never shown me photos of her, but I've seen dusty prescription bottles of Kevadon. I know that this was a muscle relaxant for pregnant women and that no one knew the effects of the thalidomide-based drug at the time of my gestation.

I know all this because there are books down here. This *is* a rec room after all. While the sunlight comes through the window opposite my mediocre bookshelf only three hours of the day, Father has provided me with a flashlight. (This has only been in the last year or so, as my pain threshold has called for me to start using electric shocks as discipline. I'd gotten past the simple things like skin piercing and hesitation cuts.)

And just because the local community is involved with treating its deformed children like pit bulls to be bet on, this doesn't mean that the board of education doesn't get involved. Occasionally, a glorified truant officer might stop by the house, to inquire if, say, the papers I was turning in to the school each month fell short of their expectations. Father would insist that I might simply be struggling over a specific civics lesson; in truth, I'm usually distracted if I am thinking of new ways to further my pain threshold. Father doesn't come down here often; I send the papers upstairs through a pneumatic tube. One of my science books says that by the 1980s there will be machines that work like telecopiers but the copies will be transmitted to another person's phone number.

The school knows about my independent studies (of *their* kind of education) because Father has told them of my progress. When he describes what I look like, it is not surprising that they choose not to descend into the "wreck room" to visit me. The rec room where I spend all my time, they are told, reading all kinds of books and playing with the games. And this pleases them. See, what it was, Father made an arrangement with the school board that I be privately taught at home, to spare the normal students the distractions and revulsion inevitably provoked by my physical appearance.

Amazing that this can still be a world where normals frown upon freaks five years after man has walked on the moon. I guess giant leaps for mankind go only so far.

What Father never tells the school board is that the books I read involve body modification and holistic healing. Years ago I was reading mysteries about Alfred Hitchcock's *Three Investigators* and *Trixie Belden,* but now I read for a different kind of release. I devour medical texts to learn about myself, then experiment with new techniques to further my pain threshold, my personal brink of controlled insanity.

Independent learning. Everything from texts by Bruno Bettelheim and Tracy Albert Knight to Gerrold Frank's *The Boston Strangler,* classics by the Chinese Yellow Emperor on pain centers, Jay Osigu's manual on pain projection, and Harwood Fassl's incredible tome on reduction of the thalamus, circa Belgrade, 1931. There is also Doolittle's book on reactionary effects while using *The Kingsburgy Techniques* on tendon-severing of live victims, and Presedo's volume of the Dramenon spiritualism of the dream wolves who lived in the southeastern regions of Valerisa during the Dark Ages.

There's even a history of this town down here. This damnable, nondescript, *American Playhouse* village born of old money and built upon family fictions. A make-believe history of children well cared for after the misfortunes that had befallen their families, devil worshiping becoming outlawed pregnancy drugs, clandestine deals with ancient deities blurred into visions of dioxin-filled maternity wards.

One would think this was one of those stories.

And this particular story always begins and ends the same way, with the pages of the book stained by droplets of blood caused by ancient paper cuts and marked by shreds of skin.

I am now missing two of the seven fingers I was born with. I have made peace with this, or whatever idea of tranquillity I should allow myself in this existence.

This is why I've been able to win at so many of the contests, although I did get hurt during a fight several years back. This was when the Vietnam War was just beginning and my opponent's father led her to believe that I was one of the gooks that had killed her older brother. That kind of crap went on all the time, this thing about parental pressure. It was worse than stories I've heard about the normal kids being ridiculed during Little League.

I learned something from that experience, though. That emotions can be fatal if one neglects their power. And it has helped me learn all the more about my opponents' weaknesses, which are more psychosomatic than anything else. The girl whose brother died in the war, I don't know how much "quality time" they had spent together before he went in-country, but that was only because I never had an opportunity to chat her up before I bludgeoned her at the ass-end of round seven. Hey, she took a good chunk of my face off with her teeth as early as round three. All because my slanted eyes and deformed skull give my face an Oriental cast.

Now I go for the jugular, metaphorically speaking. I modify my body to reflect the faults and deformities in my opponents. Maybe she taught me that.

Or maybe I learned it looking at my own reflection long enough.

When I was much younger, I looked at my warped features in the windowpanes of the main living room. This house has been here forever—one of the oldest in this section of the town, most of the furnishings were here when we arrived. I do not recall if there was a "For Sale/Sold" sign out front when Father and I arrived when I was four, although I do recall the nearest neighbor having an election sign stuck into the ground.

I have no clue as to whether Father rents this house, inherited it, or bought it outright. He never discusses what he does for a living, (though the fact of his silence about such matters will be moot before long.) What I do know is that I spent seven months upstairs, though Father denied my viewing the blond-colored Philco television in the living room. It was when I became of school age that I was exiled to the "wreck room."

And all of its attendant torture devices.

Blueprint for the damned: the room is square, the stairwell leading down angled as if installed by a carpenter prone to seizures. (Who knows, if this house was inherited, maybe he did have epileptic fits, and that would mean he was a blood relative.) The door is wooden with huge metal hinges, with an arcing border of misshapen red clay bricks around the edges of the frame.

The first thing I learned to do to myself, while in preparation for my first battle, was to break my tiny fingers by sticking them through the slit while the door was open, screaming only that first time that it swung shut. Soon I was able to waggle my fingers independently while the digits were caught tight in the frame. The first time I accomplished that, though, the tip of the little finger fell off. Father suggested I eat it.

I even tried to shove my pointed elbow joints into the frame, but they would only slide back out as if they were cheaply made wedges. I *would* gouge the skin in smooth ridges, though. Father was kind enough to break my arm that I might reach the wounded area to my mouth and lick the blood.

I owed much to him those first months. I won my first battle, with another six-year-old P'nakottian who had heavy scar tissue over one side of his face, in the second round and with little effort. Snapped his neck clean, Father beaming from the stands.

The next year I was on my own with my disciplines. Father had told me that he was there only for the first taste. With the next seven killings made in under five rounds, I was somewhat of a golden boy. Until that debacle with the lizard girl who thought I was of Asian origin.

I learned from that experience, as I've stated before. There is a square box in the center of the room. I think of an eviscerated billiards table. I have modified the insides to look like the pit where me and those my age have battle. (I am always blindfolded before I am led from the wreck room; the pit could be in the backyard, for all I know.)

I have ripped shelving units from my makeshift bookshelves and heightened the walls of my miniature battle pit. Against the far wall were receptors for Snavely prods; I ran wire around the edges of the pit, effectively electrifying it.

For three hours each day I blindfold myself and pretend I am fighting another—albeit in a more confined place—and I parry and thrust and often shock myself. But the books I have read have taught me to lose the pain. The current hums through me, making music along my bones, vibrating around those that have been broken and healed badly.

Lovely bone tunes that now play back to me with every blow that an opponent might make.

I am particularly euphoric when I am allowed a solid blow against my eye sockets.

There is another battle coming up next week, and Father told me that it will be with the younger brother of the scaly girl I killed years ago. He informed me of this just before I pulled him into the wires connecting the pit to the Snavely units. Not conditioned as I am, I expect it to be several minutes before he regains consciousness, if not longer.

Father made me too independent for *his* own good. I supposed it would come to this sooner or later, even if I wasn't going into battle with my current opponent. I had come to realize that, through it all, there was always Father. I needed to sever myself from him as cleanly as I had sliced the tendons in my wrists months back.

I will heal quickly from this, too.

Father with his perfect features. Like all the other parents. Perfect vision. Pristine dental work. The children all having excess body hair, scales, partial exoskeletons, or even two sets of teeth.

I need to know loss, like the family whose normal son went to Vietnam. Loss of my only remaining family member, to add to my collection of other losses—emotions, tendons, connective and digestive tissues.

Father would have lost me eventually, perhaps within this coming week. With his death, and my eventual one, perhaps this place will become deserted. Haunted. Perhaps it will become a preschool. Who can tell?

I will tell Father how well he taught me before I kill him. That will make him proud, to be sure.

But I think I will have fun with his body first.

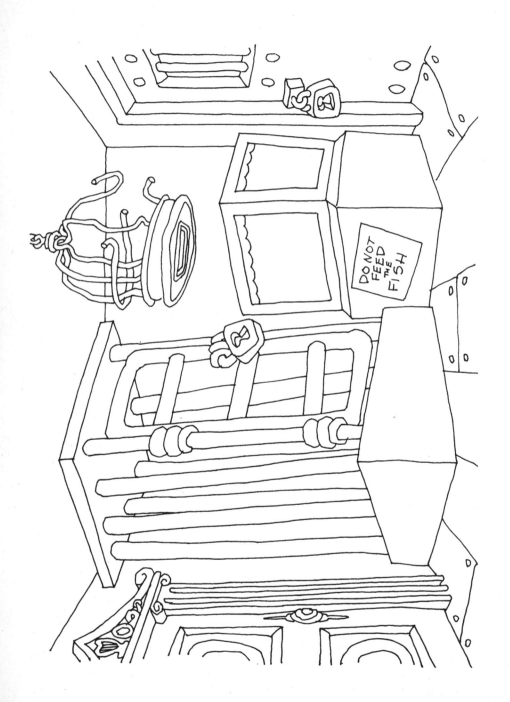

AFTERNOONS WITH THE BEASTS

by David Aaron Clark

Even Lady Julianna's maid cannot know all her secrets. I find it is a boon to my continued service to her that I indeed do not. The ignorance is necessary, for it holds the fear at bay. Fear from the terrible enough things that I do know.

Fear, yes, and other states, even more wracking influences upon the human soul, awful humors that twist the very ether of one's God-granted being. States in which a man's—or woman's—very humanity might be in question, as the muscle response shivers through a back, or loins, with the impossible assurance of some other species altogether.

This house is full of such emanations. Treacherous, evil black radiances from beneath the floorboards of certain closets. Rooms where there are cold spots and warm spots, things wet that should not be, voices heard where there is no possible throat. In such chambers, there are histories of atrocity clamoring for resurrection.

Why do I stay here then, in this mausoleum of anonymous ghosts, wherein each room is a phial to be emptied out on judgment day, a schoolroom informed by lessons in terrible, forbidden knowledges? In a fit of selfish fancy, I might claim it is to look after my Lady, as she is slight of stature, despite her clamorous dark beauty, and to look upon her in the street, you might think her easy prey for those of brutish vigor and strength.

But that would be a conceit, because the Lady does not need me to look after her. Though I have not seen them, I know that she has her guardians.

I hear them in a particular hallway, behind a certain thick steel door, its seams intaglio'd with the proof of ancient escape attempts. Others might claim what I hear is nothing more than the static that plays against the filaments of an idle set of nerves, but my ear has learned the scratch of tooth and claw, the rustle of large feather. I have heard the whisper of cold, leathery hide, large and stealthy, occupying the unseen air on the other side of the abandoned Menagerie's door, where its author could not possibly be.

I was not always cursed to serve as the unwilling library of aural terror; before this house I was a gay enough young girl, not dismayed by my station in life. Like any bright, pretty woman, I had aspirations. Having not yet even met her, I had little idea that my and the Lady Julianna's fates were linked, and that grim room was to be their final locus.

It was not long after Lady Julianna herself first came here, with me hired that very first week to see to her needs, that she set a small foot in The Menagerie. She has described it to me since then, and the tones of resigned madness that infect her musical drawl all but draw tears from my eyes.

She found herself overwhelmed by an immediately familiar sensation, one that had been haunting her since she gazed up past her fine lace veil at the jutting maw of the church whose alter she had so recently stood before.

Captivity.

She wandered to and fro through the long hall, enjoying how unusually tall she felt under its low ceilings. She picked her way around the clutter of empty cages, some of them misshapen from the insane paroxysms of bestial brains tormented into senseless rages.

Left abandoned and unrepaired, they spoke the dolorous tales of prior tenants, playing impassive host to brutal campaigns committed against dumb creatures attempting to indoctrinate them into the worship of their own death, if only because that passing might then mean a cessation from the unbearable ardor of their tortured realities.

Julianna stopped by the tiny, barred window, overwhelmed in its task of providing the sole conduit of ventilation to years of gamy stink. Sickly beams of late afternoon's gray light filtered through and expired upon the floor, leaving great patches of darkness that, against all reason, Julianna suddenly felt sure were populated.

She was not wrong. The shriek of some great scavenger bird raked the air, and she turned in a dizzying circle, seeking its cause. Her reason told her the cry must have come from outside, perhaps the roof, but the proof of her senses attested that the sound had come from within this room.

And then she lost her mind.

Or so it seemed, and her sight was transformed into a narrow geometry where objects signaled only food, pain, and danger. Her skin bristled, as if feathers were brushing the inside layers, seeking freedom. Her toes curled, easily piercing her stockings and leaving deep gouges in her leather slippers. Her head ducked of its own accord, seeking, despite the physical impossibility of such an action, to nestle beneath her armpit. From a great distance, she heard a man's voice, and did not understand the language—did not understand even what a man was, except this: a tormentor. She swooned.

When she woke, her skirts stained and torn, Lady Julianna, being of Gypsy blood and not disinclined to believe in the possibility of the fantastic, understood what had happened. She had been possessed by the dead avian soul that had been held captive in this room.

As she would now learn, the numb, insistent ghosts of stupid animal pain swarmed the Menagerie, transforming it into a constant museum of atrocity. Any visitor whose soul was attuned to the radiances emanating from more subtle planes, who was cursed with a nervous system raw enough through either nature or experience, ran the risk in this place of falling into a quivering trance, brain seized up by the leftover charges from spilled blood and brute natures driven to their final frenzies.

Indeed seeking to provoke this peculiar condition, Lady Julianna spent many of her afternoons in there, with God and myself both held at bay by the oversized bolts drawn shut on the other side of the thick, steel door.

The states she would progressively drive herself into were so extreme that she would report to me later how even the old, tattered linen of her childhood bed-gown, worn in memory of her lost parents, would feel rough against her tender, inflamed skin.

She would sink into the corner, passing through a thin, dusty beam of gray afternoon sun, feeling herself irradiated and run through by it, even as the air around her nose and mouth seemed to pulsate with the harsh, powerful breath of a great ape.

In her vision she would see, standing by the great cage, now unexploded, padlock still in place, the scientist, a chill jeer twisting his craggy features. He looked something like the architect. Lady Julianna would sometimes swoon with angry passion, her loins afire with the hatred of her captor.

Then there was the water tank. Appallingly, it was still full of a brackish paste of putrescent liquid that she suspected had never enjoyed a chemical composition as simple as water. A metallic smell of sweet rot reached from the tank to the door.

She would circle the tank on certain afternoons, imitating the impatient circuit of a caged predator fish. Swallowing all my fear, I would sometimes press my ear to the great door, and faintly hear her wandering in aimless circles for hours on end, slippers shushing against the unfinished floorboards.

She would tell me that the static electricity thus generated acted as a conductor to her nervous system, allowing her to roll like a dead leaf across the stony field of several dozen's worth of dead animals' infernal torture garden. She would collide with the eternal moments of pain and spasm endured by martyrs to science.

It was, as she told her husband Simon one day over a late Sunday afternoon lunch, "The only room in this infernal house where I feel human."

Such exchanges were not rare between the unhappy couple. She had married the Lord of the house, true. Not for love, but safety. Julianna, as I have said, is of mostly Gypsy blood, born and raised among a traveling caravan of them. She bears their unmistakable beauty and smoldering temper; her voice is velvety but her resolve made of flint.

She had been having a casual affair with the architect, a sharp-edged man whose bad humors often drove her away from him for weeks at a time.

Simon Manson was not an evil man, but certainly a venal specimen. He was the scion of some deposed nobility, somewhere—no one in the town could seem to agree on which now-liberated country had ejected his lineage.

He was also a modestly talented man, orderly and mean enough in his living to parlay the knowledge and technique imparted by a fine European academy (an education financed by appropriated peasant gold), along with the patronage of other refugees who owed his parents favors (delivered at some juncture in the escape process), into a lucrative career.

When his forbears succumbed to old age and stress, the young Lord Manson had been left free to his own priorities. Besides making money, his other preoccupation was young peasant girls, and Julianna had not been the first.

She had been, however, the first he chose to marry. Promises he had made to others, yes, the town was full of such tales, and they had indeed reached me, in the form of an admonition from my own mother to stay out of the flat-eyed rake's amatory path.

But Julianna had somehow saddled the beast, and her bit was deep in his mouth. Cold and haughty as he was, there were hardly any visible demonstrations of his amorous thrallery. But by the very act of his proposal, defying social convention and perhaps good business sense as well—what would his parents' friends, now his patrons, think of a Gypsy wife?—he had wed her.

My mother had been so dumbfounded by the event she had raised nary a protest when I applied for the job of the new Lady Julianna's maid, and my references secured the position. But I had known one truth as soon as I saw her face: The Lady did not love the Lord. How could she, any more than an eagle might lie with the sparrow, a wolf with a petulant squirrel?

After a week, the length of time it took me to earn Milady's trust and prove to her I was not a double agent hired by the Lord, she explained how the union had come about.

There were pogroms against her kind springing up in various quarters of the nation, and entire Gypsy families were regularly slaughtered by roaming parties of Village hooligans. Her own family fell victim, with her and her brother Arturo the only survivors, as they had been to the stream for water when the craven attack commenced.

Arturo had struggled against her grip to run back toward the screams of her mother and two older sisters, the shouts of her father and uncle, but Julianna had succeeded in dragging him into the brush, where they went undetected and were spared.

The incident went unremarked in the town; little attention was expended on the welfare of the Gypsies, only on their nuisance. But that night, when Lady Julianna brought Arturo by the hand to Lord Manson's gate, she knew he would glean the truth, and her fealty would be sealed, at least for the sake of her only surviving blood. At least behind the facade of this house and its middle-class owner they could find some sanctuary.

And a certain kind of sanctuary, it was. The architect's house— it was his house, and his alone, for she had not yet earned her right to be his heir as well as his wife, he told her more than once—was vast. Classic in design, as he would have had no less. Exquisite in execution, for he could not tolerate anything lax. Built in a long-ago era when the port city around it had not even been properly civilized, the mansion had passed through several hands before his.

She had discovered such in the library where the history of the house was kept in the sea-swollen journals of illiterate but wildly successful slave traders and buccaneers whose brutish hands had faded upon the pages as time passed, made delicate and given false nobility by the kiss of antiquity and decay. She would spend much of the morning in the library, as her duties were none, and any interest deemed too lively was forbidden.

She could have whatever she wanted, as long as it did not come with an excess of freedom. This life of kept indolence and forced luxury was as bad as a jail to her, but she persevered. She had married the man before God, and she did not take that lightly. Nor did she take Arturo's safety lightly. In the Lord's household, they were both safe from the pogroms still being conducted outside of the town's metropolitan safety.

Then came the day of the first nail in the sacred wood, that day that Lord Manson made his announcement.

"Lady Julianna, the boy needs an education. He needs to be among fellows his own age. And he needs to be out from under our feet. I am enrolling him in a fine academy as of next week."

"Simon, can't we keep him here? He'll be so terrified and out of place among those rich boys," she had argued on the child's behalf, before he was sent off, dour-faced, to a school several hundred miles away that built its gleaming reputation on discipline and fraternity.

"He must assimilate, darling, and you must tend to your husband. Did I not happily save you both? Simon replied, dismissing the issue. I had been collecting my lady's private laundry from her chamber, and nearly sneered at the man who hired me behind his back. If the Lady hadn't immediately melted my heart, I would have never stayed in that house for the meager salary he paid me.

Saving Julianna's brother but sending him away was the sort of spiky favor typical of Simon, an architect made up of gruff distances disdainfully expressed on pinched, ascetic features. How could he have ever hoped to move my Mistress's mixed blood, which steams with Gypsy aromas until it curls her black locks and cooks her skin olive?

He knew obsession, yes, but it was a cold, surgical passion that animated his contemptuous, lusty stares and his increasingly mistrustful ways. For he was aware that, despite her amatory efforts to persuade him otherwise, his bedroom charms were slight for the Mistress. The interrogations and litanies were constant.

"Julianna, my butler says you received a package today? What could it have been, I wonder, that you have failed to mention it nearly two hours after I've come home."

"Julianna, the butcher's brat seems to have an eye on you. I suggest to discourage his boorish leers, you will no longer accompany Rose on the shopping trips."

In their home, Simon was a bizarre suitor, given to weird strategies to force humiliating intimacies between them.

"Darling, you mustn't latch the water closet door. I am your husband, and that is in a sense like your doctor. Thus, I would be irresponsible not to monitor your bowel movements for consistency and regularity, as well as your ablutions for their thoroughness, since lack of detail to personal hygiene can lead to all manner of unpleasant conditions, some of which could keep you from the proper discharge of your wifely duty, a development I'm sure we would abhor when it came to finding the inspiration to maintain the high cost of this household."

I nearly dropped my laundry basket when I heard that speech from around the corner. Oh, the studied crudeness of his taunts, the sadistic games he played with her, simply because he could!

Was it a wonder she turned to the Menagerie, seeing in its corners the dead calm following the lifestorm, a garden of rotting animal carcasses, all soft, mossy and silent, in illustration of the quietude which inevitably follows life's bitter judgments, the sentencing by the law of other people's desires.

That bestiary, hidden in the northernmost corner of the building's third floor, had been founded to serve as a room of living trophies brought back by the house's very first owner on his frequent voyages to tropical and inordinately savage climes.

Cages were set up for fowl, fish, and mammal. Many combinations and varieties of such passed through, donated after some time to the local zoological society or sold to a passing circus. Cursing once proud beasts to dreary ever-afters.

Born of man's thoughtless vanity, the Menagerie evolved during subsequent incarnations, eventually becoming something far more perverse.

Lady Julianna learned one quiet afternoon as she sat motionless in the hollow, dry air of the library, turning each fragile page as if it were glass, that two proprietors before Simon, the owner had been a purported man of science, a wild-haired rogue who had fallen in academic disfavor during a series of scandal-ridden tenures across Europe.

12 December 19__. Progress continues, though final results are still only the shakiest conjecture. If these beasts have souls, I almost pity them. If they don't, the entire enterprise has been a grand waste of time and resources.

The gorilla's responses are the most rich; perhaps I am

influenced by the sentimentality of anthropomorphism, but the sullen creature, an obvious early, discarded template for the human race, seems capable of more than just retaining the memory of torture. Sometimes I would swear I see a glimmer of human vengeance in his eye, and when I turn unexpectedly from the laboratory table I catch him panting, and staring at me with his head cocked in an oddly reflective aspect. Perhaps he is just imitating me when I am lost in thought.

He does not touch his food for the last two weeks, no matter how tantalizingly it is prepared. The reverend, that sentimental tippler, took one look at the hairy brute and declared him a saint on a hunger strike. See what giving away your best whiskey to the clergy earns you!

The vulture is another matter; nothing but hunger, that one. His predecessors have proven on the dissection table how physically slight their brains are, I see little room in them for any higher cognitive skills. No matter how I try to apply Pavlovian technique, the great, ugly bird resists the learning arc. His beak may drip blood and his throat may work in great convulsions, but he still will attempt to eat the dead mice left beneath his perch, though every one has been impregnated with razors and pins.

The pirahna has proven instructive, and is perhaps the most perfect of these species. Even when I charge its water with mild electric shocks, its instinct still takes over as soon as I drop chum into the tank. Its response time is even swifter when I award it living vermin; I think the thrashing of the drowning mice awakens its bloodlust even more swiftly.

25 December 19__. What a vile creature, that ape! I suppose it was my fault, for leaving the door ajar while I went to use the water closet. The scullery maid was in a fit of hysterics when I came back and found that the stray cat she had adopted had ventured up into the Menagerie, and within grabbing reach of that African beast. Too bad for the silly little strumpet's sensibilities, that she had followed so closely behind her little kitty.

On the positive side, at least the ape did not need to be fed today. On the negative, who knows what disease that vermin-ridden alley prowler may have been carrying.

6 January 19__. An interesting development; the avian brain evidently is sophisticated enough to entertain the desire for suicide. When I entered the Menagerie this morning and found the vulture hanging neck-first from its perch, somehow having managed to wind its chain around the bar on which it normally hunches, I thought it a clumsy misstep, perhaps part of an escape attempt, or thanks to a start from the ape.

This afternoon, after its electroshock session, however, it performed a deliberate maneuver before my own eyes, attempting once again to, in effect, hang itself. Marvelous!

Lady Julianna later told me the sympathetic natures of the two different masters of the house were immediately evident to her.

"They are both the worst sort of sadists, hiding their joy at torment behind a cool, rational facade," she complained to me one night as I drew the water for her bath. Her smooth, nut-colored brow was wrinkled in disgust.

"If Lord Manson were not my brother's benefactor, I would leave him in an instant," she confided. This much had already been obvious to me, and I suspect, to her husband as well.

Which made the moment that came not two evenings after that pronouncement all the more apocalyptic, when after a sumptuous dinner of roast venison Simon Manson pushed his plate aside and puffed seriously on his evening cigar, staring at Julianna with some obvious weight on his mind.

There was, however, no preamble to the declaration that came next, no gentle words or warning to cushion the blow.

"Your brother has been murdered, Julianna. I'm sorry. It seems there was a ring of boys who had ostracized him because of his blood, and they one day provoked him into a fight with one of them. Then they all jumped in and beat him to death. It's a huge scandal at the school."

A huge scandal at the school. You could practically see it through her shawl; Lady Julianna's heart was molten, exuding red and yellow rays of grief, anger, hatred, torment. Arturo. His quiet eyes. His lonely smile. I'm sure she was imagining it twisted into anger by ceaseless indignities and insults, magnified in their effect by his distance from the one remaining member of his family, the only other soul who could understand his ache and solitude.

In an odd moment of telepathy, my thoughts were hers, and I could see with her the next vision dredged up by her shock: that sweet boy's face bloody, malformed by bruises and scratches, teeth missing, lip split, eyes with the vessels burst and drenched in crimson. Warm, dark childish skin gone clammy and chalky with death.

"Julianna?"

When Simon dared speak to her, I found that I could not breathe. Half out of the dining room, half not, I could only stand frozen, my mouth unceremoniously agape, and wonder at the Lady's next word or action. Insanely, I thought of their dinner's next course, growing dangerously cool in the kitchen. A good an excuse as any to withdraw. I knew what my next course of action would have been, and I did not want to witness the brooding Lady's physical attack on her husband.

"Julianna, this is a terrible tragedy. Those boys are simply monsters. Why, we ought to sue the school and their parents, for letting such beasts—"

"Beasts."

Her reply seemed almost like a parrot's echo, a senseless syllable delivered by tongue alien to speech's complications.

"Beasts rarely kill for sport, Simon. They do protect their ground and their family, however. Which makes you less than a beast, doesn't it? My brother was yours as well."

"Only because I wanted you for my wife, Julianna," Simon snapped back, before realizing the crudity of his remark under the circumstances.

Rather than reply in kind, however, Lady Julianna merely smiled at her husband, offering him the most mockingly merry of grins, a burlesque of reconciliation. Then she returned to her dinner, but rather than take knife and fork to the pheasant I had prepared, heartily grabbed the bird up off her plate, and dug her strong white teeth into its breast. The juice ran down her chin and pooled on the breast of her gown. Stifling a gasp, I left for the kitchen.

Preparing the next dish, I was distracted by a violent clatter from the dining room. Upon my return I found that Lord Manson had fled, and that Lady Julianna had flung her dinner against the wall, causing a large grease spot that trailed to the floor, pointing the way to the mess of the hapless bird's corpse. She looked over at me from her place at the huge, mahogany table, as I without remark knelt to clean away the gruesome debris.

"He doesn't deserve to continue drawing breath, not when Arturo has been deprived of his."

I chose my words carefully.

"He is a terrible man, Milady, very venal. But what are we, as mere women, to do about it? It is the horrible way of the world."

"There are other worlds, where retribution is more swift," she replied, and then spoke no more.

I took to my bed that night with every nerve-end painfully singing, feeling the evil electricity that permeated the entire house. I did not see the couple together again before bedtime, but did pass Lord Manson in the hallway of the master bedroom. He was drunk, yet attempting even in his cups to maintain the exaggerated posture and elegant walk which he so prided himself upon.

Upon spying me, he seized my shoulders roughly, his fingers filthy pincers digging through my uniform and into my flesh. The foul stink from his maw was redolent with decay, a whiff of the slaughterhouse on a Saturday afternoon.

"The bitch!" he muttered, his eyes unfocused, not even seeing the terrified expression on my face. "Now the bitch thinks she's going to sleep in that room! Used to living like an animal, I suppose, she with her sainted dead parents and that sorry little whelp. Well, now she's alone in the world, and she's going to have to learn to live like a human being. Or if she wants so badly to commune with the lower animals, I shall teach her what it truly means to be one!"

Throwing me against the wall, he lurched away, toward the third floor.

What course to take? The Lady had no champions, and the Lord no friends who cared for his welfare. Only business associates. I might call the constabulary, but it would mean my position for certain. Still, it might save Lady Julianna from a terrible beating.

I was in the downstairs hallway, cranking the telephone, when the muffled scream reached me. Though feminine in its unabashed terror, the timbre, or so it seemed, was masculine. Pain will do that to a voice, I learned when I was small and my father lost three toes to a bored horse's misplaced hoof. The agony gives raw vocal chords the depth of multiple genders.

Gathering my skirt about me, I raced up the back staircases, which afforded a more direct path to the third floor. From the other end of the hallway, I could see that the Menagerie's door was open, a dull steel glimmer in the shadows thrown by the iron sconces set into the walls on either side of it.

I approached the portal with an sense of awful resignation, sure I would carry the sight of Lady Julianna's swelled face, perhaps even her broken body, with me for the rest of my days.

At first look into the room, I could not see either of them. Then I looked back by the cage that had once held a noble but tortured gorilla, martyred under the auspices of human science, and their forms materialized from the shadows. At first I thought he was being cradled by her, in the classic aspect of the Pieta. But further observation, provoked by the hideous gnashing and tearing coming from their locale, revealed the truth.

I cannot properly describe her horrible aspect, for it was so unnaturally malformed. Her spine seemed raised and swollen, and her limbs were askew in impossible long wing-like swoops, while her posture was hunched and ape-like, and her features twisted and gaping, hungry teeth drenched in Lord Manson's blood.

She grunted a deep, soft bellow when she saw me, and then screeched in perfect imitation of the thin, piercing cry of a sated vulture. The air around her seemed thick with the stink of brine, electricity, sweat and gore. A scent that predated civilization, and native intelligence, and of the human soul itself.

The Lord himself was mauled and mangled, his flesh scored by so many tears as to make its pale hue of death as hard to confirm as the original shade of a well-used butcher block. He looked instead ruddy, and sweating copious red tears from every pore. Great pieces of him were missing, the edges of the wounds ragged and gnawed, impatiently severed. The expression on his face was an odd mix of outrage and terror, his shock somehow haughty even in a state of fresh decomposition.

Our eyes locked. Oh God save me, that was the worst! For there was in Lady Julianna's gaze no hint of recognition, and instead the alien glare of a feral beast, who in a bloodline unweak-ened by evolution has stalked, killed, and ate since the dawn of recorded time, and probably before. They were tropical river beds, opaque with the blood of weaker fish. They were a bleached desert, made alluring by the promise of sweet rot within its victims. They were pits of furious vengeance, pulsing with the beating of some great beast's massive breast.

Then those haunted orbs rolled back in her head, and she fell forward across the corpse of Lord Manson.

I have looked after her since. The Lord lays in a cask in the wine cellar, where he helps ferment what I'm certain must be a quite tart vintage, never to be uncorked. Not one friend has inquired after him, and the bank clerks accept Lady Julianna's hand on his cheques, rarely even inquiring after him. His business associ-ates have been informed that a nervous condition has necessitated his early retirement, and a little research provided me with the names of distant colleagues to turn them over to, colleagues not likely to call and thank him for the recommendation.

I take care of the housing, doing the shopping and the cooking. The cleaning, I fear, has grown sporadic, and the laundry occasional. I do feed and bathe the Lady every night, and rise early in the mornings so I may spend the day shopping and enjoying the unfettered sunlight, clean from the taint of that damned house's air.

My trips to the butcher's shop have grown frequent; more and more, the Lady demands the most raw and bloody cuts of meat, which she insists on preparing herself, while I am gone the next day. The food disappears without fail, leaving not even bone or gristle needing to be disposed.

Of what goes on during those daylight hours I am not quite sure. There has been, at certain times, evidence of visitors. I am not sure if Lady Julianna has suitors, for there is much these days she chooses not to share with me. But I do know this, for sure:

Afternoons, she spends with the beasts.

THE MONSTER LAB

by Steve Antczak

Melissa heard the clatter of the horses' hooves and the wheels of the carriage on the cobblestones announcing her uncle's arrival. She went to a window, watching through lace curtains as the ornately carved carriage rounded the cherub fountain in the center of the drive. The driver eased back on the reins, slowing the four black geldings, then stopped the carriage at the bottom of the marble front steps of the Lydecker house.

Roderick Lydecker, Melissa's father, had inherited most of *his* father's fortune, passed down from an ancestor who'd amassed riches trading in slaves from the Dark Continent. The house and property, in upstate New York, made up the bulk of the inheritance: five hundred wooded acres centered around a Tudor mansion; a stable, servants' quarters, and a guest house. Most of the buildings on the property had fallen into disrepair. A smaller portion of the fortune, in the form of a flat cash payment, went to Roderick's only sibling, his younger brother, Jacob. Melissa knew her uncle had invested his money in the shipping and warehouse insurance business in Boston, and amassed a fortune of his own.

The driver pulled down a large trunk, setting it gently on the ground, then opened the door to the carriage. A moment later he was helping a lady climb down from the carriage to the ground.

So Uncle Jacob had a lady in his life. Melissa felt excited at this notion because in all the years she'd known him, her uncle had never had *anyone* in his life but himself. However, no one else emerged from the carriage. The lady was alone, and Jacob had apparently not yet arrived.

Disappointed, Melissa went into the foyer to summon her father's only remaining servant.

"Nob!" she called. "Nob!"

A moment later she heard heavy footsteps upstairs and a large, hunchbacked, nearly hairless man appeared at the top of the wide, spiral staircase.

"A lady has arrived," Melissa told him, "and she has a big trunk with her. Please bring it in, and show her in as well."

Nob nodded obediently and came down the stairs, which creaked and moaned under his immense weight. Nob had been Roderick Lydecker's trusted servant since before Melissa's birth, and had even outlived her mother's attempts to have him discharged. Melissa's mother later died from falling out an upstairs window she was apparently trying to clean. Nob had been helping her, and for a while afterward Roderick suspected the misshapen mute of *murdering* her. Melissa managed to convince her father that without her mother around, they'd need Nob more than ever, so he eventually dropped the matter.

Next to Nob's bulk Melissa felt like a small child, although alone, or around men of normal stature, she felt womanly. Petite, yet shapely, she had pronounced breasts and wide hips, and thick curls of auburn hair fell across her shoulders. She also liked to think her blue eyes were lit with a lust for life, like her father's, where Nob's brown eyes tended to reflect his dull and docile nature.

Melissa waited until Nob went out the front door before running to the backstairs that led to the basement and her father's "workshop." She opened the door and, not daring to venture down without Roderick's express permission, called out to him.

"Father, come quick! There's a *lady* here to see you!"

A few moments later she heard a door open and close, the jangle of iron keys and the snap of a lock falling home, and her father's muttering voice.

"A lady?" he said. "To see *me*? What on God's earth . . . ? Who could she be?" All the way up the stairs he muttered, until he paused to kiss Melissa on the forehead and sigh in exasperation. He, too, towered over her, although his frame was straight and true, not warped as Nob's was. He kept his black-as-oil mustache and hair tightly trimmed. His piercing blue eyes always seemed to be looking beyond the here and now.

"Perhaps she's with Uncle Jacob," Melissa ventured, "and he's sent her on ahead while he tidies up some business back in Boston."

"Perhaps," her father said, although he didn't sound too convinced. He walked a few paces past his daughter, stopped to straighten out his shirt and coat. He ran his fingers through his hair and buffed his fingernails on his sleeve; then he continued toward the front door. Nob held it open to let the lady in.

"Hello, Roderick," Melissa heard the unmistakably soft voice of her uncle say.

"My God . . . *Jacob?*" sputtered the eldest Lydecker brother.

Melissa rushed to her father's side to see for herself.

At first she thought that the lady before her stood taller than most women, and had larger bones. She wore a long, dark green dress, a black petticoat embroidered in gold, long black velvet gloves, a dark green scarf, and a black hat underneath which Melissa saw the face of . . .

"Uncle Jacob!" she gasped when she saw *Jacob's* face smiling at her. His light blue eyes, lacking the sharpness of Roderick's, seemed somewhat glazed. His blond hair played out under the scarf; he'd let it grow to shoulder length. He powdered his face, too, like a true lady.

"Melissa, dear," Jacob greeted her. "My, you've grown! Look at you, you're very nearly a woman!" Had she not spent a large portion of her childhood hearing her uncle's voice, Melissa thought she could easily have mistaken it for a female's.

"And you, Uncle," Melissa said, "you've, umm, *changed.*"

Uncle Jacob laughed. He sounded *quite* feminine, light and airy. "I'm still your *uncle* Jacob," he said. "Don't you worry."

"But . . . but you . . . " Roderick stammered. He took a deep breath. "You look like Mother!"

"Do I?" Jacob asked. "Well then . . . thank you, brother. I'll take that as a compliment."

"What's happened?" Roderick asked. "An accident of some sort . . . ?"

"No, no," Jacob answered. "I will tell all, but first . . . " He nodded in the direction of Nob, who stood by silently, holding the trunk.

"Oh." Roderick seemed to snap out of a trance. "Right. Nob, take that up to the guest room I had you prepare for my . . . brother."

Nob, without so much as a by-your-leave, carried the big trunk upstairs. The other three watched, as if glad of the distraction. But then Nob was out of sight and down the second-floor hallway, and Melissa and Roderick turned their attention back to Jacob.

"Do you have any brandy?" Jacob asked. "It was quite a chilly ride here. . . ."

"Oh, of course." Roderick, still acting as though a real lady were in the house, rushed away to prepare the study for them, leaving Melissa alone with her uncle.

"You look very pretty," Melissa could only say.

"I know," Jacob replied. All the same, now that the initial furor over his arrival had died down, Melissa couldn't help but notice that her uncle also looked very tired. Bone-weary.

"Father's been looking forward to seeing you again," Melissa continued, to avoid the awkwardness of silence. "He's been telling me stories of your childhood together in Salem."

Jacob smiled.

"Oh, yes, our childhood together. We were the best of friends as well as brothers."

"That's what Father says. He says you did everything together."

"Oh, yes, we did." He smiled wistfully and his eyes seemed to focus beyond Melissa, beyond the present of 1908 and into the distant past.

A moment later her father called them into the study.

The pungent aroma of leather-bound books permeated the study, where Roderick had poured three glasses of brandy. Melissa realized she had been invited to sit with them for the first time in her life, probably because her father needed her for moral support. Indeed, she noticed the pallor of his face, and his skin seemed waxen. Brandy had been a good idea.

They sat, and sipped their drinks in silence for a moment.

Finally, Roderick spoke.

"I assume there's a good reason for your masquerading as a woman, Jacob?"

"Of course there is, although it may seem silly to you at first. You must trust me when I say that until I arranged my 'transformation,' my life was becoming a living hell."

"I'm listening."

"You haven't seen me in over two years," Jacob began. He paused to sip more of his brandy. "And in that time my condition has deteriorated drastically."

Melissa knew all about his condition. Jacob had suffered for a number of years from an unidentifiable malady that doctors told him would gradually siphon off his strength, shorten his breath, and render him feeble and old well before his natural time. In short, he did not expect to live beyond the age of forty, and she knew he was in his late thirties now.

"I found, as a man, that other men I had dealings with, both socially and professionally, regarded my weakened condition with contempt. I discovered that several of my close associates schemed behind my back to wrest control of my insurance holdings away from me. And these men I counted among my most trusted friends. So I devised a plan. It occurred to me that the very traits they found distasteful in me, they very much admired in *women*. Well, I realized that my physique, if you will, wasn't exactly manly anymore, and in fact I had acquired a distinctly feminine appearance, even dressed in trousers and a shirt with the sleeves rolled up. I concocted a female identity, Roderick, a *sister* who'd been married off at a young age and whom we'd not been in contact with for years, who suddenly found herself a widow and in need of male sponsorship. So I began spreading it around that I had found a potential cure for my ailments in the Far East—Katmandu or some such place—and that I would be leaving our *sister* in charge of my affairs while I ventured off to begin treatment!"

Jacob paused for a moment to sip his brandy while Roderick absorbed these revelations.

"Sister?" Melissa's father could only mutter by way of comment.

"Yes," Jacob said. "Andrea. Dre, for short. She's the baby, three years younger than me."

"I see."

"I've always wanted an aunt," Melissa said.

Jacob smiled at her. "Life got so much easier after that, I must say," he continued. "Because I was a woman with male sponsorship, my associates suddenly adopted a code of ethics when dealing with me. I even had a few marriage proposals"—Roderick gagged on a sip of brandy—"which I declined, of course. One of my suitors committed suicide, you know. Poor thing!"

"God," Roderick said, setting his drink down and rubbing his face with his hands. "Sounds like you created a monster!"

Melissa broke into a fit of giggles. They watched her, Roderick with exasperation, Jacob with bemusement, until she calmed down.

"Sorry," she said quietly.

Jacob looked at his older brother. "When I got your note, Roderick, I barely took the time to get my affairs in order. I hired a firm to take charge of things—"

"Which firm?" Roderick asked, frowning, suddenly all business.

"Boyle and Leech."

Roderick nodded his approval.

"I came right away," Jacob said. "When I read that you could cure me . . . You said, 'I am positive I have discovered the means of relieving you of your bizarre illness and can guarantee you a new life unfettered by the shackles of infirmity.'" Jacob took a deep breath. "I don't think I'll last through the winter, you know, especially if it proves to be too severe. Not in the pathetic condition I'm in now."

"Then we must begin your . . . treatment as soon as possible. Tomorrow."

Jacob's eyebrows rose. "Tomorrow?"

"Yes. Until then, however, let us sit awhile and sip our brandy, and talk of happier days. I don't think Melissa has ever heard the story of the time I wrapped you up in bandages and convinced you you had died and become a mummy. . . ."

Jacob groaned. "Does she need to hear it now?"

Roderick looked at his daughter with a twinkle in his eyes. "I also managed to convince him that he had to obey me, because whoever raised someone from the dead became their master."

"Father!" Melissa exclaimed, laughing. "You were so cruel. I'm glad *I* never had an older brother!"

"Indeed," said Jacob, "but I must say this: I am quite glad to have an older brother this day, especially one who is a genius, if a bit mad, and who cares enough about his sickly little brother to devote the vast quantities of time and money it must have taken to discover a way to cure him." With that, Jacob raised his glass in salute to Roderick. Melissa followed suit, and the three of them sipped their brandy in a silent toast.

"What else are big brothers for?" Roderick asked then, after they had emptied their glasses. He got up to fetch the bottle and refill them.

Next day, breakfast was served in the dining room at eight. The kitchen and dining room smelled of bacon and sausage and fresh-brewed coffee. Jacob came late, wearing a flowing dressing gown of linen and lace. Roderick, busy reading a book of Byron's verse, didn't notice him at first. But when he did, he stared in disbelief.

"I have no men's clothing with me," Jacob explained. "How would it look, in the event of an accident or other emergency, for a woman to be traveling alone, yet with a man's clothes in her trunk?"

"I see."

"Anything of yours would hang too loosely on me. Besides, this is quite comfortable. It's about the only thing I wear these days. I don't know why women don't rebel against the outrageously uncomfortable clothes we make them wear!"

"I'm sure I don't know, either," Roderick said. Both men looked at Melissa, as if expecting some revelation, but she just shrugged and sipped her coffee.

"So, Roderick," Jacob said, "will the procedure take very long?"

"It may take a while, yes."

"Days?" Jacob asked. "Weeks? Months?"

"The actual procedure won't take long, but the recovery period could last a while. A few months, perhaps."

"Will it be particularly painful?"

"Painful?" Roderick frowned. "Uncomfortable is probably more like it. There will be a certain amount of disorientation. Just remember at all times that you're in good hands, and not to panic. Always keep in mind what the alternative is."

Jacob nodded gravely. "Death," he said. "Slow, undignified, dishonorable . . . I do not wish to waste away like that. Rather, let me die undergoing some experimental treatment so that I may at least contribute in some small way to the cause of science."

"You sound like Father," Melissa noted. "He's always talking about the great cause of science, but I think he's just having fun. I think he *likes* tinkering around downstairs in the Monster Lab by himself."

"Melissa . . . " Roderick began in a threatening tone.

"Monster Lab?" Jacob asked. "Roderick, is that what you call your lab?"

Roderick grinned. "It seemed to be the only thing I could think of. I never told her about it."

"About what?" Melissa asked.

He looked at Melissa. "That's the name of the play lab your uncle and I had when we were children."

"We used to find dead animals," Jacob explained, "and sever their body parts and reattach them to the bodies of other animals, hoping to create living monsters. Of course we never succeeded, the poor animals being, as they were, dead already."

"What a gruesome thing for two young boys to play at," Melissa commented. "But that's boys for you."

"We never actually killed the animals ourselves," Jacob said. "Roderick used to hike all around looking for ones that were already dead. I always marveled at how he could find so many that'd been freshly killed. Still, I guess we entertained ourselves with pretty gruesome play! Luckily Mother and Father never found us out. We built the Monster Lab in a big oak tree way out in the woods, and as far as I know, no one ever knew about it."

"It sounds like *you* haven't changed much," Melissa told Roderick in a mischievous tone.

"Are you *still* performing those macabre surgeries?" Jacob asked, amusement in his voice. "You haven't outgrown *that*, then."

"Quite the contrary," Roderick said. "The work I do now is real. Not play. Someday it shall revolutionize medicine. But . . . you'll see when I take you downstairs later."

"You won't need me . . . will you, Father?" Melissa asked.

He waved the question off. "Don't be silly, of course I will. Nob, too, for that matter."

Melissa lowered her gaze to her breakfast and didn't say anything else, nor did she eat any more. Roderick and Jacob finished breakfast in silence, too. The reunion of the brothers had apparently already lost its novelty; they'd run out of things to talk about, or at least things either wished to speak of.

At the end of the meal, however, Roderick did speak. "You are free to do as you wish with your body today, Jacob. Indulge yourself with drink, food, tobacco, or anything else you desire. I have plenty of everything in this house. We shall have an enormous feast for dinner, and then I'll take you down to the so-called Monster Lab and we can begin the procedure."

That ended breakfast. Roderick disappeared downstairs. Nob worked in the kitchen preparing for dinner. Jacob asked Melissa to accompany him for a walk outdoors.

Outside, the sun peeked through gray clouds. A cold wind blew across the grounds. Jacob remarked how good it made him feel to take it all in, the place where he and Roderick had summered with their parents so long ago.

"A lifetime ago," he finished wistfully.

He told Melissa her grandfather used to do a lot of foxhunting in the rolling countryside. Now the stables held only horses for the carriage. The walk enlivened Melissa at least, but Jacob looked worn and tired by the time they got back to the house. Melissa ran on ahead, up the stairs, and waited for her uncle at the front door.

As he slowly climbed the stairs, Jacob paused, stood still for a moment, then collapsed.

"Uncle!" Melissa yelled, and rushed to his side.

Nob carried Jacob upstairs, led by Melissa. Jacob groaned and came to in the upstairs hallway, halfway to the guest room.

"The nervous new husband carries the blushing bride to the bedroom," Melissa said, smiling.

"I fainted," Jacob told her. "Please fetch me some brandy."

"Brandy," she said. "Yes, Uncle." She ran downstairs, got the bottle, and returned as Nob opened the door to Jacob's room.

"You can let me down," Jacob told the hunchback. "I'm fine." He felt Nob hesitate. "Really, I'll manage."

Ever so gently, Nob let Jacob down on his feet. Jacob had to place one hand against a wall for support, but other than that, he seemed strong enough to stand.

"Thank you," he said to Nob.

Melissa handed the brandy to Jacob. He took it with his free hand. Then she looked at Nob.

"Don't you have to finish preparing dinner?" she asked. Without so much as a grunt in reply, Nob retreated downstairs. Melissa watched the hunchback go, then turned to face Jacob.

"You know it's strange," Jacob said, "but Nob reminds me of your mother. I watched him cutting the vegetables earlier, just before we left for our walk, and he did it just the way *she* used to."

Melissa felt the expression on her face harden almost automatically. Her vision seemed to cloud.

"Ridiculous," she said, tight-mouthed, "and I would thank you not to defile Mother's memory with such disrespectful comparisons in the future! Mother was a brilliant woman, well educated, a wonderful chef; kind, noble, beautiful. . . . Nob is an ugly, brainless animal who has learned certain tricks the way a smart dog might learn how to roll over or play . . . dead!" With that last word— *dead*—Melissa broke into tears and ran to her room, slamming the door shut behind her.

Roderick seemed lively enough at supper, but he looked haggard. Jacob came to the table drunk, bringing the now half-empty bottle of brandy. Melissa felt better after a nap, and no one made mention of the dark circles under her eyes. She regretted her confrontation with Jacob earlier, and imagined leaving him there in the hall, bewildered and perhaps a little hurt by her sharp tone. She just could not face discussing her mother with him. It relieved her that Roderick chose not to mention her tirade, for she was certain he heard every word of it. Voices carried throughout the house with astounding clarity, especially when raised in anger.

Nob retired to the kitchen after serving the food, which filled the room with a rich aroma reminiscent of a holiday feast.

"Mmmm, thish ish *good*," Jacob slurred around a mouthful of roast pork, spitting bits of food with each word.

"I'm glad you like it," Roderick said, but he wasn't smiling. He sighed as his brother took a gulp of brandy straight from the bottle.

A moment later Jacob speared another forkful, but as he raised it to his lips he paused, then dropped it, and slowly slid out of his chair to the floor.

"Finally," Roderick said. He looked at Melissa. "He never could hold his brandy, but I was beginning to wonder."

Melissa said nothing.

"Now what's the matter?" her father asked.

"Nothing."

"You should be happy, you know. You'll be living in Boston before long, with a substantial monthly allowance from your uncle Jacob's holdings. I'll have enough money with *my* share to continue my work. And Jacob will be alive and *healthy* again. We should *all* be happy. *I* am happy, though I'd be happier if you were happy, too."

Melissa sighed. "If it's all the same with you," she said, "I'd rather feel miserable for now."

"You were like this with your mother," Roderick said. That comment ignited a fire in her gut, but she didn't respond to it. Roderick continued. "If only you knew how much your denial hurts her . . . but then you *do* know, don't you? She wrote you those letters, the ones you burned."

"She wrote those letters *before* she died!" Melissa practically screamed, her pent-up emotions bursting forth. "*You* told Nob to slip them under my door after you buried her body! My mother's soul is in heaven, not trapped in the body of that hunchback!"

Roderick sighed.

"How many times must I tell you, Melissa?" he asked. "The soul is housed in the *brain,* not the breast. The heart is merely a pump—"

"Then why, when I feel sad, does it ache *here?*" she said, hitting her chest with her fist. "Why, when I am happy, do I soar *here!*" She struck herself on the chest again. "Just because he knows what she knew doesn't mean he's *her!* When her heart stopped beating, her spirit left! Mother is *dead,* just like Uncle Jacob will be dead, and you're the one who's fooling himself, and that's why I can't take it anymore! *That's* why I want to go to Boston—"

Melissa broke down into sobs then, while Roderick silently watched her. Jacob groaned on the floor.

"I have to start," Roderick told his daughter. "My offer remains. If you help me this last time, you can go to Boston with no ill will, living off the money from Jacob's holdings. If you refuse to help me, I will insist you remain here until you find a husband—"

"I'll help you." Melissa regarded the place at the table where Jacob had been sitting. "He's dying anyway, isn't he?"

Roderick nodded.

"Then let's begin."

Roderick's so-called Monster Lab wasn't in the basement. It was *below* the basement. A massive iron door kept it sealed off from the rest of the subbasement, most of which Roderick never used. The dust, cobwebs, and stale air attested to that. By the dim glow of a gaslight, Melissa saw the iron door had a wooden sign glued to it, jagged-edged, with the words MONSTER LAB written on it in uneven, childish script: the actual sign from the treehouse Monster Lab years ago, Melissa's father explained.

Roderick pulled down a lever located across the hall from the lab, and the iron door opened slowly. An elaborate mechanism of pulleys, gears, and chains clanked and wheezed, echoing throughout the subbasement. Melissa sneezed as the door kicked up dust. The unmistakable stench of decay, mingled with the odor of the chemicals that kept it somewhat subdued, hit them like a sudden wind.

Nob carried Jacob's limp form, draped over his deformed shoulder. Melissa followed, then Roderick, who flipped up another lever, igniting the electric lights he'd recently installed. They hummed loudly, filling the room with as much noise as light.

Though she knew what to expect, Melissa still recoiled at the sight of what Roderick had created in the Monster Lab: an actual, honest-to-God bloody mess. Red stains smeared the walls, rivulets dripped into pools from the operating tables, unidentifiable pieces of flesh rose in lumps from the puddles on the floor, entrails snaked around table legs, while in the corners sat piles of discarded pieces of human bone. Most of the torso of a body, half again as big as Roderick, lay on the main table.

Nob set Jacob on a table across the room.

A set of cabinets lined the wall opposite the door, the drawers marked with the names of various body parts and features whose humor apparently only Roderick could appreciate—such as WARTS AND HICKEYS. Human brains floated in jars, each labeled in a manner suggesting the same peculiar sense of humor: GOOD, BAD, SICK, TWISTED, CRIMINAL, and UNIMAGINATIVE. Melissa, who'd visited the lab a few times before, didn't remember seeing these odd labels.

"Father?" she asked.

Her expression must have given her thoughts away, because Roderick explained, "I made those for Jacob, to remind him of the Monster Lab from our childhood."

She wondered what the drawer marked FUN BITS held.

"Here," Roderick said, handing her a label with the phrase MY NAME IS on it, and just beneath that her own name scribbled in Roderick's barely legible handwriting. He had one for himself and one for Nob, too, although Nob's bore the name Catherine—Melissa's mother.

"What are these for?" Melissa asked.

"Everything must be labeled," Roderick replied. He didn't elaborate. Melissa noticed a certain wildness in his eyes, and decided not to pursue the issue.

Jacob groaned and came to, slowly sitting up. He blinked at the bright lights, then looked around, taking in his surroundings with a growing expression of disbelief and horror.

"My *God*," he said. "Roderick . . . what have you done?"

"This is my Monster Lab, Jacob," Roderick told him, indicating the blood-soaked room with a sweep of his arm. "Remember when we were children? The cabinets for eyes and noses and warts and hickeys . . . Well, this is *it*."

"You weren't joking, then," Jacob practically whispered. He looked at the headless body on the operating table, then over at a severed head on another table. The top of the head had been removed, the brain and eyes scooped out.

"Like it?" Roderick asked. "That'll be you, when I'm finished. Your brain in that head, atop this body. You'll have your own eyes. . . . I'll be attaching new feet, as this poor fellow had clubbed ones, and deformed hands as well. You'll be as strong as an ox. A smaller, more aesthetically pleasing body I cannot provide, I fear, as I am not so adept at putting one together . . . yet. The more I do it, the better I get, and soon I'll have you in a body as thin and tightly wound as the one you have now, and I'll have Catherine in a delicate, petite woman's body instead of the one *she* now inhabits." He looked purposefully at Nob, then at Melissa.

"Catherine?" Jacob said, also looking at Nob and then at Melissa, as if expecting confirmation from one, or both, of them. Nob didn't react at all. Melissa's face burned, and she bit her lip, forcing herself not to speak. She lowered her head to stare at the red puddles on the floor.

"Melissa," Roderick said. "The syringe. We must begin at once. Time is not on our side."

"Syringe?" Jacob asked. Melissa walked over to another cabinet, opened it, and produced a big syringe with a long needle. It looked more suited for injecting a horse than a man.

"We must inject you with a compound that will render you unconscious so you will not feel any pain. I hope you won't mind being unconscious."

"Pain?"

"I highly recommend being unconscious while I remove your brain," Roderick explained patiently.

"Remove my brain?" Jacob looked around nervously, appealing to Melissa for support, or reason, or *something*.

"Don't be afraid," Roderick said. "The procedure worked on Catherine. She inhabits the body of Nob! Alas, I disposed of his brain. It had been damaged *in utero,* the same accident that rendered him a hunchback. But as you can see, she's fine. Oh, she can't talk because Nob didn't have a tongue, but I've been meaning to get her one soon. Maybe I'll give her yours. You won't be needing it. . . ."

"Father," Melissa said, suddenly feeling ill, "please stop."

Oblivious to the effect his words had on her, Roderick continued, "And besides, I've put a perfectly workable cow's tongue in your new head." He walked over to the severed head on the counter, near Melissa. "Would you like to see?"

As he turned the head around to give Jacob a good view inside its mouth, Melissa suddenly plunged the needle into his left buttock and pressed the plunger down about a third of the way with her thumb. A stunned expression played across Roderick's face. His eyes rolled up into his head, his lids fluttered closed, and he fell to the ground, soundly thwacking his skull on the floor and splashing gobs of thick blood onto Melissa's clothes.

"I'm sorry!" Melissa cried to her now unconscious father. Then she looked at Jacob. "I couldn't do it! He's . . . he's crazy, you see, and . . . with Mother, she was already dead, or she would have died soon enough, but I couldn't let him kill Nob because it wouldn't have worked! It wouldn't have!"

"Melissa," Jacob said. "What are you talking about?"

"Mother's brain is *not* in Nob's head," Melissa told him. "Father had Nob drugged, and was going to cut the top of his head off and remove his brain, and replace it with Mother's, but I injected him, just as I did now, and knocked him out before he started. When he awakened, I convinced him he'd succeeded, and he didn't remember because he'd been working in a delirium for several days.

"*I* taught Nob how to cook the way Mother did! *I* showed him how to write the way she did! Nob went along with my ruse, and continues to do so because I saved his life, and he knows no other world than this house and Father's employ. He killed Mother, and it was no accident. She hated him. She treated him like a slave, always beating him, even when he tried to help her clean the upstairs windows! So he pushed her out one day. She lingered for weeks, her body broken but her mind still active. She could open her eyes and see, but that was *all* she could do! So Father decided it was only fair for Nob to let Mother's brain inhabit his body. He'd been performing experiments for years, and had succeeded in switching the brains of two dogs, though they died less than a week later. But he determined he was ready to perform the operation on Mother and Nob.

"I knew he would fail if I let him proceed! I devised a plan to stop him. Then, for show, I rebelled against the idea of Mother's brain in Nob's head. It worked because I've always been contrary, so Father expected it of me! My refusal to accept his truth only reinforced his belief that he'd succeeded!"

"I think I understand," Jacob said. "But then that means his 'procedure' for curing me of my illness isn't real, am I right?"

Melissa nodded.

"And you were going to go along with him anyway, knowing he'd fail?"

Melissa nodded again.

"Why? In God's name, *why?*"

"Because, it would make him happy," Melissa answered. "And he and I had worked out a deal. You see, we'd have to declare you dead, and Father would be your beneficiary. He was going to give me enough of a monthly allowance to move to Boston—and leave this dreadful place once and for all."

Jacob considered this, then asked, "But what of our 'sister'? What of Dre?"

"Who?" Melissa asked, confused.

Jacob indicated the dinner dress he was still wearing.

"Oh, *her.* Well . . . I suppose we'd have to say she decided to stay on with Father. Or maybe got married off again or something. I don't know. I'm sure Father had something figured out for you, or her, or . . . you know."

"Melissa, why didn't you just inject *me,* instead of Roderick, as you were supposed to?" Jacob asked.

"I couldn't!" she replied. "It's so horrible, to have your brain removed like a seed from a grape! I couldn't bear the thought of him doing that to you! Not after Mother."

"But I am *dying*," Jacob told her. "My strength is being sapped from my body by the moment. Soon I'll need a nurse to care for me, to feed me and help me with my toilet. I don't want that. That's no way for a *man* to end up!"

"Do you *want* Father to remove your brain and to try and put it in the head of this . . . *thing?*" Melissa asked.

"If it makes him happy," Jacob said, "then perhaps I do. And you will benefit from it, too. Even if the operation fails—if I know my brother, you'll still get your wish. You'll be living in Boston in a month. And Roderick, well, he'll still have Nob as his success, so his failure with me will be bearable, right?"

"I suppose," Melissa said.

Roderick groaned on the floor.

"See to his head," Jacob said. "I think he hit it pretty hard. And inject me before he awakens. You can tell him he slipped in the blood and fell, hitting his head."

"This is what you want?" Melissa asked.

Jacob nodded.

"I'll miss you, Uncle Jacob," Melissa said as she refilled the syringe.

"You never know," Jacob replied, "maybe he'll *succeed*."

SOMEONE'S IN THE KITCHEN

by Nancy A. Collins

Pruitt knew the cottage was the one for him the moment he laid eyes on the slightly blurry Polaroid in the realtor's office. It was tacked onto a cork bulletin board, nestled among expensive country estates and seedy farmhouses.

"How about this one?" he said, plucking the picture free and holding it out to the realtor, who took it from him with a mildly surprised grunt.

"This one? I'll have to admit I don't know that much about the place," she replied, tapping the edge of the Polaroid against a brightly lacquered nail. "I suppose you could say we 'inherited' the house. It was one of old Garret Stroud's properties, rest his soul. He'd been handling it since the fifties, I guess. When he passed on last season, his widow called up the office and said it was too much for her to deal with alone. Since she and Garret never had kids, there wasn't anyone to take over the business, so we bought her out." She glanced back down at the cozy cottage with its white picket fence, climbing roses, and canary-yellow shutters and trim. "But to tell you the truth, Mr. Pruitt, I wouldn't have thought you'd be interested in this one—I mean, wouldn't you rather see one of the town houses? They're much closer to the shore and the nightlife. . . ."

"I appreciate your concerns, Mrs. Hardy," Pruitt said, smiling wanly. "But I've had enough nightlife in Manhattan to see me through the summer."

The cottage was as quaint and cozy as its picture. It was set back from the blacktop county road, the front yard surrounded by a white picket fence. Except for a slate-gray Cape Cod a few hundred yards away, there were no other houses to be seen. Mrs. Hardy took out her key ring, frowning at the color-coded tags.

"I know I have the key on me somewhere. However, it's only fair that I warn you, Mr. Pruitt; no one's been here to air the house out yet, so it might smell musty. . . ."

"I'll bear that in mind."

With a small cry of triumph, Mrs. Hardy located the proper key and fit it into the front lock. The hinges squeaked a bit as she pushed open the door, the wood slightly warped by the humidity. Pruitt stepped forward, sniffing the air like a cautious hound, but instead of smelling the faint odor of mildew, he detected a far more unusual—and pleasant—scent.

"Pancakes."

"I beg your pardon?"

Pruitt blinked, somewhat nonplussed to discover that he had spoken aloud. "It smells like pancakes."

Mrs. Hardy frowned, sniffed, then shot a skeptical look in his direction. "I don't smell anything."

Pruitt sniffed again. The pancake smell was gone now. "Must have caught a whiff from the people next door having breakfast," he muttered.

Mrs. Hardy looked like she wanted to tell him that, unlike Manhattan, people in her neck of the woods didn't have breakfast at two in the afternoon, but said nothing. From there on in, everything went without incident as she showed him the house.

The cottage was fully furnished, although much of it looked a bit worn. Whoever had originally owned the place had bought their furniture in the early fifties. Not the fifties "moderne" space-age stuff on display in trendy SoHo stores. No, this was solid, middle-class American furniture—well made and reasonable, if not particularly remarkable. It reminded Pruitt of his great-aunt's house in Teaneck.

There was a tidy front parlor, complete with doilies, a small dining room, a bathroom with an old-fashioned ceramic tub with curled feet, a bedroom that faced the back garden and boasted a four-poster Shaker bed, and a good-sized kitchen with an old-style range and refrigerator that sparked fond memories of Pruitt's childhood.

"Wow! I haven't seen one of these in ages! We used to have one of these when I was a kid!" Pruitt grinned, slapping the sleekly rounded top of the Kelvinator.

Mrs. Hardy glanced down at an index card she'd pulled from

her day planner. "According to what information was given to us by Mrs. Stroud, these are the furnishings and appliances that belonged to the original owner, a Mrs. Hettie Greenfield, who died in 1956."

"This place is great!" Pruitt grinned. "It's like walking back in time. The minute I cross the threshold, I'll be able to forget about everything at the office." As he tested the knob on the back door, his eye was caught by a second, narrower doorway next to the pantry. "Does this place have a fruit cellar?"

"It doesn't say anything about one on the card. But then, I wouldn't be surprised if it turned out there was one. A lot of the older houses around here have them."

Pruitt opened the door and was surprised to find that the stairs led up and not down. Attic storage, no doubt. The stairs were narrow and strangely spaced, as if designed for someone crippled with severe arthritis, and he had to bend nearly double to make his way up them.

Whatever had been originally stored up there certainly couldn't have been worth the effort of hauling it up and down the steps. There was no door at the top of the stairwell, just a hole cut in the attic floor. Poking his head into the attic, he was surprised to see a narrow bed, a chest of drawers, and what looked like an old-fashioned washbasin and commode tucked under the sharply slanting roof. A bare lightbulb dangled from the canted ceiling.

"That's odd." He sniffed as he clumped back down the stairs. "Stroud must have converted the attic into a second bedroom. But I'd be damned if anyone bigger than a twelve-year-old kid could get up and down those stairs on a daily basis—or stand to be in that room for more than ten minutes. Talk about cramped! Still, I guess it could prove handy should one of my friends decide to visit for the weekend for a taste of the country!"

"Then you'll take it?"

"Of course! How could I pass up a charmer like this?"

Pruitt's first night in his summer cottage passed without incident. He found himself growing tired by eight o'clock, exhausted by the long drive from the city and unpacking his books, cookware, and clothes. After the sun went down, he stood on the back porch for a long moment, sipping a bottle of Snapple as he listened to the cicadas drone in the trees. There was something comforting—almost hypnotic—in their singing. After spending so much time surrounded by the man-made cacophony of New York City, he had come to appreciate the sounds of nature.

He was in bed by eleven o'clock, which was actually quite early for him. Plagued by insomnia since college, Pruitt usually didn't go to bed until two or three, and even then he'd only sleep four or five hours at most. That was one of the reasons he'd always had trouble maintaining relationships. Women don't like to wake up to find their lover has vacated the bed for the comfort of a book or late-night television. For some reason they always felt as if he were slighting them; as if his inability to fall asleep meant he was unable to be comfortable or fully trust them. Even after Pruitt explained his predicament, they all still seemed to nurse hurt feelings, as if suspecting he was lying.

Maybe it was the country air, or perhaps it was just simple exhaustion after a grueling week at work, but he slept soundly until six the next morning, when he was stirred awake by the pleasant aroma of bacon sizzling in the pan and coffee brewing on the stove. He smiled sleepily as he opened his eyes to the daylight spilling into the bedroom, dappling the wallpaper with the leafy patterns of the tree outside his window.

Pruitt stretched lazily under the clean, cool sheets, thinking to himself; There's nothing like the smell of breakfast cooking in the kitchen to make you look forward to waking up in the morning. Then came a short shock of realization. Wait a minute. I live alone.

Pruitt hurled aside the bedclothes and hurried into the hall clad in nothing but his briefs. Even as he stomped through the house, his only weapon the tennis racket he'd picked up from one of the boxes he'd left in the living room the night before, he wondered exactly what the hell he thought he was doing. In the twenty-six years he had been living within the seething belly of New York City, he had never once experienced a break-in. No doubt there was irony to be found in his driving three hours from the city's homeless, junkies, and professional criminals, only to wake up and find an intruder in his newly acquired summer house.

"What's doing on? Who the hell's in here?" he bellowed, trying to sound more indignant than frightened. "What are you doing in my house, asshole?"

As he pushed back the swinging door that led from the dining room to the kitchen, it occurred to Pruitt that whoever was preparing his breakfast might not be a burglar but one of the locals, performing an act of simple neighborliness that twentieth century life had rendered obsolete in the major metropolitan areas. No doubt the story of how the big-city slicker cursed out the preacher's wife while waving around a tennis racket and dressed in his BVDs would go over big around the cracker barrel.

Pruitt was halfway to apologizing when he set foot in the kitchen—only to find the room completely empty. There was no skillet of sizzling bacon sitting on the range top, nor was there a coffeepot to be seen. Yet there was still a hint of the aroma of fresh-brewed java hanging on the air, like the perfume left by a mysterious woman disappearing into the night.

Pruitt's second weekend in the country came after a particularly dismal week. Work at the office was both tedious and unrewarding, and he'd found himself agreeing to have dinner with an old girl-friend who was, for some reason, trying to rekindle their affair. She insisted on cooking for him, knowing that he placed a great deal of importance on such things. He had always considered the willing-ness and ability to prepare meals for others as a testament of love. Four-star restaurants were all very nice, but nothing spoke the depth of a heart like home cooking.

It wasn't until he sat down to eat in her modest East Village apartment that he remembered the reason their relationship had come to an end. Despite a winsome personality, a dynamite figure, and a sex drive that wouldn't quit, the poor woman simply couldn't cook to save her life. And to make matters even worse, her idea of a home-cooked meal smacked of the weight-conscious, calorie-counting recipes found in the back of glamour magazines. The appetizer consisted of humus and baby carrots. The entrée was undercooked spinach ravioli, sans sauce. For dessert she presented him with a Sara Lee cheesecake that, considering the wretchedness of the meal that preceded it, tasted like the Holy Grail of baked goods. The dinner did little to rekindle Pruitt's passion, and he left halfway through his second cup of instant coffee.

While riding the subway home, Pruitt reflected on how some-thing he'd once taken for granted—his mother's cooking—had assumed a mythic quality in his mind. Had his mother been so gifted in the culinary arts that no woman could ever hope to match her? Or were his memories and expectations exaggerated? Or was it simply asking too much to find a woman who was both a demon in the bedroom and an angel in the kitchen?

These thoughts were still buzzing around in the back of Pruitt's head during his drive upstate, but they were hardly preoccupying his waking hours. The first night went by uneventfully enough, and he spent the next day puttering around the house, working on the novel he'd been lugging around with him for the last six years. He'd been working on Chapter Five for sixteen months now. He liked to think he was a writer marking time by working in an office until his Day of Greatness came, as opposed to being a paper pusher whose hobby was tinkering with a book he was never going to finish. It sounded better. Just like "single" sounded better than "confirmed bachelor."

However, by the time supper rolled around, Pruitt found himself no closer to the end of Chapter Five and in no mood to stick a TV dinner into the antique oven, which, despite its quaintness, was somewhat intimidating. So he decided to hop in the car and check out the local eateries.

What they provided was a companion for the night, in the form of a pretty bartender, a sociology major going for her master's who was making ends meet by pulling brew for the locals and what she referred to as "the summer people." After a greasy hubcap-sized yuppie-burger garnished with grilled onions and sautéed mushrooms and a few beers, Pruitt found himself driving back to the cottage with Elaine's slightly dented Camaro following him, the headlights glaring in the rearview mirror.

They fucked in the four-poster, which squeaked and groaned as if they were performing the sexual decathlon. Pruitt had enjoyed himself—and he felt reasonably certain the young lady had, too—but the racket of the bed certainly made things sound a great deal more impressive than they were.

He fell asleep with the sociology major's hair pressed against his cheek and did not wake up until he heard the front door slam, followed by the sound of the Camaro hastily heading down the gravel drive.

Pruitt sat up and looked blearily around the room, trying to get up to speed. He'd brought someone home with him last night. Someone who hadn't bothered to stay to find out how thick their beer goggles had been. Even though he was a grown man—some would even say a little on the mature side, nowadays—and knew the score when it came to one-night stands, he couldn't help feeling a little rejected. He yawned and got out of bed, stretching to greet the day. She hadn't even bothered to say good-bye. Or had she? He could definitely smell coffee brewing.

Pulling on last night's discarded jeans, he shuffled into the kitchen, knuckling the sleep from his eyes. There, arranged on the kitchen table, was a plate boasting a short stack and a side of bacon. An old-fashioned coffeepot—one of those metal monstrosities that looked like it belonged in a logging camp—sat atop the stove.

Pruitt was both surprised and genuinely touched. He had experienced breakfasts with one-night stands before, but usually in diners. Once or twice he'd had room service deliver breakfast in bed. He'd certainly never had one go to such trouble and then leave without waking him up. Still, it was a nice gesture, if somewhat puzzling.

He poured himself a cup of the coffee from the stove and sat down to the pancakes. He was surprised he hadn't been awakened by the sound of her working in the kitchen. He was usually a light sleeper, although last night's exertion and the beers he'd knocked back at the pub probably had something to do with him sleeping through it all. He paused for a second to admire the pancakes. They were a delicate golden brown, not the color of buckskin, which was how the pancakes at the diner on the corner always came out. They were so tender he could cut them with his fork, and so moist they didn't need butter. Indeed, they all but melted in his mouth. Pruitt was impressed. He hadn't had pancakes this good since he left home for college, twenty-five years ago. The bacon was equally perfect—crisp and crunchy without being burned. Just the way he liked it. And the coffee tasted as good as it smelled.

It wasn't until he was putting his plates in the sink that he realized that there weren't any dirty mixing bowls or skillets to be seen. In fact, come to think of it, he wasn't even aware he'd owned a coffeepot.

Later that afternoon he called the restaurant he'd gone to the night before and asked for the woman who worked the bar, suddenly realizing he couldn't remember her name.

There was a long pause and then a vaguely familiar female voice came on the line and said hello.

"Hello . . . Elaine?" Pruitt closed his eyes and prayed he was guessing right.

"Yeah. Who's this?"

"George. George Pruitt. We, uh, met last night . . . ?"

"Oh. Yeah. Hi. What do you want?" She sounded fairly distant for someone who'd gone to the trouble of fixing a total stranger breakfast.

"I was just calling to thank you for breakfast."

"Huh?"

"You know—the pancakes and bacon. That was really nice of you. I was wondering if you might be interested in going out later on—"

"Wait a minute, buddy—I don't know what you're talking about. I didn't fix breakfast for you—your mom did."

"My mother?"

"Yeah, when I went into the kitchen to see if you had anything to drink before I split, there she was—standing with her back to me at that weird old stove. Why didn't you tell me your mom was living with you? And with all the noise that damn bed made all night long—I could have lied down and died of embarrassment! I left before she could see me."

"Look, uh, Elaine, I don't have the slightest idea who or what you're talking about! My mother is living in a retirement community in Florida. I swear!"

"So you're saying I'm either crazy or lying, is that it? Well, look, George, or whatever your name is—I don't do mama's boys. Especially ones as old as you. And if you come round here again bugging me, I'll tell my boyfriend. Is that understood?"

"But—but—"

The phone buzzed in his ear for a long moment before he got around to hanging it up. If his one-nighter hadn't fixed his breakfast—then who had? And who the hell was the mysterious old lady Elaine had seen in his kitchen?

Pruitt sat up with a start, his head swiveling about as if it had come unscrewed from his neck. It took him a few moments to realize where he was. He was slumped in the overstuffed easy chair in the front parlor. He'd been watching the ball game—or at least trying to. The cottage's battered old black-and-white set was far from cable-ready and the rabbit ears could only pull in one or two stations, and the reception seemed affected by everything from sunspots to shifts in the wind. The length of the shadows in the room told him he must have dozed for an hour or two, as it was close to dark outside. The television was still on, but the picture on the tube looked like a snowstorm as viewed through a layer of gauze.

His stomach growled, reminding him that he hadn't eaten since breakfast, and here it was fast approaching dinner. He debated whether to go out for a bite, but quickly decided to stay home. The only place he knew of was the restaurant from the night before, and he wasn't eager to go back there. Last night's stand might misread his motives and sic her boyfriend on him, and trouble with the locals was the last thing he needed.

Pruitt pushed himself out of the easy chair and shuffled out of the parlor. No, tonight he'd stay home with a Swanson's TV dinner. Fewer problems that way. The strange incident involving the pancakes had slipped his mind almost entirely. Instead, as he pushed open the kitchen door, he was pondering whether to have the turkey and dressing with rubbery English peas or the roast beef and gravy with congealed instant potatoes, not the identity of his mysterious phantom cook. Which is probably why he surprised her in the act.

The first thing Pruitt noticed as he stepped into the room was the smell of cooking—the rich, redolent odor of roasting meat and simmering vegetables. The second thing he noticed was the figure of an older woman hunched over the antique stove, dressed in a drab, calf-length dress and a nondescript sweater. Although Pruitt knew he should be alarmed—if not actively frightened—to find a stranger in his kitchen, his mouth began to water.

The mystery cook did not seem to notice his arrival and continued doing whatever it was that was focusing so much of her attention. Pruitt took another step into the kitchen, holding the swinging door open behind him with one hand. He gave a slight cough into his fist, but still she did not seem to notice him. Maybe she was hard of hearing. Judging from her iron-gray hair, she was probably close to his mother's age.

Pruitt cleared his throat again, this time much louder. "Ahem! Excuse me . . . ?"

The older woman spun around to face him as if he'd goosed her with a red-hot poker. From her body language, it was clear that she was frightened, but it was Pruitt who screamed and fainted.

He came to seconds later, sprawled across the linoleum. He scrambled to his feet, trying to look everywhere at once. The old woman was nowhere to be seen. The memory of what he'd witnessed made his head start to swim again, but he didn't faint this time. That face! God, her face! It looked like a papier-mâché Halloween mask sculpted by a disturbed child, except that it was fashioned of real flesh, not old newspapers and glue. Grabbing a knife from the drain board, Pruitt undertook a thorough search of the premises, peeping behind doors and even going so far as to poke the shower curtain. He searched the entire house—even the weird little room in the attic—but could turn up no sign of the old woman, or even evidence that she'd been there in the first place.

As he prowled the front parlor for the third time, an explanation for the hideous old crone in the kitchen suddenly occurred to him. The old thing was doubtlessly one of the locals—maybe she'd been working as a cook for the people who'd rented the place before him? Yeah, that sounded possible. With a deformity as severe as hers, landing a regular job was certainly out of the question. Maybe she had a deal with the old guy who used to handle the property? That she was supposed to provide morning and evening meals—something like that. The old thing probably didn't even know the cottage had been taken over by a new tenant who didn't know the score. No doubt Mrs. Hardy didn't tell him about it because she didn't know about it herself. She didn't know about the attic bedroom, did she? It all sounded very plausible. It certainly would explain everything.

Pruitt looked down at the knife he was still clutching in his right hand and groaned, slapping himself on the forehead with his empty palm.

Stupid! Stupid, stupid jerk!

He must have frightened the poor creature half out of her wits! Life was probably hard enough for her as it was, considering her condition, without him acting like a complete and utter jerk! He put the knife down and went to the telephone nook in the hallway and thumbed through the thin volume that passed for the phone book. What had the realtor said the old guy's name was? Strucker? Strider? Stroud? That was it—Stroud!

There was only one Stroud in the listings; it had to be the one who used to own the house. The old guy's widow would know the cook's name and how to get in contact with her. He dialed the number on the ancient rotary phone, the weight of the dial pulling on his finger with each turn. The phone on the other end rang six times before someone picked up the receiver.

"Hello?" The voice on the other end was old and querulous. Pruitt glanced at his wristwatch. Nine o'clock and already in bed.

"Uh, hello, Mrs. Stroud? My name's George Pruitt. I'm renting a house your late husband handled—the one on Old Switchback Road?"

"I'm afraid I can't help you, Mr. Pruitt. My husband passed away last winter and I'm no longer handling those properties—"

"I understand that, ma'am. It's just that—well, I think there's been a mistake."

"Mistake? What kind of mistake?"

"Well, the real-estate agent didn't tell me about the lady who comes in and does the cooking here, and I'm afraid I scared her pretty bad walking in on her unannounced tonight. I just wanted to find out her name and get her number so I could call and apologize—"

"Cook? Mr. Pruitt, I have no earthly idea what you're talking about. My husband never hired a cook for the Greenfield house. Least not that he ever told me. I suggest you call up Mrs. Hardy— maybe she can help you. Good night, Mr. Pruitt."

The disconnected phone buzzed in his ear for a long moment before he finally hung up. There went his nice, logical—if somewhat farfetched—explanation, right down the drain. If the phantom cook in his kitchen wasn't some harmless local woman, then who the hell was she? He was mulling over that question as he reentered the kitchen.

There was a platter of done-to-perfection pork chops with applesauce, a crock of old-fashioned sauerkraut, and a tray of fresh buttermilk biscuits awaiting him on the table—not to mention a Dutch apple pie keeping itself warm in the oven.

Even though he knew he should take the entire mess and dump it in the trash and call the cops, Pruitt found himself sitting down to the repast set before him. He felt as if he were trapped in a dream, acting slowly and deliberately, like a man moving about underwater. He wanted to jump up and scream and run out of the house and into the night, but the delicious smell rising from the food was scrambling his brain. It all smelled so good. . . .

Pruitt woke up the next morning to find himself in bed, although he had no clear memory of undressing himself. In fact, he couldn't remember anything after sitting down to the pork chops. He almost wasn't surprised to find a breakfast of country ham, French toast, and orange juice awaiting him in the kitchen. Waste not, want not, he sighed as he sat down to eat. However, even though he was supposed to drive back to the city that evening, Pruitt knew there was no way he could return to Manhattan without finding out what the hell was going on. Screw Manhattan, he was staying put until he knew the identity of the phantom cook. He'd call in sick in the morning—what the hell, he had time coming to him.

Pruitt was sitting on an old wooden deck chair in the backyard, frowning at the hedgerow that occupied the cottage's property line and trying to think of some way of finding out exactly who—or what—his mysterious visitor might be, when his attention was caught by the sound of pruning.

It wasn't a vigorous clipping sound, as one might expect on a fine summer's day, but instead seemed rather hesitant, as if whoever was using the shears was giving a great deal of consideration to whatever it was they were lopping off. Pruitt got up and wandered over to the hedgerow, peered over the top, and saw a very old man dressed in khaki work clothes and a sweat-stained Panama hat, armed with a pair of pruning shears that looked like they had been new before Pruitt was conceived. The old man was bent almost double, his neck drooping like the wattle on a turkey, and he wore a pair of glasses thick enough to use as a doorstop. His head wavered slightly as he peered at a branch the size and length of a pencil jutting from the uniform mass of the shrubbery. After a long minute the old man lifted the shears, pumped them open with his surprisingly sinewy liver-spotted hands, then allowed the blades to snap shut with a brisk *snikt!*—leaving the offending twig to fall at his feet.

"Uh, excuse me?"

The old man's head bobbed up rather quickly. Whatever his physical shortcomings might be, deafness certainly wasn't one of them. "You that new fella what's rented the Greenfield place." It wasn't a question.

"Yes. My name's Pruitt. George Pruitt. I'm sorry I haven't introduced myself before now, but I've been busy getting settled in."

The old man straightened up as best he could, studying the younger man as if trying to read something written on his forehead. He then smiled, displaying fiercely white dentures. He extended his right hand, which was callused and missing the first two joints on his ring finger. "Name's Hogue. Folks round here call me Pappy. Me and Myrtle, rest her soul, used to come up here on weekends to build on the place since after the war." He gestured to the modest Cape Cod a hundred yards away. "Been living here permanent since I retired from the railroad back in sixty-five. Now I stay here with my granddaughter. She's been keeping me company since she got her divorce. Been all kinds of summer folks comin' and goin' over the years. Still, I didn't think they'd be renting out the Greenfield place again, what with Stroud passing on."

Pruitt brightened. "Do you know anything about the people who originally lived here? I'm trying to find out a little more about the house, just out of curiosity. These Greenfields—are they still around?"

"Lord, no!" Pappy Hogue gave vent to a dry, humorless laugh that sounded like the bark of a fox. "Leastwise, the wife ain't. Couldn't say about the husband—although he'd be a damn sight older'n me if he was!"

"The wife is dead?"

"And then some, these forty years!" Pappy's seamed face darkened for a moment. "Poor ol' Hettie. Lord, what that woman must have suffered!"

"Beg pardon?"

"She killed herself, don't you know. Back in fifty-six."

Pruitt's stomach suddenly tightened, as if the morning's mystery breakfast had suddenly been transmuted into lead. "No, I didn't know."

"I still remember Hettie Greenfield to this day—hell, it'd be hard not to, considering her, uh, condition."

"Condition?"

"Nowadays I guess they'd call her handicapped or disabled or something polite like that. But back in them days, Hettie was a freak, pure an' simple."

The vision of the crumpled, ruined face he'd glimpsed the night before swam before Pruitt's eyes. He heard himself saying, as if from somewhere far away, "What was wrong with her?"

"She suffered from some kind of weird medical condition—had it from birth. It's one of them diseases they can take care of now, but back then—well, either it killed you young or you grew up hideously deformed. I'll have to admit, Hettie was hard to look at, bless her heart. She made her living the only way she could—touring the country in sideshows. Made damn good money at it, too. She got her start when she weren't more than a tot, sitting on a stage in her Sunday best and bein' looked at by folks. She started off as the Ugliest Little Girl in the World. Then, as she got older, she was the World's Ugliest Woman. And she sure as hell was—far as I know!

"But you can't judge an egg by its shell, as my mama used to say. As hideous as she was to look at, Hettie Greenfield had one of the sweetest souls ever to walk God's green earth. There was never a kinder, gentler woman born—and that's counting my mama and Myrtle. And talk about cook! Boy howdy! That woman could whip up a pumpkin pie that'd knock your socks off—not to mention anything else you'd have a hunger for. She was a whirlwind in the kitchen— there wasn't a dish she couldn't make to perfection! She could have won any number of blue ribbons at the state fair, if she hadn't been busy working in the freak show.

"But you know what the sorry thing was about that? Hettie herself couldn't eat what she cooked, on account of her jaw and mouth bein' so messed up. Made it hard for her to talk, as well. She lived off baby food and buttermilk, mostly. It was like cooking for others was the only way she knew to make herself understood."

"So what happened to her? What made her commit suicide?"

"What makes most folks kill themselves? She fell in love with a fella that done her dirty. She met this fella name of Oliver back in fifty-two, who wanted to be her business manager. She ended up marrying him later that year. Now, this fella wasn't exactly young or good-looking, but he had the charm, if you know what I mean. And for someone like Hettie—well, I figger she must have been pretty vulnerable to a sharpie like Oliver. She was in her fifties and looking forward to retiring here permanent. She'd saved up a sizable amount of money over the years—like I said, she was something of a star attraction in those days.

"Anyways, they got married in fifty-two, and in fifty-five Hettie announced her retirement. She and Oliver moved out here permanent, although he was still handling a few carnival acts on the side. Then in early fifty-six Oliver ups and disappears, taking most of Hettie's life savings with him. The bastard pretty much left her with just the bloomers she was standin' in. Heard tell he run off with some fire-eatin' belly dancer or what not. They found her a week later—she'd gassed herself in her oven. Funny thing is, the kitchen table and all the counters were covered with pies, cakes, cookies, jams, pot roasts—like she'd spent the last days of her life cooking for someone who wasn't there. Or for her own wake."

Pruitt sat in the front parlor and thought about what Pappy Hogue had told him. He now knew, without doubt, the identity of his phantom cook. And phantom was indeed the correct word.

Although part of him still wanted to deny it in favor of a rational explanation, George Pruitt's heart and—more importantly—his stomach had embraced the unknown. Instead of feeling afraid, he felt a great sadness come over him as he thought of how it must have been between Hettie and Oliver in the tight confines of the cottage. He now knew who had lived in the tiny, cramped attic room. He wondered if Oliver had brought his trollops home to the squeaking Shaker bed, and felt a shudder of pity and shame for the hapless Hettie, banished to her narrow cot, forced to listen to her husband's rutting. No doubt he never appreciated the meals she prepared for him;

they were truly love poems as passionate and heartfelt as any penned by the great poets. No, beasts like Oliver take such gestures as their due, nothing more.

He could not bring himself to be frightened of the ghost of Hettie Greenfield, no matter how ugly she might be. Any creature capable of preparing food so heavenly could not have malice in its nature. Whatever her reason for fixing his meals, Hettie Greenfield was not out to harm him, of this he was certain.

There came the sound of crockery rattling ever so slightly from the kitchen, and Pruitt could make out the quiet *whumpf* of the stove's gas burners igniting. Instead of being anxious, he felt a sense of well-being creep over him, as if a warm blanket had been pulled over him by a comforting hand. He had not felt such inner peace since early childhood, when he could sleep soundly in the back of the car, secure in the knowledge that his father was at the wheel.

That night Hettie made Yankee pot roast with new potatoes and baby carrots, with soda bread on the side and Indian pudding for dessert. Pruitt slept long and deep, and when he woke the next morning, he called in sick. After all, he didn't want to miss lunch.

Pruitt woke up to find himself sprawled on the parlor floor. Funny. He didn't remember fainting. He used the easy chair in front of the television to pull himself upright, then stood teetering uncertainly for a long moment before sitting down again.

The TV screen was awash in snow. Pruitt couldn't remember what he'd been watching. Or if he'd been watching anything at all. A part of his brain wondered what day it was. It was hard to tell, now that he'd quit his job. At least he thought he'd quit it. Maybe he'd been fired. In any case, he was no longer going to work. Or outside, for that matter.

He squinted at the shadows creeping along the walls, trying to tell the time. He couldn't remember whether he'd eaten lunch or not. Thinking about lunch made him start to salivate and he wiped at the drool with a shaky hand.

He had never eaten better than he had over the last two weeks, of that he was certain. Hettie's love had made itself manifest in a dizzying array of delicious meals: roast turkey with cornbread dressing; Maine lobster with drawn butter and roast corn; southern fried chicken with white gravy and biscuits; honey-glazed ham with baked apples; pecan pie à la mode; sweet potato pie; Toll house cookies; shoofly pie; gingerbread men; butterscotch pudding; and divinity fudge, not to mention pancakes that all but floated off the griddle, cinnamon rolls the size of a baby's head, and whole pigs of bacon and Virginia ham.

"George. . . ? Dinnertime."

Pruitt tried to lever himself out of the chair, failed, then tried again and succeeded. He dimly wondered how it was he'd started hearing her voice lately. At first she'd been mute—as if the gap between the living and the dead swallowed all attempts at verbal communication. Maybe she was simply no longer fearful of being rejected. Heaven knew how often that exact same fear had caused him to hold his own tongue in the past.

It took him a while, but he finally made it to the kitchen, where he found her waiting for him at the table, smiling fondly. Another deeply buried part of him found it passing strange that Hettie was no longer ugly. At least not to his eyes. In fact, as the days wore on, she seemed almost . . . well . . . beautiful.

"I fixed your favorite for you tonight," she said, gesturing to the chicken dumplings, fresh corn bread, and black-eyed peas. She said that every night, and every night it was true.

"Thank you, Hettie. It looks delicious," Pruitt whispered as he eased himself in the chair at the head of the table. "What have you got planned for afters?"

"Tapioca pudding."

"Honey, you're going to make me big as a house!" Pruitt chuckled as he speared the first dumpling and raised it to his watering mouth. He looked up to compliment Hettie on her cooking, only to discover that her face had been replaced by a brightly shining disk.

They found him several days later. Mrs. Hardy had come by to see why the latest rent check had bounced, only to find the doors and windows locked. Walking around to the back porch, she happened to look through the kitchen window and saw what she assumed to be Pruitt slumped across the table. She ran back to her car and used her cell phone to call 911.

The coroner's report read that at the time of his death, George Pruitt weighed eighty pounds and that the autopsy revealed his stomach contents to consist of newspaper and cobwebs, which coincided with the sheriff's report of finding what looked to be a partially eaten *New York Times* on the plate underneath his body.

Still, they were at a loss to understand how Pruitt—an outwardly successful and stable business executive—could systematically starve himself to death. Or why, upon entering the house, the sheriff's deputies and the paramedics reported smelling the aroma of fresh pancakes.

BIOGRAPHIES

Steve Antczak was born in Salem, Massachusetts and raised in South Florida. He's wanted to write stories ever since the third grade, when he penned thirty pages of *The White Tiger*, the tale of how he and his friends stowed away on a plane to India to see a legendary giant white tiger first-hand. Although that text is lost, he has other stories that have appeared, or will be appearing, in the anthologies *Superheroes*, *Adventures in the Twilight Zone*, *Confederacy of the Dead*, *100 Wicked Little Witch Stories*, and *In Dreams* (in the UK) and in the magazines *Tomorrow*, *Not One of Us*, *Abrupt Edge*, *Deathrealm*, *The Third Alternative*, *Fresh Blood*, and *Vampire Junction*.

David Aaron Clark is the author of four novels, the most recent of which is *Into the Black*. His short stories have appeared in *Love Bites* and *Forbidden Acts*, and he is coeditor of the anthology *Religious Sex*. He lives in San Francisco with photographer J. D. Vargas.

Nancy A. Collins is the author of *Walking Wolf*, *Wild Blood*, *Tempter*, and *Fantastic Four: To Free Atlantis*. Her novels *Sunglasses After Dark*, *In the Blood*, and *Paint it Black*, featuring her punk vampire heroine Sonja Blue, have been recently collected in the omnibus *Midnight Blue* from White Wolf. Her short fiction has appeared in such anthologies as *The Year's Best Fantasy & Horror*, *Best New Horror*, *The Definitive Best of the Horror Show*, *Splatterpunks*, and *The Best of Pulphouse*. She was the writer for DC Comics' *Swamp Thing* series from 1991 to 1993. She is a recipient of the Horror Writers of America's Bram Stoker Award for First Novel and the British Fantasy Society's Icarus Award. She is also the founder of the International Horror Critics Guild and the coeditor of the erotic horror anthologies *Forbidden Acts* and *Dark Love*. She is currently working on the comics adaptation of *Sunglasses After Dark* for Verotik; the fourth installment in the Sonja Blue Cycle, *A Dozen Black Roses;* and a romantic dark fantasy called *Angels On Fire*, both from White Wolf; scripts for the comic book based on *The X-Files;* and the forthcoming DC/Vertigo series, *Dhampire*. She is also working on the screenplays for *Sunglasses*

After Dark and *Walking Wolf*. She currently resides in Denver with her husband, anti-artiste Joe Christ, and their Boston terrier, Scrapple.

Christopher Golden is the author of nine novels, including *Of Saints and Shadows, Angel Souls & Devil Hearts, Daredevil: Predator's Smile,* and the trilogy *X-Men: Mutant Empire,* featuring the world-famous Marvel Comics characters. Golden has recently entered the comic book field with work on such titles as *Wolverine* and *Vampirella,* and the acclaimed creator-owned series *Thundergod.* He has written articles for *The Boston Herald, Disney Adventures,* and *Billboard,* among others, and was a regular columnist for the worldwide service, BPI Entertainment News Wire. His short story appearances include *Forbidden Acts, The Ultimate Spider-Man,* and *The Ultimate Silver Surfer.* Golden was born and raised in Massachusetts, where he still lives with his family.

Melissa Mia Hall is a Texas author whose fiction has appeared in *Twilight Zone,* Charles L. Grant's *Shadows* anthologies, *Women of Darkness, Post-Mortem, Things that Go Bump in the Night, A Whisper of Blood, Cat Crimes III, Forbidden Acts* (in collaboration with Douglas E. Winter), and bunches more. She has been a teacher, interviewer, filmmaker, book reviewer, and film critic at various times in her career, and is a member in good standing of PEN Center USA West. T. E. D. Klein once called her Fort Worth's answer to Shirley Jackson, only she looks a lot better.

T. E. D. Klein is the former editor of *Twilight Zone* and *CrimeBeat* magazines. His bestselling horror novel *The Ceremonies* won the British Fantasy Society Award for Best Novel. One of the tales in his collection *Dark Gods* won the World Fantasy Award for Best Novella. He divides his time between New York City and upstate New York.

Kathe Koja is the author of *Strange Angels, Skin, Bad Brains, The Cipher;* and *Kink,* from Henry Holt. Her short fiction appears in various magazines and anthologies. She lives in the Detroit area with her husband, artist Rick Lieder, and her son.

Mike Lee is an author, journalist, and reviewer whose work appears in a variety of magazines and anthologies. He has written two novels, *Quentin's Amerika* and *Caught Between Lanes*. A former editor at *The Austin Chronicle, Genesis,* and *Rockpool,* Lee now divides his time between family and working on his third novel. He lives in New York City with his wife and daughter.

Anya Martin is a freelance writer/journalist, music critic, and editor specializing in horror, science fiction, comics, and rock 'n' roll. She had her first published short story in *Confederacy of the Dead,* and an essay appeared in *Splatterpunks 2.* Her latest story appears in *Dark Destiny III.* Fresh from two years of promotional writing for Marvel Comics, she is currently penning a contemporary southern gothic novel.

Gregory Nicoll is a Georgia author, music reporter, and chili chef whose short fiction has been showcased three times in *The Year's Best Horror Stories.* His work can be found in anthologies such as *100 Vicious Little Vampires, Grails: Visitations of the Night, Weird Menace, Cthulhu's Heirs, Freak Show, Deathport, Confederacy of the Dead, Still Dead: Book of the Dead 2, Cold Shocks, Chilled to the Bone,* and *Ripper!* Greg provided publicity and uncredited additional dialogue for the 1990 movie Blood Salvage, and has written numerous band bios, record reviews, and CD liner notes. When he isn't listening to loud music in a smoky rock 'n' roll club or working feverishly on his computer, you'll often find him on the shooting range with one of his beloved 1894-model saddle carbines. Known for quite some time by the nickname "Stretch," Greg officially closes the book on that pesky alter ego with his story in *The Ultimate Haunted House.*

Expatriate Englishman **Philip Nutman** is the author of the critically acclaimed novel *Wet Work.* A three-time Bram Stoker Award nominee, his fiction has appeared in nearly two dozen anthologies, including *Book of the Dead, Borderlands 2,* and *The Year's Best Horror Stories XIX* and *XX,* and has been translated into five languages. He is currently at work on a new novel and a screenplay for a major Hollywood studio.

Bram Stoker Award-winner **Norman Partridge**'s first novel, *Slippin' Into Darkness* was called "nitro-laced, in-your-face fiction for the '90s" by *Locus* and "easily the most auspicious genre debut of the year" by Stephen King. Recent projects include *The Bars on Satan's Jailhouse* (a chapbook), editorial duties on the *It Came from the Drive-In* anthology, and comic scripts. A collection of short stories, *Bad Intentions,* was published in 1996. Partridge makes his home in Lafayette, California, where he is currently working on his next novel, a suspense tale with surfboards and cacti.

Wayne Allen Sallee is a Chicago native whose first story was published in 1985. He has had eleven stories reprinted in the last ten *Year's Best Horror Stories* edited by the late Karl Edward Wagner. His first short story collection, *With Wounds Still Wet,* was published in 1995. Recent work includes *Frankenstein: 1976* and the comic book *Dream Wolves,* which has been optioned for film.

Lucy Taylor's horror fiction has appeared in *Little Deaths, The Immortal Unicorn, David Copperfield's Tales of the Impossible, Desire Burn, Dark Love, Hotter Blood, Hot Blood 4, Hot Blood 6, Flesh Fantastic, Bizarre Dreams, The Mammoth Book of Erotic Horror, High Fantastic,* and other anthologies. Her work has also appeared in publications such as *Pulphouse, Palace Corbie, Cemetery Dance, Bizarre Bazaar 92* and *93, Bizarre Obsessions,* and *Bizarre Sex and Other Crimes of Passion.* Her collections include *Close to the Bone, The Flesh Artist,* and *Unnatural Acts and Other Stories.* Her novel, *The Safety of Unknown Cities,* has recently been published by Darkside Press. She is currently at work on another novel. A former resident of Florida, she lives in the hills outside Boulder, Colorado with her six cats.

Gahan Wilson's cartoons have appeared in *The New Yorker*, as well as in *Weird Tales, Punch,* and *Paris Match*. He's written stories that have appeared in *Omni* and *Fantasy and Science Fiction*, as well as children's books, including *Hairticklers*. Recent projects include illustrating *Now We are Sick* (edited by Neil Gaiman) and *Spooky Stories for a Dark & Stormy Night* (compiled by Alice Low), and writing book reviews for *Realms of Fantasy*.

COPYRIGHT INFORMATION